YOUR MAN IS STRIKER.

You're a cop. A professional. And you know what that means.

You have to listen to shouts of 'white racist pig.' You have to make sure someone is trying to kill you before you use your gun. You have to listen to all the wisecracks about graft and see your name smeared in the paper by circulation-hungry reporters and you have to take it.

But now your partner is rolling on the ground with a bullet in his gut. He's black. His assailant is black. And suddenly you stop caring what they call you or what the rules are.

Somewhere among ten million people a killer is hiding—and you're going to find him your own way. . . .

Big Bestsellers from SIGNET

- ☐ **BADGE OF HONOR by Dallas Barnes.**
  (#Y5978—$1.25)
- ☐ **YESTERDAY IS DEAD by Dallas Barnes.**
  (#W6898—$1.50)
- ☐ **ARABESQUE by Theresa de Kerpely.**
  (#J7424—$1.95)
- ☐ **BEHIND CLOSED DOORS by Robert Woolf.**
  (#J7423—$1.95)
- ☐ **THE FRENCHMAN by Velda Johnston.**
  (#W7519—$1.50)
- ☐ **THE HOUSE ON THE LEFT BANK by Velda Johnston.**
  (#W7279—$1.50)
- ☐ **A ROOM WITH DARK MIRRORS by Velda Johnston.**
  (#W7143—$1.50)
- ☐ **KINFLICKS by Lisa Alther.** (#E7390—$2.25)
- ☐ **RIVER RISING by Jessica North.**
  (#E7391—$1.75)
- ☐ **LOVER: CONFESSIONS OF A ONE NIGHT STAND by Lawrence Edwards.** (#J7392—$1.95)
- ☐ **THE SURVIVOR by James Herbert.**
  (#E7393—$1.75)
- ☐ **THE KILLING GIFT by Bari Wood.**
  (#E7350—$2.25)
- ☐ **WHITE FIRES BURNING by Catherine Dillon.**
  (#E7351—$1.75)
- ☐ **CONSTANTINE CAY by Catherine Dillon.**
  (#W6892—$1.50)
- ☐ **YESTERDAY'S CHILD by Helene Brown.**
  (#E7353—$1.75)

THE NEW AMERICAN LIBRARY, INC.,
P.O. Box 999, Bergenfield, New Jersey 07621

Please send me the SIGNET BOOKS I have checked above.
I am enclosing $_____(check or money order—no
currency or C.O.D.'s). Please include the list price plus 35¢ a
copy to cover handling and mailing costs. (Prices and numbers
are subject to change without notice.)

Name_____

Address_____

City_____State_____Zip Code_____
Allow at least 4 weeks for delivery

See the Woman

by
Dallas Barnes

Ø
A SIGNET BOOK
NEW AMERICAN LIBRARY
TIMES MIRROR

SIGNET, SIGNET CLASSICS, MENTOR, PLUME AND MERIDIAN BOOKS
are published by The New American Library, Inc.,
1301 Avenue of the Americas, New York, New York 10019

FIRST PRINTING, JUNE, 1973

7 8 9 10 11 12 13

PRINTED IN THE UNITED STATES OF AMERICA

Dedicated to those men who paid the ulti-mate price in their efforts to protect and serve.

PROLOGUE

It was a few minutes to one, and Los Angeles had passed through another hot August Saturday night into a cooling, dark Sunday morning.

In the northwest, beyond the hills, the valley was alive with the affluent young, in their new cars and motorcycles, moving restlessly to and from their parties, discothèques, and drive-ins.

To the north, Hollywood's own unique night life seethed. The hippies swarmed its streets, peddling their sleazy underground newspapers, narcotics, and themselves, clogging sidewalks, spilling into the street, slowing and stopping traffic.

In the east, the Mexican-American community slept. Here and there a noisy, happy party punctuated the stillness.

Downtown Los Angeles sprawled away darkly from the towering City Hall bathed in chalky white light. The city, too, was still, except for an occasional screech of brakes or the sound of a wine bottle breaking on skid row.

In West Los Angeles, the rich slept comfortably. Their parties were soundproof behind walls and trees.

The Santa Monica Freeway cuts east to west through the heart of Los Angeles. South of the freeway, spread over some thirty-five square miles, lay the black community, home for more than 600,000 souls.

Of Los Angeles' seventeen police divisions, three provide service for the black community—Seventy-seventh, Newton, and Southwest divisions.

As one A.M. neared, Southwest Division had only twenty-two police officers on patrol. After spreading the two hundred and seventy-five men over four different shifts; after manning the jail, the desk, the vice squad, station security; and after counting men on vacation, men with injuries or regular days off, there was one man for every 7,400 citizens. That was all that remained to protect and to serve.

The Watts Summer Festival, an annual celebration of black achievement, was one week away. Every year, as the black community's festive mood gathered momentum, crimes and arrests increased and tension mounted.

The morning watch, working between midnight and eight A.M., had been on duty now for fifty-five minutes. They had handled three armed-robbery calls, two assaults with a deadly weapon, seven family disputes, two lost children, three abandoned children, one drowned child, one rape, two burglaries, and one murder, the result of an argument over a television show. An ordinary night.

PART

ONE

~~~~~~~~~~

"KMA-367,0100 hours," said the link, as black-and-white patrol cars throughout the city scurried about in the hot August night.

To mid-watch units, the link's announcement meant another two hours of watch. To the morning watch, it meant the end of one hour. Seven more to go.

"3A81 clear," Officer Bennett said crisply into the radio mike. Then, after releasing the talk button, "And ready for another four calls."

Steve Bennett was twenty-four years old, black, and pleased to be told he resembled Bill Cosby. He had been a policeman for eleven months, and knew he had found his place in life.

Steve's family came to Los Angeles from Columbus, Ohio, when he was still in grade school. Steve had dropped out of high school in his senior year to join the Marine Corps, and after six years had almost decided to make it a career. Then, while home on weekend leave, he met Joy.

Steve decided to marry Joy the minute they met, and after only six weeks, he asked her. Joy loved him, but she did not want to be separated from him while he returned to Vietnam for another tour of combat duty. So he chose between Joy and the Corps, and took his discharge in September. They were married the same month, and now had a six-month-old son, Martin.

Steve worked for North American for a while.

Then one evening, after a particularly bad day of tracing red, black, and yellow wires through aircraft fuselages, he got a traffic citation.

He was driving northbound on Western Avenue, crossing Slauson, when he noticed red lights in his rear-view mirror. "Oh, Christ," he breathed, as he pulled to the curb and stopped.

"Good evening," said the white-helmeted motorcycle officer, moving just to the rear of Steve's car door. Steve twisted in his seat, looked at the unemotional face, and wondered what color eyes were hidden behind the officer's sunglasses.

"The reason I've stopped you is because you failed to yield the right of way to two pedestrians who were in the crosswalk at the last intersection you crossed. That's a violation of the State Vehicle Code, as well as a danger to the two kids who were crossing the street. You'll receive a citation for the violation. Now, may I see your operator's license?"

Steve took his license from his wallet and handed it to the officer, who said, "Back in a moment," turned, and walked to the rear of the car. Steve glanced in his rear-view mirror and saw another motorcycle officer standing at the right rear of his car watching him. "Good tactics," he thought.

"Pig! Honky!" Steve turned, startled at the sudden shouting. Clenched fists gestured from a passing yellow Cadillac full of laughing Negroes. The Cad gunned off into the southbound traffic of Western Avenue.

The first officer reappeared. "I'll need your signature on the citation. It is in no way an admission of your guilt, only a promise to appear on or before the date indicated."

Steve took the citation and pen and signed it, returned the citation book and pen. The officer tore out a copy and handed it to Steve. "How many times a day does that happen?" Steve asked.

"Too many," the officer answered. "Thanks for your cooperation. Drive carefully, now."

"Guts," thought Steve. "Real guts, like the Corps." He pulled away into traffic.

"Look at all that fucking traffic. . . . Jesus, looks like it will be another wild Saturday night," said Wayne Conrad.

Steve penciled in their last two radio calls, on the patrol log. "Welcome to the ghetto, whitey," he said.

"Just keep writing, boy."

Steve smiled.

Conrad was a tall, tanned white man, ten years older than Steve, with eight years in the department. Steve liked Conrad. Working with him, he found it easy to forget that they were different skin colors. They were partners.

"3Adam81, two calls," said the soft, impersonal female voice on the radio. "See the woman a family dispute, 6305 Seventh Avenue, Apt. 7, and See the manager a 415 fight group, 3109 Edgehill."

Steve noted the calls on the pad mounted on the dash, picked up the mike. "3Adam81, Roger on two."

"That 415 fight group on Edgehill is in 3A21's area, maybe Tom will pick it up, if he heard it," Steve said to Conrad.

"No staying in your own area on Saturday night."

"The Rat Patrol." Steve smiled, as he shook a cigarette from a pack of Kools above the sun visor.

"Beep . . . Beep . . . Beep." Code Three, an emergency call for a patrol unit. They waited, stomach muscles tightening.

"Southwest units in the vicinity and 3A58, a

415 man with a shotgun and shots fired, 1341 West Thirty-seventh Place, 3Adam58 your call is Code Three."

"There's a good one for Buzz," Steve said, glancing at Conrad.

"He's got a recruit with him tonight, too." Conrad smiled. "That'll make his shit shake."

They rolled southbound on Crenshaw as Steve lit his cigarette and Conrad wove the black-and-white in and out of the heavy traffic, turning left onto Slauson Avenue.

"Check Frank William Sam-827, Partner."

"The fifty-seven Chevy?" Steve asked, turning to look.

The car passed, in the opposite direction. Six male Negroes, mod dress, probably late teens, early twenties, blue fifty-seven Chevy, Steve noted to himself. He flicked on the light on the hot sheet and ran his finger down the eight column, "817 . . . 821 . . . 825 . . . CHS-827 . . . FWS-827. . . . It's hot!"

"Okay, get a want on it," Conrad replied calmly, U-turning hard to follow the Chevy, which was now nearly a block off and moving away.

"3Adam81, requesting a want on Frank William Sam-827."

"3Adam81, stand by. 3A98, go ahead."

"Goddammit," Steve complained nervously. "Can't even get a want on a hot roller."

"He's about six cars ahead in the number-one lane," Conrad said. "I don't know if they made us or not."

"3A98, Roger, no want on suspect. 3A81, repeat your license."

Steve repeated, "3A81, requesting a want on Frank William Sam-827."

"Roger, Frank William Sam-827, stand by. 3A71, four calls. . . . See the man. . . ."

"Jesus Christ," Steve growled, the tightness in his stomach growing.

Conrad glanced at him. "He's two cars ahead of this Ford, and they've made us, they're eyeballing us now."

Steve heard the tremor in his partner's voice now and felt relieved that he wasn't the only one.

"I hope he doesn't rabbit in all this traffic." Conrad leaned forward slightly.

"3A81, Frank William Sam-827 is a West Hollywood stolen," the radio said. "A blue 1957 Chevrolet, serial number C5711L074, with a hold for prints, or hold all occupants, and notify West Hollywood detectives."

"Bingo!" Conrad passed a car on the right to fall in line behind the Chevy.

"Roger," Steve replied into the mike.

Joy got up from the couch and turned off the television set. She watched Ed McMahon and a can of dog food fade from the darkening screen. Tossing the *TV Guide* onto the coffee table, she went to the baby's room and adjusted the blanket, even though it was undisturbed. Then, kneeling beside the crib, she reached through the bars and put her hand on the baby's back, felt him breathing through the blanket. "Sleep tight, Baby Martin."

Helen Conrad was busy in her kitchen chopping celery for potato salad. Tomorrow would be the annual family reunion, and as usual, she was stuck with the potato salad. It was a hell of an hour to be making potato salad, but some friends had dropped over, and it couldn't wait until the next morning, because that was Wayne's day off. She would rather spend the time with him.

"Tell Communications we're following the vehicle and we'll stop them at Slauson and LaBrea." Conrad spoke without taking his eyes off the suspect vehicle.

Steve picked up the mike. "3A81, we're following Frank William Sam-827, westbound on Slauson, approaching LaBrea. Six male Negro suspects in the vehicle. This unit will be Code Six-Adam at Slauson and LaBrea."

"Roger, 3A81," said frequency three. "All units, 3A81 is Code Six-Adam with a stolen vehicle, Frank William Sam-827, a blue 1957 Chevrolet, with six male Negro suspects at Slauson and LaBrea."

Conrad flipped the red lights to the on position, bathing the Chevy ahead in red light. The three men in the rear of the car were clearly visible now, twisting to look back at the police car.

Steve could see their mouths moving in argument. He said nothing. He knew Conrad saw it also.

The heavy traffic on Slauson yielded to the flashing red lights. Steve picked up the shotgun from the rack in front of the seat and worked the pump action to put a round in the chamber, the gun's action sounding strangely loud in the police car. There was no conversation between the two partners now. Both knew other black-and-whites were rolling toward Slauson and LaBrea.

The Chevy's right-hand turn signal was on, moving from the left lane toward the curb.

"How about that shit," Conrad said, "driving a stolen car; but he doesn't want a ticket for failing to signal a lane change."

The Chevy pulled to the curb and stopped.

Steve was breathing fast; he could feel the blood

pounding in his ears. His right hand was on the door handle, his left on the shotgun.

Conrad stoppèd, pushed the selector to park, unsnapped his pistol, drew it, and opened the car door in a smooth, practiced motion. "Watch your ass," he said.

Traffic on Slauson had slowed to watch. Some of the passing faces laughed and jeered, and some showed just curiosity.

Conrad and the driver of the Chevy, a tall slender Negro with a moustache, both left their cars at the same time. Conrad didn't even see the gun before a forty-five slug tore into the base of his neck. He felt a sharp burning sensation as his revolver, by reflex, fired three times. Two of the bullets struck the driver in the chest. The third streaked into the darkness of the early-morning sky. Conrad fell backward to the pavement. He was dead.

Two more men rolled out the right side of the Chevy as Steve shouted, "Freeze."

The short, fat one raised his arm, and Steve saw the pistol. He jerked the trigger on the shotgun. Its blast pierced the darkness like a bolt of lightning. Both men jumped backward, like rag dolls, their mouths open in disbelief as the window glass in the Chevy exploded. They collapsed next to the open car door, their blood pouring onto the curb.

"Don't shoot! Don't shoot! We give up," shouts came from inside the Chevy.

"Come out, you bastards, or I'll kill you where you sit!" Steve shouted.

"We're coming, don't shoot, please don't, we're coming! We don't have any guns."

Steve crouched behind the door of the black-and-white, shotgun leveled through the open car-door window.

Traffic was now stopped on Slauson. Steve could see bright headlights, hear shouting, screaming, and crying from the gathering crowd. He glanced across the front seat, saw the toes of Conrad's shoes. "Oh, damn . . . oh, goddamn . . ." Tears streamed down his cheeks, and he felt cold. His stomach jerked. "Oh, Joy, Joy, help me. . . ."

"We're coming, man. Don't shoot. Don't shoot, man."

"Keep your hands where I can see them, or I'll kill both of you."

Two men climbed from the rear seat, moving clumsily with hands outstretched as they stepped over the bodies crumpled near the door, and stood facing him with their arms stretched skyward. They were young, only seventeen or eighteen. One of them, wearing white Levi's, had a wet crotch.

Steve straightened quickly. "Move over to that house and put your hands on the wall."

The two men crossed the sidewalk cautiously, eyeing Steve as they moved, and placed their hands on the wall.

"Police Department, may I help you?" droned the officer working the complaint desk in Communications.

"They're shooting across the street! Oh, dear God, they're killing each other!"

"Now, calm down, lady," said the officer flatly, "and tell me where you're at."

"They've shot a policeman, and he's lying in the street," she replied.

The officer's pencil scribbled. "Where are you?"

"I'm Esther Washington, I live on Slauson. My God, man, don't you care what's going on down here?"

"Where on Slau—"

"If you don't hurry, we'll all be killed."

The officer's voice tightened. "Mrs. Washington, just tell me where you live on Slauson, and I'll send help."

"At 5206 West Slauson."

As soon as he heard the address, he wrote it on the pad in front of him, tore off the sheet, and placed it on the conveyor belt on top of the complaint desk. It traveled the length of the complaint desk and was picked up by the officer working the link position.

The link picked up the slip. "Son-of-a-bitch," he said, keying the switch for all police frequencies in the metropolitan area.

"Southwest units in the vicinity and 3A71, officer needs help, shots fired, officer down, 5206 West Slauson Avenue, 3A71 your call is Code Three."

Hearing the link's broadcast, jaws and stomachs tightened in black-and-whites throughout the city. "3Adam71, roger," the officer shouted into the mike over the sound of siren and engine as his partner snaked their car through the snarl of traffic on Crenshaw Boulevard.

Lieutenant Bowen, the morning-watch commander, was already headed out of the station, thinking of a similar call two years ago; remembering that when he arrived at that scene, his younger brother lay dead, his stomach torn away by a shotgun blast. He had been a policeman only three months.

"Spread your feet. Don't move," Steve warned, "or I'll kill you both."

"Hey, man, we're just hitchhikers. We don't know these dudes. They just picked us up back on Western."

"Shut up." Steve stood trembling, holding the shotgun on the two, thinking, "If they move, I'll kill them. . . . Come on, guys, come on. Where in the hell are you?"

"Harry, you stay in this house," cried Wilma Casner, while her husband rummaged wildly through dresser drawers.

"You stay out of this, woman," said Harry, grabbing a twenty-two revolver. "That officer needs help."

"You fool, you go messin' around and get yourself killed," Wilma cried. But Harry was already at the door.

"I'll be careful, hon," he said, stepping out into the darkness on the porch, trying to force a left slipper onto a right foot.

"You call the police, Wilma, and tell them to send help." He was gone.

Steve felt the burning pain inside his stomach before he heard the shot. His legs buckled under him, a sudden taste of salt filled his mouth, and he fell forward, down into a roaring, buzzing sound. "Joy, help me. I don't want to die." He heard his shotgun roar and felt it jerk as his face hit the cool, damp grass.

The two young men spread-eagled against the house screamed. Their fingernails scraped the stucco wall as they fell, their bodies sawed through with pellets.

As Harry Casner rounded the front of his house, he saw the man in the rear seat of the Chevy sit up and shoot the officer. The officer fell forward, his shotgun firing as he struck the ground; the two men leaning against his house crumpled in blood. He heard his wife screaming inside the house. "My God," he thought, "this can't be happening." And then he was dead. The bullet struck him high on the forehead just below his receding hairline. He never heard the shot.

As Casner slumped to the ground, the man climbed from the rear seat of the Chevy, gun in hand. He was a big man, over six feet tall and weighing at least two hundred and twenty pounds. He wore a sweat-stained white T-shirt and faded Levi's. He walked to where Steve lay, knelt, and pulled Steve's pistol from its holster.

Flashes of pain caused lights to dance in Steve's eyes as the big man pulled at the pistol belt. Opening his eyes in the blur, Steve saw the big ugly face. "Fucking black pig!" the pockmarked, round face snarled, wrinkling the wide purple scar on the bridge of his broad nose.

The big man moved a knee to the small of Steve's back, shifting his weight to it; blood bubbled out of Steve's mouth, and he made a gurgling sound. The man's image blurred as the intense pain drove Steve into unconsciousness.

Patting the cop's buttocks, the big man pulled a black wallet from Steve's rear pocket, stuck it into his waistband, and stood up.

He turned to run, then hesitated, turning back. "Slave!" he growled angrily, and puckering his heavy lips, he spat on Steve. "Filthy black slave!" Then he ran for the corner and disappeared.

"KMA-367; 0115 hours," the car radio announced. But the men assigned to 3Adam81 didn't hear it.

By the time Lieutenant Bowen arrived, at least six other black-and-whites were there. Slauson Avenue was blocked now. Air-3, the division's police helicopter, clattered overhead, flooding the entire area with intense blue-white light. Sergeant Chuck Johnson, a short stocky Negro with piercing brown eyes, was shouting orders. He looked up as Bowen reached him.

"It's Conrad and Bennett," Johnson said. "Conrad's dead, and Bennett looks bad." Though Johnson spoke without emotion, Bowen noticed that his eyes were red and glazed.

The city ambulance screeched to a halt beside the patrol car where Conrad's body lay, and two uniformed attendants scrambled out, one carrying a first-aid kit. The driver of the ambulance looked at the bleeding bodies strewn about the two cars and the lawn. "Jesus," he breathed.

"Anderson, over here," shouted Lieutenant Bowen. The officer had been standing over Conrad's body. Now he moved. "I want you and your partner to maintain security on both cars, on Conrad's and the suspects'. I don't want anybody touching either one. We may need prints from both of them."

"Got it," said Anderson. He started back across the street toward the two cars.

Bowen crossed the street to the rear of the ambulance as the men slid the stretcher in. He looked at Bennett's motionless face, a trace of blood at the corner of his mouth.

"He's alive," said Sergeant Johnson.

"Good."

"Wilson, you ride with Bennett in the ambulance," Johnson said.

"Right, Sarge."

One attendant climbed into the rear with the officers. The other swung the doors closed. From across the street an officer waved and shouted. "Hey, wait. One of these guys is still alive." One of the men cut down by Bennett's shotgun was stirring, moaning.

"That's a goddamn shame!"

"Let the son-of-a-bitch die; Bennett can't wait."

The ambulance driver stood motionless, looking at Bowen.

"Pick the son-of-a-bitch up," Bowen said, "and hurry."

The two attendants quickly removed another stretcher from the ambulance and moved toward the two bodies near the house.

"Lieutenant," said Sergeant Johnson, "71's got a wit or a suspect in their car over there. They haven't been able to get anything out of her, though. She's hysterical."

"We think that's her old man over there on the lawn," Johnson added.

"Okay, Chuck," Bowen said, surveying the scene. "I've got two men on the black-and-white and the suspects' car. I want you to seal off the whole damn block. Put men on every intersection. I don't want a goddamn cockroach to get in or out of here. The only people I want moving are policemen. Everybody else, I want in their house.

"After you've got it sealed off, organize search teams and sweep through the shooting scene. When you locate anything that looks like any kind of evidence, put a man on it, but don't touch it or move it. Get a log started, so we know who's assigned to what and who we've got down here.

"I'll get back to the station, call the skipper, and get the detectives down here to start putting this mess together so we'll know what the hell happened. Any questions?"

The sergeant, busy making notes, looked up. "I'm going to need the whole damn watch to cover this, so we'll want help from someone, to watch the store. And another thing, somebody should go get Bennett's wife to the hospital. If he's going to go, she should be there."

Bowen put an unlit cigarette between his lips and then removed it. "I don't want his name broadcast on the radio, because the newshawks are no doubt listening. Send a unit to the station to get his address, and then have them pick up his wife. And have them take Shirl from the desk. They'll need a policewoman to stay with the kid."

The ambulance pulled away, the siren drowning all talk.

Bowen watched, along with the others. The blinking red and amber lights of the police cars cast a firelike glow on the black surface of the street, around the men. Six people lay dead, one a policeman. The dead officer's police car sat quietly, the motor still idling.

"Pardon me, Lieutenant."

Bowen turned and saw the press pass clipped to the shirt collar of a large, broad-shouldered Negro. A portable tape recorder hung around his neck; a mike was in his hand.

"Lieutenant, I'm Charles Mann, from KBCA-TV, and I wonder if you might brief me on what has happened here," said the reporter.

Bowen eyed him for a moment. He wished he could tell him to go to hell. "The only facts we have available at this time are that we have six people dead of gunshot wounds, one of those six a Los Angeles police officer. In addition to that, we have two other men critically wounded and en route to the hospital. One of those is another Los Angeles police officer. That's all the information I have available right now, and I won't answer any questions at this time."

"Thank you very much, Lieutenant," replied the

reporter, switching off the machine. He made no move to leave.

"If you intend to stay," Bowen said, pointing, "stay at the command post Sergeant Johnson is establishing over there."

"No, sir," said the reporter. "I'll leave, but before I do, could you tell—"

"I said, no questions now."

He watched the reporter walk away. "He'll interview the neighborhood and have his own version on the evening news before we even start to figure this thing out," he thought angrily. "Stupid son-of-a-bitch." Bowen crossed the street, put the unlit cigarette in his mouth, and patted his pockets. Searching for a match, he walked to where Conrad lay.

He took the unlit cigarette from his mouth as he looked down. Conrad's eyes and mouth were open. Bowen's face was expressionless. He replaced the cigarette between his lips, turned, and walked to his car.

"Johnson," he said, "tell 3A71 to take that woman to the hospital and get her calmed down."

Johnson nodded.

Bowen climbed into his car, started it up, then took the tired cigarette from his mouth, tossed it out the window, and drove away.

Sharon Gunning heard the telephone ringing and shook her sleeping husband. "Dave . . . Dave . . . get the phone."

Gunning groped in the darkness, picked up the telephone in the middle of a ring. "Gunning. . . ."

"Captain, this is Lieutenant Bowen," came the voice over the phone. "We've had an officer killed. . . ."

Gunning sat up. "Who? . . ."

"It was Conrad, Skipper," Bowen said. "Bennett got hit, too, and he's at Daniel Freeman Hospital in critical condition."

"Is the suspect dead?"

"We've got six D.B.'s at the scene," Bowen said.

"Six!" Gunning shouted in disbelief.

"Yes, sir," Bowen said, "and we don't know what in the hell happened. They had a hot roller, but one of our D.B.'s is wearing a bathrobe and house slippers. We don't know where in the hell he fits in."

A pause.

"Any suspects get away?"

"We don't know, Captain. Sergeant Johnson is down there now, with the area sealed off. He's got men knocking on doors looking for wits, and 3A71 has a wit or possible suspect, but she's too damn hysterical to talk now."

"Okay, Jim, I'll be down in about fifteen minutes. . . . On the radio in about five, if you need me."

"Right, Captain." Bowen hung up.

Sharon Gunning lay quietly in the darkness as her husband placed the phone back in its cradle.

"We've had a shooting," Gunning said as he swung his feet to the carpeted floor. "We've got one officer dead and another close. . . . We've also got five other people dead. Jesus Christ, this'll be a big mess, no matter what happened. . . . Watts Festival coming up in a few days . . ."

Sharon pushed the blankets aside, reaching for her robe. "Why you, Dave?" she said in a bitter tone. "Don't the detectives handle these things?"

Gunning flashed her a heated look, not answering. He switched on the light on the dresser, pulled on his watch, picked up a blue shirt, and walked toward the bathroom. "Son-of-a-bitch," he said as the bathroom door closed.

The phone rang in the watch commanders' office. Annoyed by the interruption, Bowen picked up the phone. "Lieutenant Bowen."

"Lieutenant, this is Wilson, at the hospital with Bennett."

"How is he?"

"Bad. He's in surgery now. It doesn't look good. But, the main reason I called, Lieutenant, is because Bennett's gun is missing."

"What?"

"I said, Bennett's gun—"

Bowen cut in, "I heard that. Where in the hell is it?"

"I checked the ambulance, it's not there. . . . I don't know."

"Okay, I'll call Johnson on the radio; maybe they've found it," Bowen replied.

"Another thing," Wilson added. "This place is crawling with reporters bugging the hell out of me about what happened. What should I tell them?"

"I could suggest something, but you and I would be out of a job," Bowen said. "Don't tell them shit. The skipper is on his way, and he'll decide what to tell them. Stall them for a while, Wilson."

"Okay, Lieutenant." Wilson hung up.

"Bennett's gun is missing," Bowen said. The group gathered in the watch commander's office stared.

Joy woke up when she heard car doors slamming. The lighted clock on the nightstand read one-forty. Someone coming home from a night out. She closed her eyes, trying to think of the last time she and Steve had been out on a Saturday night.

She was dozing off again when the doorbell rang.

"Who is it?" She stood in the darkened living room. "Police officers, Mrs. Bennett." She opened the door to two uniformed officers and a policewoman.

A rush of sudden fear left Joy breathless as she studied the sober trio. "Please . . . come in," she managed in a shaken tone.

"Mrs. Bennett, I'm Shirl Baker," the woman said. "These officers work with your husband."

Husband! The word exploded in Joy's head. "Steve!" she screamed. "My God, what happened?"

"Your husband has been shot, but he's alive. . . ."

"3L30 to 3L90, go ahead."

Bowen recognized Sergeant Johnson's voice. "3L90 to 3L30," Bowen answered. "The officer transported by the G-unit is missing his weapon. Do you have any information on its location?"

"3L30, negative. No information now. Let me check with my people down here and give you a call back."

"3L90, roger," Bowen answered, and put down the mike. He put an unlit cigarette in his mouth and then removed it. "Conners," he called to the officer working the front desk.

"Yes, sir."

"Screen all my calls. I don't want to be bugged with anything not priority. I've got a number of calls to make, and I don't want to be interrupted."

"Right, Lieutenant."

Bowen put the unlit cigarette back into his mouth, picked up a pencil, and began to write:

8/20/0150 A.M.; Notifications.

Divisional Commander
Homicide

Prints
Photo Lab
Communications
Divisional Detectives
Officers' Families

Bowen stopped writing, sat back in his chair, and surveyed the silent faces of the six men watching him. He searched his pockets for a match; finding none, he removed the cigarette from his mouth.

"Anybody know Conrad's wife?" he asked.

The station sergeant for the night said, "I do. He was a classmate of mine in the academy. We used to go to the drags with our wives, but I haven't seen her for a year or so."

"Okay, you're it," Bowen said. "Jesus Christ, we don't even have a policewoman to send with you."

"I worked with Conrad quite a bit," said another officer. "I'll go along."

"Okay, fine," Bowen said. He wrote their names on the pad in front of him. Then he said, "See if you can find a neighbor who knows her well; you'll need a woman's help. After you get there, give me a call."

The sergeant and the officer nodded and left.

"Who in the fuck's got a match?" Bowen asked, his voice angry.

Sergeant Johnson, standing at the rear of his black-and-white station wagon, wrote on the yellow pad in front of him:

0150; 3L90 reports Officer Bennett's pistol missing. Requests command post check for same at scene.

Finishing, he looked up and called, "Lewis."

"Right here."

"Lewis," Johnson said, "go around and check with everybody down here and see if anybody picked up Bennett's gun."

"That's going to take some time."

"It's not going to take more than five minutes, Lewis," Johnson said.

"Right, Sarge." The officer turned and disappeared into the darkness.

Bowen ran his finger down the department telephone directory spread before him. "Communications Division," he said, squinting as his finger located it on the directory. "2614," he repeated as he dialed the number.

Bowen drew heavily on his cigarette.

"Communications, Sergeant Watson," said the voice.

Bowen exhaled the smoke from his lungs. "Watson, this is Lieutenant Bowen, Southwest; we want to know where our help call came from."

"Right, Lieutenant," replied the sergeant. "We were just about to call you. It was a citizen's call, a Mrs. Esther Washington of 5206 West Slauson; she's your person reporting."

"What was her address again?" Bowen made notes on the pad before him.

"5206 West Slauson," the sergeant said. "We've got her phone number if you want it."

"No, we'll go see her." Bowen crushed his cigarette and started to hang up the phone.

"Lieutenant . . . ?"

"Yeah."

"Lieutenant," the sergeant asked, "we were wondering, how's the other officer?"

"He's alive."

"Okay, Lieutenant, and if we can do anything, give us a call."

"Right." Bowen hung up.

"Lieutenant," the desk officer called, "Wilson from the hospital on eight-two."

"Right." Bowen turned back to the phone. "Yeah, Wilson," he said.

"Lieutenant, I've got some news."

Wilson's voice was unsteady. Bennett? Bowen steeled himself. "Let's have it, Wilson."

"The suspect that rode down with us is dead," Wilson said.

Bowen felt relieved. Bennett must still be alive.

"That's not the good part, Lieutenant," Wilson added carefully. "The suspect was J. D. Ward, Councilman Ward's kid."

"Christ," Bowen said, and then, urgently, "How do you know it's him? You could be wrong."

"One of the nurses down here knows his family," Wilson said, "and she recognized him."

"Okay," Bowen said, as his mind churned with the possible situations that the death of the councilman's son could create. "Has the councilman been notified?"

"Yeah, the nurse that knows them called," Wilson answered. "But she didn't tell them their son was dead. Just that he had been shot. He's on his way here now, Lieutenant."

Bowen scribbled notes on the pad as he asked, "How's Bennett?"

"They're still working on him, Lieutenant, so I assume he's alive."

"Good . . . good," Bowen said, and asked, "Has his wife arrived?"

"No, sir," Wilson answered, "but 3A71 showed up with some screaming broad. The press ate that up, took a helluva bunch of pictures."

"How many reporters do you have there?" Bowen asked.

"About eight."

"Do they know it's Ward's son?"

"No, sir," Wilson replied. "They don't even know he's dead yet."

"Okay, Wilson, stick with it. I'll try to get a sergeant down there before the councilman shows. Keep me posted. . . . What a goddamn mess," Bowen said, slamming the telephone down.

The black-and-white jerked to a halt at the hospital's emergency entrance, and a group of men moved down the ramp toward the patrol car.

"Stand back, goddammit," the officer said, opening the rear door for Joy.

"Who's this?"

"A suspect?"

"You under arrest, lady?"

They pushed forward; flash bulbs went off. Joy held a Kleenex to her face as cameras flashed. One of the officers took her by the arm.

A reporter shoved a microphone into her face. "Do you have any comment on the slayings?"

"Get the hell out of here." Joy's escort guided her firmly through the swinging doors, reporters streaming along behind. Cameras clicked and flashed. A nurse passed, walking quickly, carrying a tray of instruments covered with a white towel.

"Down here, we've got a room for her," someone yelled. A door opened. Joy hesitated at the door of the lounge. A patrolman came over to her.

"I'm Officer Wilson, Mrs. Bennett. I rode down here in the ambulance with your husband. He's in the operating room now, and I'm sure they'll let us know as soon as there's any news."

Joy drew a deep breath. "Where did Steve get hit?"

"In the lower back," Wilson said. "It could have been a lot worse."

Joy closed her eyes tightly and bowed her head.

"You okay, Mrs. Bennett?" Wilson asked.

"I'll be okay," Joy said without looking up. She wished she could be alone.

Another officer stuck his head in the door. "Excuse me; Lieutenant Bowen wants you on the phone at the receiving desk," he said to Wilson.

Joy sat huddled in her chair. The room was silent, bright with light, and smelled of antiseptic. She was cold. Her lips felt numb; she began to shake. "Steve . . . oh, Steve . . ." she thought. "Don't die. Honey, please don't die." Suddenly the tears poured out. She began to sob loudly.

"You holding a call for me?" Wilson asked the nurse behind the receiving desk.

"Line three," she said without looking up.

Wilson reached over the desk and punched the blinking light. "Wilson," he said into the receiver.

"Wilson, this is Bowen, I just talked to Lieutenant Clark, the Seventy-seventh Division watch commander. I briefed him on the situation and asked him to come and help you at the hospital."

"Good," Wilson replied, watching the cluster of newsmen gathered around a coffee machine.

"I think the shit will hit the fan when the councilman finds out his son was killed," Bowen said.

"No doubt about that, Lieutenant."

"Any word on Bennett?"

"No, sir," Wilson replied, adding, "His wife is here now."

"Good," Bowen said. "And tell Rice and Homes to stay with her."

"Okay."

"Has 71 got anything out of that woman yet?"

"Not yet, Lieutenant," Wilson said. "There's only two doctors on duty here, and they're both working on Bennett."

"Okay, Wilson, Clark should be there soon. Oh . . . Wilson."

"Yeah, Lieutenant."

"See if you can't get a room somewhere down there that has an outside line, so we can get you without going through that goddamn switchboard."

"I'll get right on it, Lieutenant," Wilson said. The patrolman assigned to keeping reporters away from Joy Bennett came down the hall. "Mrs. Bennett's getting pretty bad," he said to the nurse. "Could you come take a look?"

"Of course." The nurse rose instantly. The three started for the room, and the reporters followed.

"What's going on?" asked the *Times,* sipping his coffee.

"How the hell should I know?" answered the *Examiner.*

"Maybe another one died."

Joy was crying hysterically now.

The nurse put her arm around Joy. "Come on, honey," she said. "Let's lie down on the bed."

"Leave me alone," she screamed.

The nurse lifted Joy onto one of the beds, covering her. Joy drew up her knees and sobbed, small, animal-like cries from deep inside.

"Watch her for a minute, fellows. I'll get her something to calm her down," the nurse said as she pulled the bed rail up into the lock position. The officers nodded silently as the nurse left the room.

"3L30 to 3L90," Sgt. Johnson said into the hand-held mike as he stood at the rear of his station wagon. He turned to the tall, slender officer at his side, "Fisher, give me that F.I."

"3L90 go ahead 30," Bowen answered.

"3L30 to 90, negative on the location of the pistol. Unable to locate it; but we have turned up an eyeball wit," Johnson said.

"3L90, roger on the gun," Bowen said. Then he asked, "Who's your wit, and what info have you got from him?"

"3L30," Johnson replied, reading from the field interview card, "the wit is Melvin O. Lewis, of 5213 West Slauson. According to the officers who talked to him, he was putting his car in the garage when 81 made the stop. Anyway, to make a long story short, the wit says we've got an outstanding suspect. And that the suspect took Bennett's pistol."

"Goddamn."

"Yes, sir," Johnson said.

"Any description?" Bowen asked, disregarding radio procedure.

"3L30," Johnson answered, "the wit's only description is that he's a big ugly dude."

"That's not enough information." Bowen's voice was ragged with anger. "Get a better description and put out a crime broadcast as soon as possible."

"Roger, 3L90," Johnson said.

"3L30," Bowen added, "you've got another wit at 5206 West Slauson. She's the one that put in the help call. Her name is Esther Washington."

"Roger," Johnson answered, "and further, 3L90, wit Lewis reports the D.B. wearing the robe and slippers is his neighbor who was trying to help the officers. Lewis says the outstanding suspect shot him and Bennett."

"Poor bastard," Bowen said. Then, "Roger, 3L30, I'll call 71 at the hospital and tell them. Apparently that's his wife they've got there."

"Roger, must be," Johnson answered. "I'll get a team over to interview her right away and call you back. And I'll get out a crime broadcast as soon as possible on the outstanding suspect."

"Roger, 3L30, what's the situation with the press down there?"

"About six reporters here now," Johnson replied. "Central homicide, prints, and the coroner are here, too."

"Roger." Bowen sighed. "You'll know what to tell them."

Dave Gunning pulled his Oldsmobile into the parking space marked, "Commander," at the rear of the Southwest Division Station, and glanced at his watch as he slid out of the car. It was two-ten A.M.; the morning air was crisp and cool, and for a brief moment he enjoyed it.

"Good morning, Skipper."

"Good morning, Green." Gunning walked quickly toward the watch commander's office. There was an attractive, mini-clad Negro woman sitting on the bench at the rear of the holding tank behind the heavy protective shatterproof glass. She smiled at him as their eyes met. He wondered how she would be. On the door of the holding tank hung a rectangular blue slip of paper. On it Gunning read, "0145, Susie Smith; 647B; PC. Prostitution; Williams and Clayton; SWD/Vice." He hadn't needed to guess.

Lieutenant Bowen was hanging up the telephone as Gunning entered.

"'Morning, Captain," Bowen said. "The situation has—"

Suddenly the radio blared with many voices.

"You fucking pig, let him go."

"Kill the pigs," a woman's voice screamed. The radio crackled.

"Officer needs—"

"You bastard."

The officers stood frozen, staring at the radio.

A man screamed, "He's hurt!"

A hysterical female voice shrieked over and over, "Let him go!"

"Officer needs help! Slauson and Overhill. Get us some . . ."

The link's voice overrode urgently. "All units, officer needs help. Slauson and Overhill. Any unit in the vicinity identify and handle, Code Three."

Instantly, an excited voice answered, "12A27 will handle the call." In the background the siren began to wail.

"12A27, roger," replied the link. "Your call is Code Three."

The officers standing in the watch commander's office took off, headed for their black-and-whites.

Other uniformed officers ran down the hall past the office and out the rear door.

A voice on the radio shouted, "3A9, shots fired at Slauson and Overhill. We need more help. We've got about two hundred people here pelting us with rocks and bottles."

"3A9, roger," said the link. "Units in the vicinity, OFFICER NEEDS HELP, a major 415 with shots fired, at Slauson and Overhill. Any units available to handle, identify."

"3T34, rolling to Slauson and Overhill."

"Roger, 3Tom34, your call is Code Two," the link answered.

"13A43, responding to Slauson and Overhill."

The link responded, "13A43, roger, back up 3Tom34 at Slauson and Overhill, Code Two."

"3A98, we've got an officer injured. We need

an ambulance." The voice on the mike was harsh and broken.

The link answered, "3Adam98, roger. 13A43, use caution. Other units responding Code Three to the location."

"3A9, advise units responding to Slauson and Overhill that the crowd has Slauson blocked east of Overhill, and they should approach Slauson on Overhill from the north or south. And further, the crowd took the injured officer's shotgun."

"Roger, 3A9," the link said. "Units responding to Slauson and Overhill be advised, Slauson is blocked by a major 415 east of Overhill, and 3A9 advises a north or south approach on Overhill. Additional 3A9 reports the injured officer's shotgun was taken by unknown suspects in the crowd."

"What in the hell is going on, Bowen?" Gunning said angrily, thinking something had been kept from him.

"I don't know," Bowen said defensively. "This has—"

"Call communications and tell them we're going to a tactical alert," Gunning interrupted. He started for the door. "I'm going to my office to call the duty deputy chief and advise him what we've got. Right back."

Bowen picked up the telephone, "He jumps on my ass . . . goddammit," he mumbled.

Gunning opened the door into the front hallway and lobby. As always on a Saturday night, it was full of people. The pimps in their sharkskin suits, there with their bail bondsmen to bail out their whores. The wives and mothers in their bathrobes and hair curlers, there to bail out a drunken husband or son, after a call in the middle of the night; worried parents, here to pick up their teen-ager who just took his first joy ride in a stolen car or dropped his first red; the swollen-faced wife, here with her crying, frightened children to make a crime report against the husband who beat her; the well-dressed businessman, here to report his car stolen or his wallet picked clean by a prostitute. They all sat thrown together in the station lobby, waiting to tell their problem to the desk officers.

Crossing the crowded lobby, Gunning smelled the heavy odor of perfume, sweat, and cigarette smoke.

"Hey, there's some brass," the *Times* said as Lieutenant Clark entered the emergency room through the swinging double doors.

"Yeah, maybe he'll have more brains than that other dumb shit, Wilson," the *Morning Sun* added.

Clark, seeing the newsmen moving toward him, crushed his Marlboro in an ashtray on the receiving desk.

Clark had been a lieutenant for only four months. Being a police lieutenant was tough, but being a black lieutenant had its own special problems. Clark had learned to handle the problems. The men assigned to his watch at Seventy-seventh Division thought of him as a lieutenant who just happens to be a Negro, not a Negro lieutenant. That was the way Clark wanted it.

"Lieutenant," called the *Times*.

"I'll have some information for you in just a few minutes," Clark said. They closed around him.

"That's what we were told forty minutes ago," the Santa Barbara *Press* yelled angrily.

Clark turned sharply, looking at the reporter. The reporter looked self-consciously at the notepad in his hand.

"I'm sure you can appreciate the department's position in this situation," Clark said carefully, not

taking his eye off the reporter. "The families of the
victims are our first consideration. It takes time to
evaluate the circumstances surrounding this incident. You will no doubt have questions about the
condition of the people that are here at the hospital,
and what role they played in the incident. So if you
will excuse me, I'll check on that and be back
shortly." He pushed through the circle of reporters.

"Give one of them a little rank, and it goes right
to his head," said a reporter as Clark walked down
the hall.

Wilson flicked on the light in the doctors' lounge
and picked up the telephone. When the lounge door
opened, Wilson turned. "Yeah?"

"I'm Clark, from Seventy-seventh Division,"
Clark said, extending a hand to Wilson. "Your
watch commander asked me to come out and lend
you a hand."

"Glad to have ya," Wilson said, grasping
Clark's hand, wondering where this man's loyalty
would be once he knew the situation.

"Okay, this is it. Watch for 15528." Sergeant
Robinson drove the black-and-white slowly down
Donovan Way. He and Stewart had been silent
the whole ride from the station.

"That's it," Stewart said, "the one with the
hedge."

They pulled to the curb and sat silently looking
at the house, a large two-story brick partially
covered with ivy. A curved walk led to the front
door, where a bicycle lay in the wet grass.

"Well, let's do it," Robinson said, opening the
door. Stewart walked up the path of the house
next door and rang the bell, while Robinson waited
on the sidewalk. A plump woman in a bathrobe

and a short balding man came to the door. Robinson saw the woman bury her face in her hands. After a moment the two came down the walk with Stewart.

"This is Mr. and Mrs. Wagner; they're friends of the Conrads," Stewart said.

Robinson nodded.

They walked slowly up the flagstone path to the Conrads' door, making an arc around the front wheel of the bicycle. Robinson shivered as he rang the bell. A small dog began barking inside the house.

"That's Smoky," Mrs. Wagner said. The door swung open. A young blond boy smiled widely at them. "You guys work with my dad?" The poodle stuck his head between the boy's legs.

"Get back, Smoky." He pushed the dog with his bare foot.

"Who is it, Jeff?" Helen Conrad came into the room, tying her robe.

"It's the fuzz and Mr. and Mrs. Wagner."

When she looked at them, her lips turned white. "Jeffrey, take Smoky and go to your room. Don't wake your brother."

"What's wrong, Mom?"

"Do as I say, Jeffrey." The boy picked up the dog and ran up the stairs, calling, "Mom, ask them if they work with Dad."

"Wayne told me a long time ago how it would be," she said softly to no one in particular. "I'm just not ready. I mean, it's too sudden. I just ironed his shirt . . . today's . . . I'm just not ready."

Mrs. Wagner put her arms around Helen's shoulders and led her to a chair.

"What will I do, Ruth?" Helen said without looking up. Tears were streaming down her face. "They killed my Wayne, Ruth. They killed my husband,

and I wasn't ready. They . . ." She began to scream. "They killed him, they killed my husband. . . ."

The car's three radios came to life as Bowen twisted the ignition key.

". . . Back to your location, 3L30," the radio said. "That's a roger, 3A58." Bowen recognized Johnson's voice. "There's maybe 300 in the group now, 3L30."

"KMA-367, 0225 hours. Attention all units, all divisions," the link said. "This is a tactical-alert broadcast. There is a major disturbance in Southwest Division at Slauson and Overhill. The following divisions are now on tactical-alert status: Southwest, Newton, Seventy-seventh Street, Wilshire, and A.I.D. Stand by."

"Okay, Jim, let's have it," Gunning said as they swung on to LaSalle Avenue.

Bowen was abrupt. "Councilman Ward's son is one of the suspects, and he's dead."

"Jesus Christ," Gunning muttered. After a second, "What a goddamn mess. Does Ward know this yet?"

"He knows the kid's been shot, but not that he's dead or that he's been shot by the police," Bowen said. "I've got Clark, the Seventy-seventh watch commander, out at the hospital, helping our people," he added, slowing to a stop for a red light. There was no traffic in the intersection, and Bowen went on again, through the red light.

"How's Bennett doing?" Gunning asked.

"I talked to Wilson while you were in your office," Bowen said. "He's at the hospital, and the only information he had was that they were still working on Bennett."

"How about notification to Conrad's family?"

"We've taken care of that. Bennett's wife is at

the hospital now, too." Bowen turned right onto Slauson Avenue. "We've got Shirl from the desk staying with his kid."

"Good. Do we have any outstanding suspects?"

"We've got one," Bowen said matter-of-factly. "The suspect took Bennett's gun. Confirmed. Eyeball wit. Johnson put out a broadcast."

"Okay," Gunning said. "Now, what's causing all this shit at Slauson and Overhill?"

Bowen slowed the car as they approached Slauson and Crenshaw. Slauson and Overhill was still eight blocks away, but traffic on Slauson was at a standstill. Cars and people clogged the street. Bowen turned northbound on Crenshaw.

"Pigs . . . Pigs . . . Honky mothers. . . ." came from a group of Negroes standing on the corner.

"Goddamn apes," Bowen muttered, watching the group fade into the darkness in the rear-view mirror. "Johnson stationed a black-and-white at Slauson and Overhill. He put them there to divert traffic around the scene. They were routing the westbound traffic on Slauson, north and south on Overhill. A crowd gathered. Then, some goddamn drunk threw a wine bottle at their black-and-white. It broke the windshield. Anyway, they bagged him out of the crowd, got him cuffed and in the rear of their car when the crowd decided to rescue him." Bowen paused. "So they rescued their drunken brother," he continued. "They also beat the one officer severely. The sons-of-bitches also took the shotgun from the car. Anyway, that was what we heard on the radio when the officers were trying to request help."

"Who are the officers?" Gunning asked.

"3A9," Bowen said, "Edwards and Miller. Edwards took the beating."

"What about the shots fired?"

"Johnson said Miller told him the suspect that took the shotgun fired it in the air," Bowen said, turning the car south onto Overhill.

"They should have shot the bastard."

"According to Johnson, Miller would have, but the bad guy ran into the crowd," Bowen said.

They could see the red and amber lights of the police cars flashing in the darkness around the intersection of Slauson and Overhill as they approached. Bowen pulled to the curb behind a black-and-white. The two men got out and walked around several police cars parked at various angles in the street. Their radios filled the morning darkness with loud, crackling static.

The two walked to the intersection, where a group of policemen were gathered around a black-and-white. The men moved back when Bowen and Gunning approached. The windshield was shattered, broken glass scattered over the front seat and floor. The shotgun was missing from its rack. The rear seat was splattered with blood. Beside the car lay a crushed police hat.

Gunning trembled with rage. He could feel the heat mounting in his ears and face as he fought to control the urge to curse.

Bowen stood silent, waiting.

"I was just about to form a line and clear those people out of there," Sergeant Johnson said, looking at Bowen and Gunning.

For the first time since their arrival, Gunning heard the rising shouts and taunts behind him. He turned to face the growing noise of the crowd stirring restlessly, about three-quarters of a block away. He estimated their number at two hundred.

"So, you silly bastards want to play war," Gunning said, eyeing the mob. "Okay, Sergeant, I'll take over. How many people do you have here?"

"Thirty-eight, Skipper."

"Okay," Gunning said, his thoughts racing ahead, laying out strategy. He glanced about at the faces surrounding him. They were sober, angry, some young, some old, some he knew, some he had never seen before. "Men, we're going to clear these people off the street and restore order, before this thing has any chance of snowballing. I want each of you to keep in mind that we're not going to act as individuals. We're going to work as a team. I don't want any overreaction. I know you're angry. We've taken a couple of hard punches this morning, but, goddammit"—his voice was beginning to show the anger he felt—"we're professionals, and we're going to act like it. Now," he added looking over the group, "get your helmets, and we'll go to work."

The group moved to their cars, opening the trunks, snapping on their helmets.

"Bowen," Gunning said, "you take the left flank; Johnson, you take the right. I'll take the center. I don't want anybody taking any individual action," he cautioned. "Our job will be to keep the men in a straight line and to assign the reserves when arrests start being made. Any questions?"

"Yes, sir," Bowen said. "How about the dispersal order?"

"Screw it," Gunning said with authority. "They've taken a prisoner from us, beaten one of our men, and stolen a shotgun. . . . Screw the dispersal order. Let 'em take some lumps."

"Lieutenant!" an officer shouted, running to Bowen. "Look down there. They're starting a fire!"

They saw the red ball of fire (it looked like a burning gas can, Bowen thought), traveling in a high arc, then dropping and crashing through a plate-glass window of a dress shop. Immediately the window display was engulfed in flames. The crowd roared its approval.

"Johnson," Gunning ordered, "get on the radio and report the fire. Have communications tell the fire department to come to our location and stand by. Under no circumstances are they to go to the fire directly. Make sure they get that clear."

"Yes, sir," Johnson said, turning to the nearest black-and-white.

"Okay, Bowen," Gunning said, watching the fire growing inside the dress shop, "get 'em lined up. Put twenty-five on the line, and keep the rest in reserve."

"Right, Skipper," Bowen said, snapping the chin strap to his helmet. "Okay, guys, line up on the street."

The group of white-helmeted officers moved, forming a line across Slauson Avenue. They stood with batons in a port-arms position, facing the crowd. Rocks, bricks, and bottles traveled through the air, falling, smashing on the street, short of the police line. The yelling and taunting grew louder.

"Come on, pigs. . . . Waiting on the machine guns, pigs. . . . Where's the gas for the women and children, pigs? . . . Pigs eat shit."

The helmeted line moved forward slowly, the jingle of handcuff keys and the twisting of leather its only noise.

A hush fell over the crowd as the helmeted line advanced, and their numbers diminished as the line approached. They slipped away, down side streets, between houses, over fences, silently. Now the dominating noise was that of the dress-shop fire, which had already broken through a skylight, sending glowing embers into the darkness of the morning sky.

The police line drew nearer. The remainder of

the crowd broke into a run, retreating. The white helmets maintained their same rhythmic, disciplined pace.

Jacob D. Ward, Sr., had been a city councilman for eight years, and had long ago established himself as the voice of the black community. This year, he was running for mayor. Though the fight against a popular white incumbent was an uphill battle, political observers acknowledged that no one had a better shot at becoming the first black mayor of Los Angeles than the councilman.

Ward sat quietly staring ahead as his deputy, Russell LeBlanc, drove the black Cadillac south on the San Diego Freeway through West Los Angeles.

"How in the hell could he do it?" he wondered silently. "Probably another fight over some whore. When did I last see him? Was it last month, or the month before?" He couldn't remember.

"Did they say how serious his injury was, Russell?" Ward asked his deputy.

"No, sir, they didn't," LeBlanc said in his usual businesslike tone.

"Damn, I hope it's not serious. Things are going too well to have anything go wrong now, Russell."

"Yes, sir, things are going very well. I thought your handling of the audience tonight was excellent, and I'm sure it's going to help our campaign in the valley," LeBlanc said confidently.

Ward glanced at his slender young deputy. "Thank you, Russell. Thank you."

LeBlanc loved Ward as a father. Ward was everything he ever wanted to be. Tall, broad-shouldered, with straight black hair graying at the temples. A sincere, honest face, a voice that could keep you on the edge of your seat with a low whisper, or make you tremble as it shook with rage.

He had first met Ward when the councilman sat in on a round-table debate, while LeBlanc was still in law school. The topic was "Is a Police Review Board Necessary?" LeBlanc remembered how the councilman had creamed one of his opponents, a white police sergeant, during the debate. LeBlanc learned two things that day. One, that words used properly could accomplish practically any goal, and two, that Councilman Ward would be the black leader of the decade.

For four years LeBlanc had worked long and hard trying to impress the councilman, and during the last Council election he had really proven his worth.

In the closing weeks of the campaign, the polls showed Ward's opponent, Tyron Brown, to have a slight lead. After many nights of digging, LeBlanc finally found that Brown had a white mistress. With a payoff to the white girl, he had been able to obtain pictures.

At first, Ward had rejected them, saying that he could win an election without blackmail. Day after day, LeBlanc pleaded with him. The polls indicated trouble, and besides, if Brown would sleep with white, he'd sell out to white. When his standing in the polls continued to slide, Ward finally told LeBlanc that what he didn't know wouldn't hurt him. LeBlanc understood.

Two days later, Brown withdrew from the race and announced his support for Ward, and Ward won the election by a landslide. The next day, a *Times* headline read, "MASSIVE SUPPORT SHOWS WARD A RISING BLACK POLITICAL FORCE."

After the election, LeBlanc became his chief deputy, and now he was his campaign manager. The mayoral campaign was going extremely well.

The press had been providing excellent coverage, invitations for speaking engagements poured in, and most important of all, Mayor Abbott was in trouble with the City Council over the new Rapid Transit Railway and the threat of a refuse workers' strike.

The report of Ward's son being shot had reached them as the councilman concluded an address to the valley's WECAN organization.

Women-Effecting-Changes-in-America-Now was a strong political force in the valley area of the city, and LeBlanc had long sought their support. It seemed that the councilman's fiery address tonight, blasting Mayor Abbott's do-little administration, had finally won them that support.

As the Cadillac left the freeway at Century Boulevard, Ward reflected on his relationship with his son. Since his election to the City Council, when J.D. was ten, Ward had had little time for his family. But it was during the boy's senior year at Crenshaw High that things had begun to fall apart. J.D. had begun staying out late, sometimes not coming home at all until the next afternoon. Ward had been maintaining a strenuous speaking schedule and would hardly have been aware of his son's absences if it had not been for his wife, Sarah. She pleaded with him to talk to J.D., to find out what was wrong, and a long series of bitter arguments between Ward and his son began.

The arguing ended on Jacob Jr.'s graduation day. Ward had accepted the senior class's invitation to speak at the ceremony, and Sarah had made dinner reservations for four—J.D. was bringing a girl friend, and this would be the first time the Wards had ever met her.

But on the day before the ceremony, Ward was shocked to learn from LeBlanc that he was scheduled to address a group of prominent party leaders and financial backers in Sacramento on graduation night. The fund-raising dinner was too important to miss.

Sarah's eyes turned cold and stony when he tried to explain. Jacob Jr. was furious, finally screaming in his father's face, "You'd sell your own mother if it'd buy you a lousy vote!" Ward struck his son hard across the mouth, and J.D. ran from the house.

Soon after graduation, the boy moved to his own apartment, and Sarah informed Ward that she had decided to spend the summer with her family in Philadelphia. He could not change her mind.

LeBlanc turned the polished Cadillac into the hospital parking lot, and both men saw the three police cars at the emergency entrance. Many other cars were parked around them, most with press signs on their windshields.

"I don't like the looks of this, Russell," Ward said.

LeBlanc said nothing as he eased the big car into a parking spot. He eyed the newsmen around the emergency entrance with growing fear.

"Hey, there's Ward now," shouted the *Chronicle*.

"That's him, let's go, Ben," a cameraman said, shouldering his heavy equipment.

Coffee cups were hurriedly set down, and cigarettes crushed out as the group of reporters pushed through the door.

Ward saw the familiar faces. He adjusted his tie and straightened his back.

The floodlight of a television camera caused Ward to squint as the group of reporters closed around him. Microphones were crowded in front of his face.

"Councilman Ward," said Bill Hart with professional smoothness, "on behalf of KBAC, I'd like to extend my deepest sympathy to you and your family. Do you have any idea at this point whether your son's death will affect your race for mayor?"

Ward's face opened in shock. The only sound was the electric whir of tape recorders and cameras. "Dead . . . ?" he said in disbelief. Cameras flashed; pencils scribbled.

"Councilman," Hart asked with wonder in his voice, "are we to understand that the police department has not informed you that a policeman has shot and killed your son?"

Tears rushed to Ward's eyes. He raised his hand awkwardly to his face. "I'm certain . . ." His voice quavered. Cameras flashed. "I'm certain . . ." His voice broke, and tears poured down his face.

LeBlanc interrupted sharply. "Gentlemen, I'm sure you can see that this tragic news has come as a complete shock to the councilman."

The microphones moved to LeBlanc as Ward removed a handkerchief from his pocket. More cameras flashed.

"How did you learn of the shooting?" the *Times* asked.

"The councilman addressed the WECAN organization this evening in Van Nuys," LeBlanc said, adjusting his horn-rimmed glasses. "At the conclusion of the meeting, I received a phone call from the councilman's maid, who told me that a nurse"—he paused dramatically—"a nurse, not a police officer, called and said she had seen Jacob Jr., here at the hospital, and that he had been shot. She had no report on his condition at that time."

Pencils raced. "When the councilman heard that his son had been injured, he left immediately for the hospital."

"Councilman Ward," another reporter questioned, "has your son ever had any problems with the police?"

"No." Ward replaced his handkerchief in his pocket. "N-No, of course not." Then he said slowly, "Every time a black man reaches for his comb or wallet, he's gunned down by some scared police officer."

"Councilman," a reporter interrupted.

Ward went on with quiet intensity. "Let me say this. My son and I were extremely close. I know he respected the law and the police. And I know he has never carried a weapon of any kind." His voice strengthened, and he looked at each reporter carefully. "I will not permit his death to be swept under the rug with the rest of the black skeletons."

"Councilman . . . Councilman Ward . . . What action do you intend to . . . ? When did you last see . . . ?"

"No more questions now, gentlemen," LeBlanc said as Ward pushed his way toward the receiving entrance. The group of reporters swarmed around them as they walked. Cameras continued to flash.

Lieutenant Clark stood at the receiving desk watching the group approach. He had prepared himself to break the news to Ward, but when he saw Ward crying, he knew that somehow the reporters had it figured out and told Ward. He wondered what he could say now.

Ward pushed open the double door and strode toward him, making no attempt to hide his anger. The group of reporters crowded in to hear.

"Councilman Ward," Clark said, "my name is Lieutenant Clark, and I'd like to talk to you in private, sir."

Ward stared. "Did they think that a black lieutenant telling me that they'd killed my son would make it better?"

Pencils scribbled.

Clark's expression remained unchanged. "Sir, I'm sorry you had to learn of it the way you did; but I cannot discuss it here. I've arranged for a room—"

"To hell with your room, Lieutenant," Ward said angrily. "You killed my son in public. Now I want to know why in public."

Cameras flashed. Several reporters raced to the phone booths.

"Sir," Clark said, "I'm sure, if you weren't—"

"You're goddamn right, I'm upset," Ward shouted as he pointed a finger into Clark's face. "This is one black death that you're not going to bury on page thirteen."

Clark pushed through the circle of reporters.

The *Times* wrote on his pad, "Police refuse comment on shooting death of councilman's son."

LeBlanc took Ward's arm, "Come on, sir, let's go home. We can't do anything here. I'll take care of everything."

They walked off. Several reporters followed.

Firemen swarmed around the charred, smoking cavity of the dress shop as Bowen and Gunning returned to their car.

"Who's running the show down at the shooting scene, Jim?" Gunning asked.

"Stryker," Bowen mumbled, as he cupped his hands around a burning match and lit a cigarette.

"Stryker." Gunning hesitated, then said flatly, "Well, he'll get the job done." He disliked Stryker. He couldn't really put his finger on it—maybe it was Stryker's disregard for police policy or procedure; maybe it was jealousy. Gunning couldn't think of anyone who felt neutral about Stryker. You either disliked him or thought he was the best cop in the world. He didn't like the way Stryker got things done, but Stryker's argument was always, "Show me another way, and I'll do it."

Gunning shrugged off the thought and turned to the car. "Let's go down there and see how things are going."

"Hey, goddammit! Get that shit off that car!" A uniformed officer had left a notebook on the hood of the stolen fifty-seven Chevy. Detective Sergeant John Stryker had seen it.

The officer snatched the notebook, then stood silently as Stryker approached.

"Brilliant, just goddamn brilliant," Stryker said.

The officer was a good three inches taller and thirty pounds heavier than Stryker, but he was scared. He knew the detective with the angry, piercing blue eyes, and wanted no part of an argument with him.

"I'm wearing gloves, Sergeant," the officer said.

"I'm impressed," Stryker snarled. "Jack the Ripper wore gloves; fruits wear gloves. So what? I'm not worried about the print you put on the car, I'm worried about the print you may have just screwed up, or wiped off. There may be only one print on that whole goddamn car that's worth anything. So we don't want anybody messing it up, right? You look like a policeman, so act like one, dammit. Think before you move."

"Right, Sergeant."

Stryker smiled a small, tight grin as he walked back across the street.

He was drawing a sketch of the shooting scene in his field officer's notebook when Bowen and Gunning arrived. He looked up at the two, completed his sketch, and returned his notebook to the inside of his suit jacket. "Now, what do you want?"

Gunning noticed that Stryker's tie was loosened, as usual. "What have you got?"

"The way I see it," Stryker said, "is that the black-and-white stopped where she sits. The driver of the Chevy came out shooting. He used a forty-five automatic. He fired one round. It got Conrad in the base of the neck. Conrad got off three rounds. Two of those were good shots. They got the driver dead center. We don't know where the third one went. Too bad Conrad didn't shoot first. If he had, he could tell you the story.

"Now, Conrad and the driver are down, dead or dying. Two more bad guys, from the front seat, come out the right side. One of them had a six-inch thirty-eight. We don't know which one. Prints will show us that. Anyway, Bennett smoked them when they showed the gun. They didn't get off a shot," he said with satisfaction.

"After that, according to our wits, Bennett got two more out of the Chevy, from the back seat. He put them against the wall of the house, and then some boy-scout citizen came out to help. A suspect was still hidden in the Chevy.

"The bad guy, in the car, sat up and shot Bennett in the back. Bennett fell, his shotgun fired, and he got the two standing against the house. Damn shame, right?" Stryker smiled sarcastically. "Then the bad guy shoots the boy-scout citizen who eye-balled all this.

"Our bad guy has got to be a one-hundred-per-cent asshole, because after he did all this shooting, he got out of the car and took Bennett's wallet and gun."

Stryker paused, seeing the coroner's deputy and several detectives lifting Conrad's body onto a stretcher, covering it with a black rubber sheet.

"Anyway," Stryker said, "the bad guy got away.

Our wits can't tell us where the hell he went, and we haven't got much in the way of a description. You know, none of these A-1 citizens ever see a fucking thing . . . unless it's white."

"Where do we go from here?" Gunning asked.

"Well," Stryker said, "our bad guy is hot. So he's not going to foot it too far. I've got a hold for prints on all vehicles stolen within twenty blocks of here. I sent two men down to the morgue to get prints from the bodies so we can find out who they are. Once we know that, we'll have some idea who their playmates are."

"Good."

"We'll run them through R and I," Stryker said, "and maybe we'll get some addresses to check. This clown has got to come down somewhere. The bad guy came out of the back seat, so it's very likely he used the center post on the right side of the Chevy to pull himself out. Prints is going to get right on that.

"I've had photos taken of everything from all angles. The photo lab said they'd hand-deliver them in less than an hour."

There were no questions, and Stryker went on. "I've got all the weapons found here at the scene. I'll run them for wants as soon as we get back to the station."

"I'll call West Hollywood sheriff's and see what they've got on the Chevy. My partner is banging doors right now. As soon as he gets back, we'll go to the hospital to handle the bodies there."

"Sounds like you've covered it all," Gunning said.

Stryker smiled tightly, running his hand over his thinning brown hair. If he had forgotten anything, it wasn't worth remembering.

"Jim," Gunning said to Bowen, "get somebody to

drive 81's car back to the station. That is, if Stryker is done with it."

"Sure." Stryker smiled.

"Have them put it in the garage," Gunning called as Bowen crossed the street.

"Right, Skipper."

Stryker and Gunning watched as the tow truck hoisted the front of the Chevy off the ground. The operator of the tow truck, a slim Negro wearing a ball cap, placed a gloved hand on the Chevy's bumper as it raised to waist level.

"Hey, fella, get your hand off that car!" a voice shouted from the darkness.

The tow-truck operator jerked his hand away. A tall uniformed officer appeared beside the operator. The officer looked directly into the face of the tow operator. "How long have you been running this tow, fella?"

Stryker and Gunning watched from across the street.

"I'm wearing gloves, man," the tow operator complained.

"I'm impressed," said the officer. "I'm really impressed. Jack the Ripper wore gloves; fruits wear gloves; so what? I'm not worried about you putting prints on the car. I'm worried about you screwing up what's already on there."

"Okay, officer," the operator promised, "I'll be careful."

"Now, there's an alert young officer," Gunning said.

Stryker was smiling.

The tow truck pulled away, its muffler roaring loudly in the morning's stillness.

"Something amusing?" Gunning asked.

"No . . . nothing amusing. Nothing at all."

"Skipper," Bowen said as he approached, "do

you want to maintain the command post here, or drop it?"

Gunning looked at Stryker. "Your people about finished here?"

"Yeah, we should be out of here in about five minutes."

"Okay, Jim," Gunning said, "have Sergeant Johnson pick up and clear out. If we leave, there'll be nothing left to draw a crowd. Tell Johnson to maintain heavy patrol in the area, but not to be pushy."

"Hey, Bowen, have all your people that were involved in this caper report to the station so we can interview them," Stryker called.

"Right." Bowen walked off.

"You ever see one this bad before?" Gunning asked.

"Nope," Stryker said flatly as he shook a cigarette from his pack, offering one to Gunning.

"No, thanks, wife made me quit."

"Too bad, we had one human killed," Stryker said as he lit his cigarette.

"One of the dead is Councilman Ward's kid," Gunning said.

Stryker smiled. "Worth about fifty thousand votes."

Gunning breathed, "See you at the hospital." He walked away.

Stryker walked toward the house where he had last seen his partner. He was entering the front yard when West called, "Hey, Sherlock, I've already been in there."

Stryker turned back to the sidewalk, looking. "Where in the hell are you?"

"What's wrong, old man, you going blind?" West said.

"No, it's just that you're hard to see in the dark. Smile so I can find you," Stryker shot back.

"Very funny, white man."

The first thing you would notice about Grant West was ⁺hat he was big—six-three, with broad shoulders. The second thing was that he was black. He had been Stryker's partner for three years, and they were one of the best homicide teams in the city. West always told Stryker he was lucky to have him around to bail him out when things got physical. Stryker agreed. West, at 210, outweighed Stryker by 40 pounds.

"How'd you make out?" Stryker asked.

"No good," West said. "Lot of people heard the shooting, but by the time they got their ass in gear, it was all over."

"Yeah. Well, let's make a run to the hospital; maybe Bennett can help us."

"If he's still alive," West said. Stryker glanced at his watch. It was three-fifteen A.M.

"Pardon me," Bowen said to the nurse at the receiving desk.

The nurse looked up. "Yes, may I help you?"

"Could you tell me where Officer Wilson and Lieutenant Clark are?"

The nurse smiled. "Down at the end of the hall, in the doctors' lounge."

"Captain Gunning," a reporter called, approaching the two men.

"I'm James Hill, with the *Examiner*. I wonder if I could ask you a few questions?"

"Go ahead."

"Why does the department refuse to comment on why Councilman Ward's son was killed?" he asked.

Bowen saw anger growing on Gunning's face.

"Let me tell you something, fella." Gunning stepped closer to the reporter. "I'd like to know why I've got one policeman dead, and I imagine his wife and three kids would like to know, too. I'd like to know how another one of my officers got shot in the back, and I'd like to know if he's going to live. I'd like to know why the councilman's son was riding in a stolen car; but I don't. We can't give you people answers we don't have, but you can do what you usually do, you can make something up."

The reporter, now red-faced, said, "I'm sorry . . . I . . ."

Gunning and Bowen walked to the end of the hall and pushed open the lounge door.

"Good morning, Captain," Wilson said.

"Hello, Wilson."

"Captain," Bowen said, "this is Clark from Seventy-seventh."

Clark, rising out of a soft brown leather chair, extended his hand to Gunning.

"Thanks for coming over," Gunning said, disappointed to find Clark was black. He hoped it wouldn't create a problem.

"How's the coffee?" Bowen asked, seeing a small pot on a hot plate.

"Hot and wet. That's about all it's got going for it."

"Skipper, you want a cup?" Bowen asked, pouring himself some.

"Yeah, black," Gunning answered, sliding into one of the soft chairs. "Ward been here yet?"

"Yes, sir, about twenty minutes ago." Clark straightened in his chair.

"How did he take it?"

"Well, before he got here," Clark said, clasping his hands together, "the reporters found out about his son. When Ward and his deputy arrived, they laid it on him in the parking lot. By the time he got inside, he was really boiling. I asked him to talk to us in private. He refused and made several threats. I walked away from him then."

Gunning sat quietly for a moment, sipping the black coffee. "Do you think it was wise to walk away, Lieutenant?"

"Yes, sir, I do," Clark said strongly. "He was throwing a lot of abuse at us. I couldn't argue with him in front of the reporters, and even if I had, no matter what I would have said, we would've come out looking like the bad guys. I asked him to talk in private, he refused. There was no more to say."

"I agree," Gunning said, gaining confidence in the black lieutenant. "I only asked because a lot more people up the line will be asking you the same thing."

Clark nodded.

"Any word on Bennett?" Bowen asked.

"Not yet," Wilson answered.

"How's his wife?" Gunning asked.

"She got pretty bad at one point, so they gave her a sedative."

"What about that woman 71 brought down?" Bowen said, as he poured himself some more coffee.

"She's really out of it. She's been admitted."

"What woman is that?" Gunning asked.

"She's the wife of the citizen killed trying to help," Bowen explained.

"You know, Captain, by noon today," Clark said, leaning forward to rest his elbows on his knees, "everybody in this city is going to know about this caper."

Gunning said nothing as he continued to sip his coffee.

Clark continued, "Right now, at least fifty rumors are flying around out there. Every militant in this city—black, white, green, or purple—is going to close ranks and join the cause. We've got some long weeks ahead of us."

The phone rang.

Wilson picked it up. "Daniel Freeman Hospital. Yes, sir, just a moment, please." He put his palm over the mouthpiece. "For you, Captain; it's Deputy Chief Ross."

Disturbed, Gunning set his coffee down and took the phone. He wasn't ready to talk to Ross yet. He'd wanted time first to decide how to break the news. "Good morning, sir."

"Good morning, Dave. I thought I'd call and see how things were going." The voice on the phone was calm.

"Well, sir, we're slowly getting things pieced together," Gunning said, trying to be pleasant.

"Good . . . good. . . . How's the wounded officer doing?"

"They're still working on him, sir."

"What are their names, Dave?"

"Conrad's the one that was killed, sir. Bennett is the one here at the hospital."

"Any children?"

"Yes, sir. Conrad had three. Bennett has one."

"Damn shame . . . damn shame. How'd the problem at Slauson and Overhill turn out?"

"We had a crowd of about three hundred there. They burned down a dress shop. No problem clearing the area. Most of them were just curious. No arrests."

"Very good. Very good."

"I'm glad you called, sir. I was about to call you. . . ."

"Yes? Well, go on."

"Well, sir. One of the suspects killed turned out to be Councilman Ward's son."

There was a pause. Gunning listened to the static on the line. Then: "To say this is going to create problems would be the understatement of the year, Dave."

"Yes, sir."

"The press got this yet?"

"Yes, they sure have."

"Ward?"

"He raised hell. The press loved that."

"Goddammit. . . . Look, Dave, I'm going to make a few phone calls. Are you going to be there for a while?"

"Yes, sir."

"Okay, I'll call back."

Gunning paused, studying the silent phone, then carefully hung up.

"So, here's where you're all hiding," Stryker said as he and West pushed open the door to the lounge, sniffed. "Ha, no wonder, you've got coffee."

"Hey, man, what's happenin'?" West said. He and Clark were occasional sparring partners during their workouts at the academy.

"Catch, Gomer," Stryker said, tossing a coffee mug back over his shoulder without looking.

West lunged and caught the mug inches from the carpet.

"Keeps him awake," Stryker said to nobody in particular. He poured himself some coffee. "We took a look at the body," he added, pouring sugar into his cup. "Ward's kid caught one pellet behind the right ear."

"One small pellet for Ward. . . . One giant step for LAPD," Wilson said, his voice trailing as he caught an icy look from Gunning.

A nurse pushed open the door. "Your friend is

out of surgery now. The doctor will talk to you in a few minutes."

"How is he?" Bowen asked.

"I don't know. You'll have to discuss that with the doctor."

"Oh, nurse." Wilson jumped up as the door started to close. "Are you going to wake Mrs. Bennett now?"

"Yes, I was," she answered, holding the door.

"Well, her neighbor brought these things for her." Wilson handed her a brown shopping bag. "I think she's wearing a bathrobe now."

"Okay, thanks." She took the bag, and the door closed slowly behind her.

"Hope the hell he can talk," Stryker said, easing himself down in one of the soft chairs, balancing his coffee.

"That would help," West said.

"And if he can't?" Gunning asked somberly.

Stryker sipped his coffee. Then, thoughtfully, "I don't know."

"If Bennett can't talk, we're betting the whole ball of wax on prints," West said.

Gunning nodded. "How long will it take them to go over the Chevy?"

"Three, four hours," Stryker answered, looking into his coffee cup, displeased with its taste. "If nurses make love the way they make coffee, I'm glad I'm a cop instead of a doctor."

"Mrs. Bennett, Mrs. Bennett . . . wake up." The nurse shook Joy gently.

"Hmm . . . what . . . ?" Joy opened her eyes.

"Your husband is in the recovery room now; you can see him."

Joy sat up, blinking.

"Your neighbor brought these for you." The

nurse smiled. "You can change in that bathroom there. I'll wait for you."

The bright light of the bathroom hurt her eyes, but the icy water on her face was cool and refreshing. Her heart was beating fast; her hands shook as she stuffed her robe and nightgown into the bag.

She opened the door. "I'm ready," she said, and the nurse smiled. Joy smiled back weakly, her lips trembling.

The doctor pushed open the door to the lounge, pausing when he saw the five men. "Good morning," he said.

"Want a coffee, Doc?" Stryker gestured for the doctor to sit.

"Yeah, please." The physician smiled as he sank into the soft leather chair. "Black will be fine," he said.

Stryker handed the steaming cup to the doctor.

"Ah. . . . Damn, that tastes good."

Stryker shook his head in disbelief.

The doctor looked about at the waiting faces, smiled. "Well, gentlemen, barring no complications or serious infection, your healthy young officer should be back to work in about . . . oh . . . maybe sixty days."

Gunning sat back in his chair, breathing a heavy sigh of relief.

Bowen nodded. "Outstanding."

West slapped Clark on the back. "Hey, that's a blood for you. Right, brother?"

Clark smiled in agreement.

Stryker smiled his tight grin, his index finger massaging the thin scar on his cheek.

"The bullet," the doctor said, "entered the lower left back, penetrated the main lower back muscle, grazed the top of the hipbone, punctured the large intestine in several spots, passed through the abdominal muscles, and exited just to the right of the navel." He set his cup down on a small table. "Anybody have a cigarette?"

Stryker tossed him his pack and matches.

"Thanks," he said, shaking one from the pack. "You know, over ten thousand doctors have quit smoking, which proves I'm an individualist, right? Now, as I was about to say, your young officer is very lucky. If the bullet path had varied a quarter of an inch in either direction, it would have been an uphill battle."

"Doc," Gunning said, "was our suspect dead on arrival?"

The doctor exhaled a slow stream of smoke. "No, he wasn't; but I'm the only surgeon here. I examined him. He was still alive in the sense that his heart was still beating; but the nature of his wound indicated to me that it would be fatal. So . . . I chose to work on the other."

"You chose right," Stryker said bluntly.

"If I had thought there was any chance," the doctor went on carefully, "I would have had him transferred to another hospital or called in another surgeon. It was shortly after we got your man into the O.R. that a nurse reported the vital signs on him gone."

"Can we talk to Bennett, Doc?" Stryker asked.

"No. Not for about . . . oh . . . an hour, hour and a half, maybe. He won't make any sense for at least that long."

The lounge door opened. "Excuse me, Dr. Marthouse," the young nurse said, "but we've got an attempted suicide that just came in, and she's bleeding badly."

"Okay, I'll be right there." He shrugged, smashed his cigarette in an ashtray, and left the room.

"Thanks, Doc," Bowen called as the door swung shut.

"Wonder if he knows the suspect was Ward's kid?" West said.

"He's got enough problems now," Stryker answered. "Anyway, he'll find out soon enough." He stood. "Come on, West, let's go to work."

"Right, we'll see you people," West said, following Stryker.

The phone rang. Gunning picked it up quickly. "Captain Gunning."

"Dave, this is Deputy Chief Ross."

"Yes, sir."

"I just talked with the chief. He advises we set up the mobile command post at your station and maintain the tactical alert."

"Yes, sir."

"I've assigned Inspector Foster to the command post as the OIC, but you are still to act as field commander."

"Yes, sir."

"Foster will handle all details on getting things set up, so you can continue to run the show without interruption."

"I appreciate that, sir," Gunning said, masking his dissatisfaction.

"The chief would like a briefing phoned to the emergency control center from your division every half-hour starting at 0430."

"Very well, sir."

"We should have things set up by day-watch roll call. You and Foster should handle that roll call."

"Yes, sir."

"He should be at your station within the hour. How soon will you be returning?"

"I should be out of here in less than half an

hour. Bennett is out of surgery now, and the doctor says things look pretty good."

"Excellent, Dave, excellent. I'm sure the chief will be pleased to hear that. Well, I'll let you go now. I'm sure you have things to do. Good luck to you, Captain."

"Thank you, sir.

"Deputy Chief Ross," Gunning said, replacing the phone back. "We're setting up the mobile command post at the station. Inspector Foster will be OIC. He'll be at the station in less than an hour."

"I was hoping we wouldn't need it," Bowen said.

"Me, too," Gunning grunted, "but they didn't ask for our opinion."

"Captain, if you guys don't need me anymore, I'll get back to where I belong," Clark said. "I know my people are waiting on some news about what's happening."

"We certainly appreciated your assistance, Lieutenant," Gunning said, extending a hand.

Clark took the hand. "My pleasure. That doesn't fit, does it?" He smiled. "Glad I could help out, Captain."

"Anytime we can do anything for you, give a yell."

"We'll see ya, Jim," Clark said to Bowen.

"Right, thanks a lot."

"Here we are." The nurse stopped Joy near the end of a long, quiet hall. "The doctor's busy right now, so you can see your husband first. He should wake up soon, so please push the call button when he does, okay?"

Joy nodded. She was breathing hard, and found herself feeling strangely frightened, as if she were meeting Steve for the first time.

"I'll be around every few minutes," the nurse said

quietly. "You can go in now." And she pushed the door open for Joy.

The door swung in silently. Joy entered the dimly lit room very slowly. When her eyes adjusted, she saw him. He lay perfectly still. "Steve . . . oh, Steve." She started to cry. The door hissed closed behind her.

His face was sober; his lips were very pale. She wanted to hold him, to let him know that she was here and would never let him go again.

"That'll be a big help. Thanks a lot," Stryker said in satisfaction, replacing the black phone in its cradle.

West was still busy on the other phone, across the desk. Stryker tilted his chair back on two legs and reached for his cigarettes. The detective squad room was busy for a Sunday morning. Ten minutes of six. He wondered what normal people did at ten to six on a Sunday morning. He couldn't remember.

Across the room two patrol officers sat at a table working on reports. On the other side sat two Negro youths, maybe thirteen or fourteen. One of the two leaned far to the right in his chair, sleeping. One hand lay limp on his lap; the other hung at his side. The second youth sat slumped in his chair watching his toe as he wriggled it through a hole in a tattered sneaker.

Stacked in front of the youths were several small transistor radios, a tape recorder, and a broken brick. "Window smash," Stryker thought, exhaling a puff of smoke.

West hung up the telephone. "Listen to this. CII shows a want on the forty-five automatic. Their records show it stolen in a 459 last Thursday, in

West Hollywood. I've got the sheriff's file number. We can get further on it from them."

He paused.

"Go on," Stryker urged, drawing on his cigarette.

"On the thirty-eight, they show a want by St. Louis P.D."

Stryker let his chair down on all four legs. "For what?"

"Murder."

Stryker crushed his cigarette into a tin ashtray, smiled. "Murder, huh. . . . No wonder those assholes came out shooting." He straightened a yellow tablet in front of him. "Okay. Here's what I got from West Hollywood sheriff's.

"Their watch commander pulled the reports for me. They show the Chevy stolen Thursday night around eleven o'clock. They had a 459 at the Safaria Gun Shop, 4927 Sunset Boulevard, on Thursday night at about eleven. The gun shop has a silent alarm. When the alarm went, a sheriff's unit rolled on it. When they pulled up next to the shop, a sixty-six Buick split from across the street. The sheriff's went in pursuit of the Buick and bagged it about three miles away.

"Now, here's the interesting part." Stryker pointed a pencil at West. "The guy they catch is some whip by the name of Johnny Grear. He's a male Negro, nineteen, from St. Louis. The Buick is a St. Louis stolen. He's got no loot in his machine, so the unit that got him asked for another car to check the gun shop. By the time they get there, the bad guy, or guys, are gone. The Chevy was stolen from behind the gun shop. The gun shop took a four-thousand-dollar loss. About twenty guns, the sheriff's say."

"That's where the forty-five came from," West

said, picking up the steel-blue automatic from the table.

"Right," Stryker agreed. "Now, that punk the sheriff's snatched up is eating up the taxpayers' money, sitting in the bucket at the county jail, so let's pay him a visit and find out who the hell his playmates were."

West grinned. "Sounds like a winner."

"First," Stryker added, "let's get off a teletype to St. Louis and see what they can tell us about this want on the thirty-eight."

"Right."

"And tell them we've got their gun and a couple of bodies to go with it."

A patrol officer entered the squad room. "Sergeant Stryker?"

"Right here."

"Sergeant, the captain wants to see you in his office," the officer said.

"Okay, I'll be right there," Stryker said, downing the remains of a cold cup of coffee. "Hey, Guy, how about riding herd on this artillery until my partner comes back?"

The patrol officer at the next desk answered, "Sure thing, Sarge."

Stryker walked from the squad room into the station's long rear hallway. It was strangely quiet; as he passed the large clear windows in the watch commander's office, he saw a penciled note taped to the glass: "Bennett's out of surgery and doing fine." Bowen was back at his desk.

"It's open," Gunning called when Stryker knocked. "Sit down," he said, pushing some papers aside.

Stryker slid into one of the comfortable chairs, the padding a welcome relief from the hardwood in the squad room.

"Stryker, I've got to phone a report to the emergency control center every thirty minutes."

"So?"

"So, I want you to keep me advised of any developments," Gunning said.

"Every half-hour is inconvenient," Stryker said. "We don't carry phones in the field."

Gunning leaned forward, resting his forearms on his desk. "Every half-hour it is," he said flatly. "Use smoke signals if you have to; but every half-hour I want a report on where you're at and what you're doing."

Gunning always meant what he said. Stryker grinned. "Every half-hour, right?"

Gunning relaxed in his chair again. "Have you come up with anything yet?"

"Yeah, as a matter of fact, we have," Stryker said. "Both the weapons recovered at the scene have wants on them. The forty-five was stolen Thursday night in a West Hollywood 459. The thirty-eight has a homicide want on it from St. Louis. West's working on a teletype to St. Louis right now, to get more background on it."

"Good," Gunning said.

"The Chevy," Stryker went on, "was stolen during the Hollywood burglary. The sheriff's arrested the lookout man. He was driving a St. Louis stolen. It was taken about six weeks ago. So I think they've been in L.A. long enough to have established a pad. West and I are going over to the county jail and talk to the suspect the sheriff's have. I think he knows who our suspect is and where the hell he's at."

"Sounds good," Gunning said. "Don't let me keep you."

"I won't." Stryker pushed himself up out of the

comfortable chair. "Talk to you in half an hour," he said sweetly.

As Stryker closed the door behind him, Inspector Foster and a lieutenant that Stryker didn't know approached.

"Good morning, Stryker," the gangly inspector said in his soft Kansas drawl.

" 'Morning, Inspector."

"How's your handball game holding out?"

"Not bad, sir, about upper twenty-five percent."

The inspector smiled. "We'll have to try another match someday soon. Give me a chance to get even."

"Anytime, sir." Stryker smiled.

The inspector's expression turned serious. "John, you got any idea how Ward's kid got involved in this thing?"

"No, sir. Not clue one," Stryker said.

The inspector nodded, rubbing his chin with the back of his hand. "It'll be interesting to see what develops," he said. The silent lieutenant with him opened Gunning's office door, and the two entered.

Stryker walked back to the detective squad room, where West was downing the last of a pint of chocolate milk. "Come on, Garbage Gut. Let's get out to the county jail."

West tossed the container in a high arc into the wastebasket. "Man cannot live by cigarettes alone, as you'll learn someday."

"Christ," Stryker said, "here it comes, another bit of advice from Dudley Straightarrow, clean, healthy, but not so bright boy next door."

"Hey, Sherlock"—West smiled—"you keep it up, and I'll move into your neighborhood."

"Okay, okay." Stryker laughed. "I know when I'm licked." He pushed the forty-five and thirty-eight to West's side of the table. "Here, lock these up."

West locked the two weapons in the desk drawer.

Stryker was squinting in the August-morning brightness as they crossed the parking lot.

"Going to be a warm one, partner," West said, glancing at the cloudless sky.

"In more ways than one."

As the two climbed into their green Plymouth, several trucks towing large blue vans pulled into the lot. The mobile command post.

Stryker studied the notes he had made as West sped through the light freeway traffic. West was silent; he knew his partner was running the information he had through his mind over and over again, searching for leads.

Turning into the county-jail driveway, they stopped at the high wire gate adjacent to the watch-tower. A speaker mounted on a post at window level on the driver's side said, in an impersonal static-filled voice, "Your names, organization, and purpose."

"Stryker and West, LAPD, interview of an in-custody."

"Thank you," the speaker said. The high gate rolled aside.

"And one bonus burger with secret sauce," Stryker called as the car rolled forward through the gate.

"Push button for service," said the sign on the counter in the jail lobby. Stryker leaned on the button. An attractive Negro deputy in a crisp, well-fitting uniform appeared behind the counter.

"May I help you, gentlemen?"

"Sure can," Stryker said. "Is your watch commander awake?"

"We don't go to bed on duty," she said. "If you think—"

"You go to bed off duty?" Stryker interrupted.

"I'll get my watch commander," she said, turning away.

"How would you like to lay some pipe with that?" Stryker smiled at West.

"Be all right. . . . A little soul patrol," West whispered.

"Good morning, gentlemen. My name's Lieutenant Bean. What can I do for you?" said the lieutenant approaching the counter.

"Good morning," Stryker said. "I'm Stryker, and this is my partner, West. We're from Southwest's detectives. We had an officer killed and another wounded last night, and you've got a prisoner that we think could help us find our outstanding suspect. We'd like to talk to him."

"Yeah, I heard about the shooting," the lieutenant said. "Damn shame. You people are in for a rough time with Ward's kid dead. . . ."

"Yeah, we know," Stryker said dryly.

"Who's the prisoner you want to talk with?"

"Johnny Grear," Stryker said. "We haven't got his booking number, but we know he's in for 459PC, from West Hollywood."

"Okay," the lieutenant said. "I'm sure we can locate him for you. Come on inside." He opened the gate beside the counter. "You can use one of our interview rooms."

Stryker and West followed the lieutenant across a wide desk-filled office to a short hallway, West turning to eye the deputy again.

"Don't step on your dick," Stryker cautioned.

"Fuck you," West answered.

At the rear, the lieutenant opened a door, turned

on a light in the windowless room. "I'll have somebody get Grear."

"Thanks." Stryker and West entered the small room.

The room was crowded and smelled stale. Stryker and West sat in two of the room's three chairs, and Stryker pulled open the drawer of a small wooden table.

"What are you looking for?" West said.

"An elephant."

"You won't find any in there," West advised. "They like privacy."

The door swung open. "This is Grear," the sheriff's lieutenant said flatly, gesturing for the young Negro with him to enter. "Give a shout when you're done with him, fellas."

Stryker sat quietly, his hands folded on the small table. West sat with his chair pushed back on two legs, leaning against the wall.

Grear stood staring at the two. He was clean-looking, about five-eleven. He wore a pink shirt with a wide collar, and black striped bell bottoms. "You want me to sit down?" he asked.

Stryker and West said nothing.

"Hey, man. The old silent treatment, huh?" Grear sounded disgusted. "You clowns been watching too much TV."

Stryker and West said nothing.

Grear slid into a chair across the table from Stryker. "What are you?" Grear said to West. "This paddy's interpreter?"

No answer.

"You clowns bother me on Sunday morning just to talk about that humbug burglary the sheriff's hung on me? *Man!* Well, man, I had nothing to do with that gun-shop caper. I don't need no gun to protect myself." Grear shifted nervously in his chair, eyeing Stryker and West.

They waited.

"If it's about that Buick, man," Grear said, trying hard for a confident tone, "I didn't know it was stolen. Is that it, man? Is that what all this shit is about? Hey, goddammit," he shouted suddenly, striking the table with his fist. "Say something."

Stryker and West sat.

Grear picked at some dirt under his thumbnail. "I can prove I didn't steal that goddamn car." He stood up.

"Bullshit," Stryker said, flattening his hands on the table. "We ripped off your playmates, and guess who they tell us deserves credit for one count grand theft auto?"

"Them motherfuckers. . . . Which one . . . ? Tell me, man . . . which one of them motherfuckers told you that?"

"We won't tell you that," Stryker said soberly.

"I know which motherfucker done it . . . fucking snitch . . . he'd piss in his mommy's ear if it'd help him get out from under a beef. . . . That motherfucking Red."

"I said we won't tell you who it was," Stryker repeated.

"You don't have to," Grear said angrily. "I know it was Red Pepper. He's the only one that'd snitch on me . . . and just 'cause one motherfucker says it's so, doesn't make that motherfucker right. Does it?"

"That's for the court to decide," Stryker answered, hoping to fire Grear's anger.

Waving his hands and looking to the ceiling, Grear continued his rage. "That's motherfucking justice. One motherfucker says you did it, so twelve other motherfuckers sit down to decide who's the best motherfucking liar."

Stryker and West waited.

"What ya bust 'em for?" Grear asked.

"That's not important," West answered.

"Shit!" Grear barked. "That bitch get him busted?"

They said nothing.

"Biggest paddy whore on Normandie Avenue, staying in cockroach heaven, the Rocket Motel. Yeah, that's it. I know that white bitch got him busted. Now he's gonna roll over on me to save his ass."

West smiled broadly.

"Whatta you smiling at, slave?" Grear snarled.

"Red Pepper staying at the Rocket Motel on Normandie." Stryker smiled. "That's what he's smiling about."

"We both wanna commend you on your ability to keep your mouth shut," West added with sarcasm.

Realizing his mistake, Grear slumped into his chair. "You mothers think you're clever bastards, don't you?" he snarled. "You bunch of pricks. . . ."

"Look, Grear," Stryker said sharply, "your playmates got in way over their heads last night, and five of them are gone. . . . Dead. . . . Finished. Along with one cop. So we're not talking this horseshit humbug burglary anymore or GTA. These people you came out here with from St. Louis are wanted for murder back there. Did you know that, punk? So, if you've got—"

"Screw you, you goddamn paddy pig!" Grear shouted angrily at Stryker, jumping up, knocking his chair over backward.

Stryker raised a foot and pushed the table hard toward Grear.

The table caught Grear in the midsection, sending him sprawling backward hard against the wall.

"I'll kill you," Grear screamed, scrambling to his feet.

West moved for Grear like a big cat. Catching his arm as he lunged at Stryker, West twisted hard, pushing the arm high into the middle of Grear's back, forcing his face against the wall.

"When I let you go, punk," West whispered into Grear's ear, holding him against the wall, "I want you to be nice to my partner. Both of your feet couldn't fill one of his shoes. So you mind your manners. Like your mother taught you. Okay, brother?"

"Okay, man. Okay," Grear mumbled, his face twisted with pain.

West released the arm. "Pick up the chair and sit down."

"Now," Stryker said calmly, "who came out with you from St. Louis?"

"I know my rights, and I'm not saying nothing," Grear said soberly, massaging his shoulder. "I want to talk to my lawyer first."

"Okay, partner," Stryker said firmly. "Let's put him back. We've got what we came for."

"Right." West opened the door and left the room.

Grear continued to massage his arm. Stryker watched.

"How many times you been busted before?" Stryker asked.

"Two times," Grear said, breathing hard, but managing a reasonable tone. "Once as a juvenile, and this time. Both humbugs."

"Let me give you some advice, Grear," Stryker said in an icy tone. "I don't know if you realize what you've got your ass into or not. That doesn't matter much. What matters is what you're going to do about it now. I've seen a lot of you come down the line. Not many make it back. It's a one-way street. My advice to you is to just lay it on the line and take it as it comes. Don't try giving anybody a snow-job or playing the bad guy."

"Go to hell, pig."

Stryker saw tears welling up in his eyes.

West opened the door. "Let's go, Tiger."

Grear got up slowly, looking at Stryker.

"Come on." The sheriff's lieutenant was standing outside the open door. Grear turned and left.

"Well, what's next, Sherlock?" West said, standing in the doorway.

Stryker pushed his chair back from the small table. "Let's call the station and see if any of our guys got anything from the bodies, or maybe some prints off the Chevy, before we do anything else."

"Southwest Division, watch commander's office, Lieutenant Bowen speaking."

"Bowen, this is Stryker. Have you seen any of my people?"

"Yeah, Douglas and Sims called. They said SID got a lot of prints off the Chevy, but none they've been able to make yet."

"How about Kline and Cook?" Stryker asked. "They went to the morgue. You heard from them?"

"Let me find my notes."

"Did they call?" Stryker asked impatiently.

"Yeah, goddammit. Just a minute," Bowen said. "Okay. The suspect that Conrad killed was Jack C. Woods, his driver's license showed a St. Louis address. The two suspects that Bennett shot were Ralph Dukes and Leon Wray. Both of them also had I.D.s showing St. Louis addresses."

"Okay, I've got that. Go on," Stryker urged.

"The kid in the back seat with Ward's son was

Preston Kennedy. He shows an L.A. address of 3706 South Dublin."

"It all fits together except Ward's son and this Kennedy," Stryker said.

"Yeah, I can't figure that either," Bowen agreed. "But listen to this, Stryker. We got a return teletype from St. Louis. They say the thirty-eight was taken in a bank robbery on July 23 this year from a security guard who was killed during the 211. They've got four named suspects with descriptions."

"Let's have them."

"Jack C. Woods," Bowen began. "That's the one Conrad killed. Next, Ralph Dukes, and finally, Leon Wray. Bennett killed both of them."

"Got them. Go on."

"Here's the biggy," Bowen said in a pleased tone. "Sounds like our boy. His name is Frederick L. Pepper. He's a male Negro, thirty-two years, six-two, two hundred and thirty pounds, with a large scar on the bridge of his nose. He's got a street name of 'Red Pepper.' "

"Sounds like him, all right," Stryker said. "Now, all we have to do is find the bastard."

"Right. I've already phoned the information to communications, so they could get it on the air. I also directed any arrests or information on him to Southwest detectives."

"Good," said Stryker. "I'm at the county jail now, and we have a lead on where he may be holed up. It looks like he came out here from St. Louis with the rest of them in a stolen car. He mentioned a guy named Red—must be Red Pepper. I think he's at the Rocket Motel on Normandie. That whore-hole, you know?"

"Yeah, sounds good."

"Here's what I want," Stryker said thoughtfully.

"Number one, tell Gunning what we've got. He wanted a report every half-hour, and I'm late."

"I know." Bowen chuckled. "He's been bitching."

"Second, I want four of your black-and-whites and a sergeant to meet me at Vernon and Normandie in ten minutes. I know it's near end of watch, but I'm sure your guys will welcome the chance to bag this asshole."

"I'll have them there."

"And another thing," Stryker said. "How about calling communications and have them broadcast a Code Five for Normandie Avenue between Forty-sixth Street and Fifty-second Street? We don't want anybody spooking our suspect if he's still at the motel."

"I'll do it right away."

"Talk to you later." Stryker hung up the phone.

"3A71 and 3X73 meet 3W6 at Normandie and Vernon," said the female voice on frequency three.

"3A71, roger. 3X73, roger," the two units responded.

"3L30 meet 3W6 at Normandie and Vernon," the female voice continued.

"3L30, roger," Johnson said into the mike, turning the black-and-white station wagon south on Normandie from Exposition Boulevard.

"3A58 and 3A21, meet 3W6 at Normandie and Vernon."

"3A58, roger."

"3A21, roger."

West and Stryker arrived at Normandie and Vernon as the last black-and-white rolled into the gas-station parking lot.

"How ya doing, Chuck?" West said.

"What have you guys got going?" Johnson asked.

"We've got a clue," West said.

"Anybody got a piece of chalk?" Stryker asked.

"I'll get a piece from my car," an officer said, turning quickly to his black-and-white.

The group of eight uniformed officers stood in a rough circle around Stryker, waiting. Stryker looked at his watch; seven-thirty-five. Twenty-five minutes, and these guys were end of watch. He looked at their faces. Tired.

"Here ya are, Sarge." The officer tossed the chalk to Stryker.

"Okay." Stryker knelt on the asphalt. "Here's what's going on." The circle tightened. "We've got some scoop that our outstanding suspect is holed up in the Rocket Motel at 4708 South Normandie."

There were murmurs around the circle. Everyone knew the Rocket. He drew a rectangle on the black asphalt. "This is the motel. We don't know which room he's in, so we'll have to cover the whole thing."

Stryker looked up at the circle of faces. "Okay, who do we have here?"

"3A21," one of the officers volunteered.

"Okay, 21, you and your partner cover the south side of the motel. I want one of you at the southwest corner, and one at the southeast corner."

"Right, Sarge."

"Next."

"3A71," another answered.

"71, you and your partner take the west end of the building." Stryker made notes on his chalk drawing. "One of you take the south end, and one of you take the north end."

"Got it."

"Who else?"

"X73 here," came the reply.

"Okay, 73, you and your partner take the north side of the building. Again, cover both ends. One of you at the west end, and one at the east end."

Stryker added the assigned positions to his drawing on the pavement.

"58's next, Sarge."

"Okay, 58, you and your partner have the east side. Cover both ends north and south."

"Right."

"Okay, now," Stryker said, looking up. "West and I and Sergeant Johnson will go to the motel office, which is located here on the first floor in the northeast corner, after all of you guys are in position. After we learn which room our boy's in," Stryker said, standing up, "we'll let you know before we make any move. That way you'll all know where we're going to be."

He looked around the circle of officers. The fatigue was gone, replaced with eagerness. "Our reason for deploying around the building," he said, "is that it gives us some insurance in case this guy smells us coming before we find out where in the hell he's at. Any questions?"

"Do we stay put after you find out what room he's in?"

"Damn right," Stryker said. "Maybe he's alone, or maybe he's got the Fifth Marine Division in there with him. We don't know. If he gets by us, you're our insurance. Okay?

"Now," he continued, "once we find out where he's at, we'll pass the word to 58, and they can pass the word on around the building to the rest of you."

"Let me say this," West said. "This guy is hot. He's already shot one cop in the back, so watch your ass. When you're getting into position, don't pass any windows, and hug that goddamn building like it's a naked broad. If he sees that pretty blue uniform before you see him, he's going to be putting holes in it."

They smiled.

"Okay, guys," Stryker said. "We're going to take my car and Johnson's wagon. So get your shotguns and get back here, and we'll get to work."

The group moved quickly to their black-and-whites.

Stryker pulled out his cigarettes, shook one from the pack, and lit it. West rubbed the chalk diagram from the pavement with a foot.

"Traffic's beginning to pick up some," Johnson said as he stood beside Stryker watching the cars pass by on Normandie Avenue.

"Yeah," Stryker agreed, exhaling smoke. "Sunday morning, and all the welfare Christians are driving their new Cadillacs to church."

Johnson turned away.

"Hey, man. What's happened, somebody get killed?" a small voice asked.

Two young Negro boys were parked on their bicycles at the curb. The smaller boy struggled to keep his bike standing as his short legs stretched to touch the pavement.

"Hey, you guys detectives?" the older asked.

"Must be a big caper for all this." The younger gestured at the parked police cars.

"Just a little investigation." West smiled.

"Aw, don't give us that snow-job."

"Yeah, we watch *Adam 12*. We know what's happening, man."

"You guys got a Code Five down here?"

West walked to the two and knelt. "Look, fellas," he said soberly, "since you know police work, you can help us out. I'm going to deputize you."

Their faces lit with excitement.

"We're going down the street in a minute, and we can't leave anybody behind to guard our cars and equipment, so you can help out by providing security here at the command post."

The boys listened, breathless.

"You patrol around the cars here until we get back," West said, standing. "Under no circumstances are you to leave your post. Unless it's to go home. You're not to follow us. Is that clear?"

"Yes, sir," the two assured him fervently.

"Okay, men, go to work," West said, fighting to control a grin.

"Let's go, Sherman." The older pedaled toward the cars.

"Wait, Howard . . . wait up . . . you never wait on me." The small boy struggled to get his large bike into motion, and wobbled off.

"Very shrewd, Dr. Spock," Stryker said, smiling his small grin. The officers had regrouped, each now carrying a shotgun, muzzle skyward. There was little conversation.

"Okay, let's do it," Stryker said, taking a final puff of his cigarette. "Five of you with Johnson, and three with me."

The two boys waved as the cars rolled from the gas-station lot onto Normandie Avenue.

They traveled the few blocks to the motel. "In back of that pickup." Stryker indicated a parked truck just short of the motel.

West pulled the Plymouth to the curb and stopped. Johnson moved the black-and-white station wagon quietly in behind.

The men poured from the two cars.

"Okay, you know where you belong. Let's move."

A dog began barking in the alley at the rear as Stryker, West, and Johnson moved toward the motel driveway, Johnson carrying the shotgun from his station wagon.

It was a two-story building, a bland colorless

stucco, rectangular in shape, with a black, littered, asphalt parking lot in the center. Near the driveway entrance, an overhead neon sign proclaimed, "Rocket Motel," and underneath was a smaller sign, "Free Ice, Mix, and Chewing Gum."

As they waited for the officers to move into position, Stryker counted nine cars in the parking lot, ranging from a new Eldorado to a rusty fifty-two Buick. A sixty-five Ford with its windows down. Near the back window of the Ford lay a brown baby doll. Stolen car, he thought. The parking lot was strewn with beer cans, broken bottles, and yellowed newspapers.

The morning air in the court was heavy with the stale odor of wine, beer, and barbecue sauce.

Stryker gestured to West and Johnson, and they moved into the court, watching for any movement. Inside the court they followed the motel wall to the right, to a small office. Stryker pushed the button for service. West and Johnson stood back of him watching the court. Stryker pushed the button impatiently. "Come on, goddammit."

"Yes . . . yes. . . . What is it?" A wrinkled, unshaven, sleepy face appeared behind the heavy wire mesh.

"Police officers. Open up."

"Whatta ya want?"

"Open this goddamn door before I kick it in," Stryker growled.

"Hey, now, Officer, there's no need for this," the man said, unlatching the door. "I run a respectable place here."

Stryker pushed the door open. "I know what kind of dump you run here, Gross," he said, "you and your goddamn herd of pigs, so don't give me any shit or I'll have the vice squad crawling over this garbage pit like the cockroaches are doing right now. Is that clear?"

The manager peered at him, recognized him. "Yeah, Stryker, I understand. I understand. You won't have any problems." He stood wringing his hands.

"Where's your registration book?"

Gross moved quickly to a shabby desk covered with papers and picked up a brown ledger, handing it to Stryker. "Here you are."

"I'm looking for a fat man, Gross." Stryker was paging through the book. "He's about six-two, two-thirty, big scar on his nose. His name's Pepper. Red Pepper."

"Yeah, yeah. I know him," Gross said. "He's been here about a week. Him and some other dude. He called himself Packard—Joe Packard, that's what he called himself."

Stryker threw the book back to Gross. "What room?"

Gross thumbed nervously through the pages. "Here it is. Joe Packard, room thirty-six. That's upstairs on the west side. The bum owes me twelve bucks on the room."

"Okay, Gross, go back to bed," Stryker said, walking to the door.

"You're not going to do any shootin', are ya, Stryker?" Gross said, nervously following him to the door. "Ya know it's bad for business."

"We won't start it," Stryker said as he opened the door.

"Is he here?" West asked without turning around.

"Yeah, he's here," Stryker breathed. "He's in room thirty-six, upstairs, and he's not alone."

"I'll tell the troops," Johnson said, moving toward the driveway.

"How are we going to do it?" West said, glancing at Stryker.

"We'll knock on the door and see if he's home."

"Who gets to knock?"

"Got a coin?"

West dug in his pocket. "Call it." The coin spun in the air.

"Heads." Stryker smiled, reaching to grab the coin in the air, slapping it to the back of his hand.

"Sometimes I think you cheat, partner," West complained. "Give me my dime back."

"We're ready," Johnson whispered.

"After you, sir." West gestured to Stryker.

The three moved cautiously to the stairs that ran up the outside of the building. Stryker led them up the steps.

At the top of the stairs was room thirty-two. They moved cautiously to the left: thirty-three, thirty-four, thirty-five. They stopped; Stryker motioned West past him. West moved quickly beside the door to thirty-six, flattening his back to the wall, near the room's large picture window. The beige curtains inside were closed.

Stryker signaled Johnson to stay to his right. He inched himself near the door's edge, keeping his back to the wall. Reaching inside his coat, he removed his four-inch from his shoulder holster. West, also, held gun in hand.

They listened. From inside came the faint sound of rock music. "Sleeping with the radio on," Stryker whispered.

Stryker nodded. West acknowledged. Turning to Johnson, he whispered, "Here goes." Johnson held the shotgun at port-arms.

Keeping his back to the wall, Stryker reached with his left hand and knocked heavily on the door.

The music stopped. Silence. Stryker's breathing was rapid now.

"Who is it?" a male voice called from inside.

"Police officers. Open the door," Stryker ordered.

A pause. "Okay . . . just a minute, man," the voice said.

They waited.

"Hey. Fool, what are you doing?" a female voice screamed. "You'll get us killed!"

The three pressed closer to the wall.

"Get away, bitch."

"Put that gun down. They'll kill us if you don't."

"Let go, slut."

A shot rang out. The girl was crying and screaming hysterically.

"Let go, you fucking whore."

"No . . . no . . . no," she cried.

Stryker motioned to West. They moved quickly to the front of the door.

"Cover us, Johnson," Stryker ordered.

Stryker and West raised their feet and kicked in unison, falling to the floor as the door swung in, splinters flying.

Johnson stepped to the center of the open door, leveled the shotgun into the room. As the man whirled to face the door, they saw the automatic in his hand.

Johnson's shotgun roared. The girl screamed. The suspect cartwheeled to his left, crashed into the cheap blond dresser, and fell face-down on the far side of the bed, dragging blanket and bed sheet with him. The sharp bark of the shotgun echoed momentarily in the courtyard.

A panty-clad white girl lay on the bed, still screaming.

Stryker and West scrambled up from the floor as Johnson stepped quickly into the room.

"Sure as hell makes your ears ring, doesn't it?" Stryker said.

Johnson kept his shotgun aimed at the fallen suspect.

Stryker and West followed, guns in hand. Johnson motioned silently to a closed door in the corner. The two men moved to it, one on either side. West nodded. Stryker and he leveled their pistols at the door. West, using his left hand, turned the knob, pushing hard on the door. It swung open with no resistance, and banged loudly, striking a glass shower door. The girl screamed louder.

"Empty," West said, looking cautiously into the small bath.

"Okay," Stryker said, returning his pistol to its holster.

"Shut up," Johnson shouted. The girl curled her body tighter, but her screaming stopped.

Stryker picked up the nine-millimeter pistol from the floor. The dead man lay sprawled idiotically across the bed, half caught in sheets and blankets.

"Is he dead?" Johnson asked. He made no move toward the body.

"If he's not, he soon will be," Stryker said, calmly removing the clip from the automatic. He pushed the clip into his back pocket, then pushed the pistol's slide to the rear. A live round ejected from the chamber and fell to the linoleum floor.

"Put these on," West ordered, picking up a bra and yellow mini-dress from a chair. He tossed them to the girl on the bed. Her sobbing was muffled by a pillow, and her body continued to jerk spasmodically.

"Go out and get some fresh air," Stryker suggested to Johnson as he picked up the cartridge from the floor.

"Yeah. Think I will," Johnson answered, his

voice trailing away. He turned toward the open door.

"Need any help, Sarge?" a patrol officer said breathlessly as he appeared in the room's doorway.

"No, everything's under control," Stryker said. "Keep everybody away from the door."

"Sure thing," the officer said, looking at the dead suspect and the girl on the bed.

"Okay. Now you've seen it. Get out," Stryker said.

"Yes, sir," the officer said, turning away.

"Chuck, let me have the shotgun. Homicide will want to eyeball it," West said as Johnson moved toward the door.

Johnson said nothing, handed the gray, bitter-smelling shotgun to West, and walked out the door.

"Is he okay?" Stryker asked, glancing at West.

"Yeah," West said, watching Johnson lean on the balcony rail outside the room and look up at the morning sky. "Yeah. He'll be okay, as soon as he calms down a little."

Stryker nodded. Now, for the first time, he looked at the body, the girl still tightly curled on the bed. West saw the change. He spoke to the girl.

"Come on, woman. Get your clothes on. We've seen enough of your body."

She didn't move.

"Get dressed, goddammit, or I'll dress you," West snapped.

Her hand moved, grasping the bra and dress.

Stryker knelt at the foot of the bed, looking at the dead man. "It's not Pepper," he said. "God-dammit."

"Who, then?" West asked, leaning the shotgun against the wall.

"Damn if I know." Stryker didn't look up. "Too small for Pepper."

West watched the girl lift her heavy breasts into the cups of her bra. They strained forward as she leaned over to hook the bra in the back. Standing, she slipped the short dress down over her head. West felt a tingling in his groin.

Johnson came to the doorway. He could smell the acrid odor of the burned gunpowder and the reek of sweat in the small room. The wall next to the bathroom door was pocked and cratered by the shotgun blast; clunks of plaster and paint, the size of half-dollars, littered the floor. The mirror, a special-interest item, mounted on the wall beside the bed, showed a scarred and jagged diagonal crack.

"Chuck, you'd better get back to the station." West was crisp. "Homicide's going to want you secluded."

"Right," Johnson agreed. "I'll go."

"Hey, Johnson," Stryker called after him. "Tell the watch commander what we've got down here and that we'll need a homicide team to handle it."

"Right," Johnson said. "See you people at the station."

Johnson was glad to get out. "Nine years. I wonder if I could have done it any other way. Maybe, if I'd yelled at him. No, I didn't have any choice. 'Maybe' gets you killed. 'Maybe' gets your partner killed. I had to kill him . . . had to. There was no other way."

"You people killed somebody and ruined my business. I hope you're happy."

Johnson glanced at the man at the bottom of the stairs. It was Gross, the manager, standing holding his robe closed at the throat with both hands, looking up at him. Johnson said nothing as he walked by.

"Warn her," Stryker said, shaking a cigarette from his pack.

He studied the girl and thought of that black body crawling over her white body. It made him shiver. He couldn't understand it.

West pulled his field officer's notebook from an inside jacket pocket. "What's your name?"

"Marlene Craig." She spoke without looking at him. She was nineteen or twenty, with a good figure, thick hair, frosted blond, and very white teeth.

West said, "You have the right to—"

"Could you zip me?"

He pulled the material together at the top and ran the zipper up.

Stryker drew in on his cigarette, wondering if West would climb in bed with her. He decided West would.

She turned to face him. "Thank you." She smiled through the tearstained, makeup-streaked face.

"Okay, now listen," West said, looking into her reddened eyes. "You have the right to remain silent; anything you say can and will be used against you in a court of law. You have the right to speak with an attorney and to have the attorney present during questioning. If you so desire and cannot afford one, an attorney will be appointed for you without charge before questioning." He paused. "Do you understand each of these rights I've explained to you?"

"Yeah, I understand," she said, sitting down on the edge of the bed.

"Do you wish to give up the right to remain silent?"

"Sure, I don't have anything to be silent about." She brushed a strand of hair from her forehead.

"Do you wish to give up the right to speak with

an attorney and have him present during questioning?"

"You cops really do it, don't you?" she said seriously. "I mean, that rights shit. I thought they only did that in the movies."

"Yeah, we really do it," West said. "Now, do you wish to give up the right to speak to an attorney and have—"

"Yeah, yeah," she interrupted. "I don't want any goddamn attorney."

"Fine," he said, putting the notebook back inside his jacket. "How long have you been here?"

"Since about eleven last night." She looked to the floor.

"Is that your man?" West asked, gesturing.

"No," she said, without turning to look at the body. "That fool isn't my man. You know why I'm in here. I told that ass to open the door when you knocked. But he gets the gun. I knew he'd get killed."

"Who is he?"

"I don't know."

"Don't give me that shit. You spend eight hours in the sack with him, and you don't know his name."

"His name is George," she said. "That's all I know. Just George. I don't know his last name."

"Where'd he pick you up?"

"On Slauson."

"Slauson's a long street. Where on Slauson?"

"Near Fourth Avenue."

"Who was with him?"

"Two other dudes."

"What'd they look like?"

"One was big. You know, tall and fat, with a big scar. Here, on his nose."

"Did he have a name?"

"They called him Red."

"What about the other?"

"He was tall. Kinda good-lookin'. Ya know. He had a moustache."

Stryker felt the heat growing on his neck and ears. "Kinda good-lookin' "—he wanted to punch her in the mouth.

"He have a name?" West asked.

"I don't remember."

"Try."

"I don't know."

"What kind of a car were they driving?"

"A Chevy."

"Color?"

"Blue."

"What year?"

"I don't know."

"How'd you know it was a Chevy?"

"I rode in the middle. It had those little flags on the horn button. Ya know? Those little cross-flags."

"Was it old or new?"

"The horn button?"

Stryker smiled.

"No, the car," West said.

"It was old, I guess."

"Don't guess, dammit."

"It was old."

"Where'd you go?"

"We went to the liquor store at Fifty-eighth and Western. Then we came here."

"Whose idea to come here?"

"Supernigger," she said, pointing to the bloody body on the floor.

"Did the other two come in?"

"Yeah."

"For how long?"

"Hour, maybe."

" 'Maybe' won't do."

"Till about twelve-thirty, one o'clock. I don't know."

"What did they talk about?"

"Me."

"What else?"

"About gettin' another car."

"Did they say why?"

"No, but I knew."

"Knew what?"

"I'm not dumb, ya know."

"What did you know?"

"The Chevy was hot."

"How did you know that?"

"The ignition was punched."

"Did they say where they were going to get the car?"

"Yeah. The one with the moustache said that Baldwin Hills had nice homes, shiny new cars, and no cops."

"Why didn't he go along?" West said.

"Because he wanted me. That's why."

"Did they say when they'd be back?"

"No."

"How long you been knowing these people?"

"I've seen them around."

"Where?"

"Black Saddle on Crenshaw Boulevard."

"How long ago?"

"About a month ago. Maybe."

"You shack with them then?"

"No."

"What did you do?"

"Me and some other girls went nightclubbing with them."

"Which one were you with then?"

"There was five of them then. Ya know? The one I liked was Johnny Grear."

"Where's he now?"

"Red said he's a dummy and that he's in jail."

"For what?"

"I don't know."

"Bullshit."

"I don't know."

"You don't have any idea?"

"No."

"What kind of car did you ride in when you went nightclubbing?"

"A Buick. It had out-of-state plates on it."

"What state?"

"I don't know."

"Well, well," a heavy voice interrupted. "Might have known who'd be raising hell on a Sunday morning." A stocky, graying man stood in the door, surveying first Stryker, then the body.

"Hello, Price." Stryker smiled. "Sorry to screw up your breakfast."

"Stryker, West, this is my partner, Bishop," Price said, as a slender, balding man followed him into the room.

They shook hands.

"What have you got?" Bishop asked.

"We had some info that the asshole from last night's shooting might be holed up here," Stryker said. "But he wasn't here."

"Who's this?" Price asked, running his fingers over the damaged wall.

"One of Pepper's playmates."

Price grunted. "This his gun?" he asked, picking up the nine-millimeter from the dresser.

"Yeah." Stryker took the pistol clip from his rear pocket and tossed it to Price.

"You killed him," Price said flatly, glancing at Stryker.

"No, Johnson did," Stryker said, digging in his pocket for the other cartridge. "He's back at the station waiting for you people." He handed the cartridge to Price.

"Fine," Price said, examining the pistol.

"That hole in the ceiling is from the nine-millimeter," West added.

Price and Bishop looked at the ceiling.

"We didn't look for the empty," Stryker said. "We wanted to leave something for you people to do."

Price smiled wryly.

"That's the shotgun Johnson used," West said, pointing. "Here's the other live rounds." He handed the three red shotgun cartridges to Bishop. "The empty shotgun shell is around here somewhere."

"How come you didn't kill her?" Bishop asked.

"Johnson can't shoot worth a fuck," Stryker said, looking at the girl. She turned to West, her eyes showing fear. West didn't smile.

"She's Marlene Craig, a local businesswoman," West said. "She helped save our ass. Dipshit over there was about to shoot through the door, but she stopped him. That's how the hole got in the ceiling."

"She's been warned and is willing," Stryker said. "We don't think she's involved, so you people tread softly, if possible."

"Sure, sure," Price said pleasantly. "Always willing to help those who help us."

The girl glanced at Stryker and forced a frightened smile.

Stryker did not acknowledge it.

"Bishop," Price ordered, "go down and call the

coroner, photo lab, and . . ." He paused. "You want prints, John?"

"Yeah," Stryker answered. "We'd like to prove asshole's been here."

Price nodded. "And prints."

Bishop left.

"Why don't you two go on back to the station?" Price suggested. "We'll get your statements later."

"Right," Stryker said. He and West moved toward the open door. "We'll see you."

"You gotta go?" the girl asked in a voice edged with fear.

"Look, I know he's big and ugly," Stryker said, "but he's harmless, hasn't had a hard-on in years. He'll take good care of you."

West winked at her.

She smiled. The two left the room.

"Hey, Stryker," Price called as they started down the stairs.

"What?"

"Take your army with you," Price shouted.

"Right."

A patrol officer stood at the bottom of the stairs. "That your partner on the door?" Stryker asked.

"Yeah."

"Go around and tell everybody else to go back to the station," Stryker ordered. "Then, you and your partner stick with it, until those people upstairs leave."

"Right."

"I'll tell your watch commander," Stryker added as they walked toward the driveway.

West opened the door to their car. "Any clue on where we go next?"

Stryker slid into the Plymouth. "No, I don't know what in the hell we'll do now."

"Looks like five of them came out from St. Louis in that hot Buick," West said, starting the car. "They were strangers in town, so I'd think they'd stick together."

"Maybe," Stryker said absently. He was still brooding over the girl. Disgusting. Fucking whore, he thought.

"What's wrong?" West asked, pulling into the light Sunday-morning traffic.

"Can't figure it," Stryker said, slouching in the seat. "Good-looking paddy whore climbing in the sack with dudes."

West glanced at him sharply, then smiled. "She just knows who can get the job done."

"Yeah, if you like being screwed by a donkey dick," Stryker said without humor. "Bastard stunk like six dead elephants."

West slowed for a traffic signal. "Little competition never hurt anybody," he said pleasantly.

"Competition isn't the goddamned point," Stryker said angrily. "You ever see a dog screwing a cat, or a horse fucking a cow? That's the goddamned point."

West studied him for a moment. "You ever lay a black girl?"

Stryker laughed defensively. "No, I've never had an identity problem."

"You've met some you would," West said.

"I'll give you that," Stryker agreed. "There's some good-looking black women, but I haven't crossed the line."

"Maybe that's why you're upset," West said slowly. "They've experienced something you haven't had the nerve to try."

"Don't use that psychology horseshit on me, college boy," Stryker warned. "And don't tell me I don't have any fucking nerve. I just don't have any taste for dark meat."

"I've tried the white meat," West said deliberately, "so I can understand why you might be wondering if the dark meat isn't better."

Stryker glared. West looked away.

Several car horns sounded behind them. West glanced at the traffic signal. They were sitting through the green. West rolled the car forward. Stryker relaxed to his slouched position, silent.

Finally, after several blocks, West said, "Let's let it slide, John."

Stryker said nothing.

On Sunday morning, the *Time*'s headline read, "COUNCILMAN WARD'S SON SLAIN BY POLICE; POLICE REFUSE ANY COMMENT."

Bill Hart of KBAC-TV hosted an early-morning special newscast called, "Crisis in Black." Hart's news team had found four eyewitnesses to the shooting. Their stories contradicted each other, but Hart didn't seem concerned. He explained that excitement and fear caused the differing points of view. The eyewitnesses all sat with their backs to the television cameras during their interviews.

The other major television stations in the city also aired special newscasts. KCEN and KTXN ran the taped interview of Councilman Ward's arrival at the hospital. They showed Lieutenant Clark, but his brief statement had been edited out. When the commander of public affairs called the stations to ask why, news editors explained that it didn't contribute anything of interest to the general public.

The chief of police announced that he would hold a news conference at Parker Center at one o'clock.

Shortly afterward, Councilman Ward's field deputy, Russell LeBlanc, announced a news conference at the councilman's campaign headquarters on West Adams Boulevard at three o'clock.

Sunday morning passed slowly as the temperature climbed. The mobile command post was now in operation at Southwest Station.

Stryker, West, and Johnson gave their statements to homicide late in the morning. Johnson went home wondering if he'd be able to sleep. Stryker and West dove into the multitude of reports they had to complete, after Gunning informed them they would not be able to talk to Bennett before Monday.

It was nearly one o'clock when two officers who were handling a family-dispute call returned to their car. "ASSASSINS" was scrawled on the sidewalk in red paint. The car was in flames.

Chief of Police James Peck sat in his quiet office on the sixth floor of Parker Center studying the typed statement he was soon to deliver.

Los Angeles spread away in all directions below Peck's window, still and lazy in the afternoon sun. He sat quietly, trying to relax. A gray pigeon soared from one rooftop to another with little effort.

The intercom buzzed. Peck turned his chair around. "Yes?"

"Mayor Abbott on line twenty-six, sir."

"Thank you, Lieutenant." He pressed the blinking button. "Good afternoon, Mr. Mayor."

"Hello, Jim," the crisp voice of the mayor answered. "How are things going?"

"Well, sir, my last situation report, which I received just ten minutes ago, shows no major problems yet. We've had one police car burned in Southwest Division, and several windows broken in

Seventy-seventh. No arrests relating to either of these instances."

"Uh-huh, well, let's hope we can continue to keep control."

"We're doing our best, sir," Peck said. And thought: "What the hell do you mean, *we?* The goddamned election."

"I've been getting complaints about overreaction with your heavy deployment, Jim, and the fact that you've set up the mobile command at Southwest."

"Well, sir, you know my policy. The only way to control a riot is to prevent it. It wouldn't do a damn bit of good to increase deployment after something blows up."

"I agree with that, Jim. But what can we use for justification?"

"Past experience. The assassination of Dr. King, the raid on Panther headquarters, and many others. During those times, deployment was increased and order was maintained. If it hadn't been, there is no doubt we'd have faced major disturbances. Intelligence is satisfied that the deterrent was our show of force."

"Yes, I'll agree with that." The mayor sighed. "Have you been able to get any more details on the shooting?"

"No, sir."

"For your information, Jim, I called Councilman Ward to offer my sympathy and suggest we suspend all campaigning for a month."

"Any reaction?"

"I didn't speak to him directly. His man LeBlanc told me that Ward had nothing to say to me. I doubt that he even told Ward I called. I don't like LeBlanc."

"I don't know him, Mr. Mayor. But I do know

that Ward can lead us into a real disaster or show us the way out of the woods in this matter."

"You're right about that, Jim. He's going to swing one way or the other. But I doubt he'll repeat the theatrical display we saw at the hospital last night."

"Sir, how would you have reacted if it had been your son?"

There was a pause.

"I see your point, Jim."

After hanging up the phone, the chief looked at his watch; twelve-fifty-five, time to get downstairs, he thought.

The auditorium on the first floor of Parker Center hummed with activity. Heavy gray cables snaked over each other to the television cameras. Two hundred reporters pushed toward the front of the auditorium. Major newspapers, radio, television— all were represented in the crowd that milled about drinking coffee and sending clouds of blue smoke toward the high ceiling.

"You think Peck can keep the lid on the black community *this* time?" said a graying reporter from one of the major networks.

"Jesus Christ," another said caustically, "did one of your script writers hand you that?"

"Just what the hell is that supposed to mean?" The first reporter's face reddened.

"Save it for the League of Active Mothers," answered the second. "You know goddamn well the whole rhubarb began with criminals; not the police. Furthermore, we wouldn't be here today if Ward's son hadn't been one of those killed. You're acting as if the police are on trial. Maybe that sells your show, but this isn't showbiz. I think it's time the mayor and every other so-called leader in this city got their fat asses off the fence and called for

restraint and calm. Let 'em lay off the cops for
once."

"Frank," said the first, "you're so goddamned far
right it's a wonder you don't fall off the world.
People have a right to be angry. The cops kill the
son of a prominent black leader—unarmed, not
resisting, and shot in the back. And the police"—
he raised his voice—"refuse to give any information. This is one time Peck's not going to . . ."

"Is that the ACLU line, or did you get it out of
the thoughts of Chairman Mao?"

"May I have your attention, ladies and gentlemen," the public-address system crackled. "If you
will please take your seats, the chief of police will
be here in a moment."

The crowd shuffled to the auditorium's comfortable seats, while soundmen, cameramen, and photographers clustered around the rostrum.

Chief Peck, dressed in a dark blue suit, appeared
from the right side of the platform, walking briskly
to the rostrum. His gray wavy hair was combed
back on the sides; as always, several strands hung
down on his forehead. He carried his slender, six-
foot frame with an athletic style.

"Arrogant bastard," the Wilshire *Press* whispered
to a reporter beside him.

Peck spread his papers on the rostrum and looked
to the audience. Several cameras flashed. The television lights flared on. Peck squinted briefly, and
his green eyes swept across the crowd, found several familiar faces, and felt a bit of comfort in
knowing that he had a few friends in the audience.

Whether or not they agreed with him didn't
matter. It was just comforting to know some of
the people on the other side of all those damn
lights.

"Good afternoon, ladies and gentlemen," Peck

began in a tone the *Times* described as big-brotherish. "I would like to begin by reading a statement that I think will answer most of your questions." Pausing, he brushed the stubborn strands of gray hair from his forehead.

The audience listened quietly and intently, some scribbling hurriedly, others holding recording microphones, while Chief Peck recounted the shootings in detail and listed the victims.

"The seventh victim was Harry W. Casner, the citizen I mentioned before, who came out of his house to assist Officer Bennett. He was shot once in the head by the suspect who was hidden in the back seat of the Chevrolet.

"Now, I'll take your questions."

"Chief Peck, when . . . ?" "Chief Peck, was . . . ?" What was the motive for . . . ?" A multitude of questions came from the group simultaneously. Peck pointed to a particular reporter, who stood up and said, "Chief, what was Councilman Ward's son doing in the car, and isn't it true he was unarmed?"

"In answer to the first part of your question, sir," Peck said in an icy tone, "the two officers didn't know the identity of anybody in the car. All they knew was that they had a stolen car with six people in it. Second, Officer Bennett never had the opportunity to search the suspects. Two of the six suspects had been armed, a fact he knew too well; he had probable cause to believe that the two suspects he ordered from the car might also be armed. For this reason he placed them in a position against the wall to give him an advantage until assistance arrived. It was at this time that Officer Bennett was shot in the back. He fell forward. When he struck the ground, his shotgun fired. The blast was fatal to young Ward and his companion. That shooting was accidental, but unavoidable. . . . I repeat, *unavoidable.*

"As to why Councilman Ward's son was in the vehicle, we don't know that."

"But is it true that young Ward was unarmed?"

"Yes," Peck answered. "Next question.

"Mr. Williams." Peck designated a small man seated near the back of the room.

"Chief Peck, you've said that Officer Bennett was shot by a man hidden in the back seat of the Chevrolet. Yet earlier you also stated that Bennett had radioed that he and his partner were following a car with six men in it. How do you account for a trained police officer's failure to remember that there had to be a third man in the back seat?"

The auditorium buzzed loudly. Peck's jaw muscles tensed while he wailed for silence.

"Officer Bennett didn't miss the sixth suspect because he is a bad policeman," he said slowly, removing his black-framed glasses from an inside pocket. He seldom wore them in public, but his eyes burned from the bright camera lights, and his left eyelid had begun to twitch. He had been awake for eleven hours after only two hours' sleep.

"In a matter of two or three minutes, he had seen his partner shot to death; he had been faced with two men jumping from the car, one—and possibly the other—raising a gun to kill him; he had then shot both men to death." He paused. "You must try to put yourself in his position, Mr. Williams. He had just watched two people die, one a close friend; he had just killed two people, and very narrowly missed being killed himself. I do not believe that he can be criticized in any way for his actions in this case."

He put a finger under his glasses and rubbed his left eye.

"Yes." He pointed to a reporter from the *Times*.

"Sir," the reporter said, standing, "could you comment on the riot following the shooting?"

"Mr. Townsend"—Peck looked him steadily in the eye—"we did not have a riot. We had a major disturbance which was very short-lived. I'm certain if you call Rumor Control, you'll be told by an anonymous recording that six black men were executed last night for no other reason than because they were black." Peck's voice rose in anger as his grip on the rostrum tightened. "There's no mention in the recorded message of an officer being shot to death and another seriously wounded; but this incident, according to Rumor Control, will trigger the start of the long-awaited black revolution."

He paused, breathed deeply, and went on. "What really occurred was this. In order to protect the crime scene until our investigation was completed, it was necessary to seal off the area. One of the roadblocks established was at the intersection of Slauson and Overhill. Two uniformed officers in a black-and-white were assigned to this intersection and advised to divert traffic north and south on Overhill in order to bypass the crime scene on Slauson. Traffic on Slauson Avenue is very heavy on a Saturday night, and in a very short time a large crowd gathered. Someone in the crowd threw a bottle, smashing the windshield of the police car. The officers observed the suspect and effected his arrest. The suspect was handcuffed and placed in the rear of the police car. The crowd surrounded the black-and-white and took the prisoner from the officers. Officer Richard Edwards was beaten severely by the crowd, and is presently at Central Receiving Hospital. He suffered a broken nose, a two-inch laceration on his left cheek, and three broken ribs.

"Fortunately, his partner suffered only a few bruises. There was heavy damage to the police car, and the shotgun was stolen. Someone in the crowd fired it twice after removing it from the car. It has not yet been recovered.

"During this incident, the two officers requested help. Units responded, and thirty-eight police officers, under the command of Captain David C. Gunning, commander of Southwest Division, cleared the area with little trouble."

"How many arrests were made?"

"None," Peck said. "Both of our injured officers were en route to the hospital, so we had no idea who our suspects were. Our immediate concern was to clear the area and prevent any further threat to life or property, and we did just that.

"The individuals responsible for injuring the officers, damaging the police car, stealing the police shotgun, and for the arson of a dress shop, will be found through investigation. They will be arrested and prosecuted.

"The young lady in the green dress," Peck said, pointing to an attractive female reporter.

"Chief Peck," she said with practiced charm, "wouldn't you say it was poor judgment for these two police officers to try to effect the arrest of six suspects? Couldn't they have waited for assistance before stopping the car?"

Peck returned her smile woodenly.

"Miss," Peck said, "let me give you some idea of what the circumstances were like last night at the time of the shooting. Southwest Division covers roughly eleven square miles. One hundred and eighty-four thousand people live inside its boundaries. To protect and serve all those people, there are only two hundred and seventy-five policemen, who must be divided among three different watches.

Then there are the many necessary staff positions, and police officers do need days off, and they do need vacations, and they do get sick. So last night, to protect and serve the one hundred and eighty-four thousand people of Southwest Division between the hours of midnight and eight A.M., there were only twenty-two police officers on patrol, or eleven police units."

Peck removed his glasses, gesturing with them. "At one o'clock this morning," he explained, "communications division had a backlog of twenty-seven calls for police service for Southwest Division alone. Conrad and Bennett, although only on duty for an hour, had already handled four radio calls and had been assigned another two very shortly before the shooting. When they radioed that they were stoping the stolen car at Slauson and LaBrea, there were no other units in the division clear to assist them. Just moments before, there had been an attempted murder on Thirty-seventh Place, involving a drunken husband with a shotgun who had tried to kill his wife. So, in answer to your question, miss, no, the officers did not use poor judgment. They knew there was danger involved. They knew it was a busy night and that not many, if any, units would be clear to offer assistance. But they were both sworn to perform their duty, and they did." Peck tried another smile. "I hope that answers your question?"

"I hope so too," the woman said, sitting down.

"Mr. Flute," Peck said, acknowledging a well-dressed, bearded Negro reporter from the South Los Angeles *Grit*, a widely read Negro weekly.

"Chief-of-Police-Peck," Flute said, spreading the words out slowly as he stood, and gesturing with his yellow notepad, "what was the race of the slain suspects?"

"Negro, as you know, Mr. Flute."

"All black, Chief?"

"All Negro."

"Do you suppose that these two officers, Chief Peck," Flute asked, "may have been suffering from what we in the black community refer to as the police-ghetto jitters?"

Peck straightened. "Mr. Flute, you are suggesting that these two officers overreacted. But Officer Conrad's 'overreaction' was too late to save his own life! Is that ghetto jitters, Mr. Flute?"

The two men glared at each other. The audience waited.

"As for Officer Bennett," Peck said, "he's been living in Southwest Division, or the ghetto, as you call it, for ten years. Or didn't you know he was black, Mr. Flute?"

"No. . . . No, I didn't," Flute said, apparently surprised.

"Does that make a difference?" Peck asked.

"Well, yes," Flute stammered, "yes, that does make a difference." He sat down.

"Right on," someone yelled, and there was a spattering of laughter.

"Yes, sir," Peck said, pointing to one of the many raised hands in the audience.

"Frank Clary," the reporter said as he stood. *"San Diego Sun.* Chief, I understand there was a second shooting at about eight this morning. Could you confirm this and did it relate to the shooting of last night?"

Peck nodded agreement. "Yes, there was a shooting at the Rocket Motel, located at 4708 South Normandie at about eight A.M. this morning. One suspect was slain in that shooting. We had . . ."

"That's seven black men killed by the police in

less than eight hours," a voice interrupted. "How many more can we expect today?"

Peck recognized the voice as Flute's. His stomach churned with anger, as he spoke.

"Mr. Flute," Peck said, "I would appreciate your saving your comments for your paper. But if you insist on interrupting, make sure your accusations are correct. The death of the suspect at the motel was number six, and it wasn't the color of his skin that got him killed. It was his threat to someone else's life. He would have been slain if he were green, blue or red. And, incidentally, since you seem concerned about it, this suspect also was killed by a black officer."

Flute looked down at his notepad.

"Well, Peck just blew it with the black press," the *Examiner* whispered to a reporter beside him.

"What the hell else *can* he say?" the other whispered back. "He's a horse's ass, all right, but his story sounds straight."

"Thank you, William F. Buckley," said the *Examiner*.

"Now, Mr. Clary, to finish with your question," Peck said, returning to the reporter, who was still standing. "One of our detective teams from Southwest Division learned that our missing suspect from the shooting had been staying at the Rocket Motel on Normandie Avenue. The motel manager confirmed that the suspect did in fact have a room there. The officers deployed around that room and announced their presence.

"They heard a struggle inside the room, a female voice screaming, followed by the sound of a pistol shot. This gave the officers reason to believe that a life was in danger, so they forced open the door. At that, the suspect, armed with a nine-millimeter pistol, aimed it at the officers. He was slain before he was able to fire."

"What happened to the female, Chief?" the reporter added.

"She was not injured and not involved in the crime. She was not arrested."

"So then, the outstanding suspect from Slauson and LaBrea is dead?"

"No, the man killed at the motel was not involved in any way with the shooting at Slauson and LaBrea; but he was a companion of our suspect from the shooting there," Peck answered. "His name was George Rowe. He, too, was a newcomer to our city from St. Louis.

"Like Dukes and Wray, he was wanted for homicide in St. Louis, and it appears he was involved in the burglary of the gun shop in West Hollywood and the theft of the fifty-seven Chevy."

"What was the girl's name, and what was she doing in the motel room?" a reporter called.

"She's a witness who will help us convict our outstanding suspect, so I can't comment on that at this time."

"Can you tell us who you're after, Chief? And has this outstanding suspect been identified?"

"Yes . . . yes, he has," Peck said again, brushing the hair back from his wet forehead. "The description obtained from the witness we had at the scene, and fingerprints lifted from the stolen car, confirmed that the suspect is Frederick L. Pepper, a male Negro, thirty-two years old, six-foot-two inches tall, and weighing about two hundred and thirty pounds. He has short-cut black hair, brown eyes, a ruddy complexion, and a large jagged scar on the bridge of his nose. He has a street name of Red Pepper, and he used the name of Joe Packard when he registered at the Rocket Motel several days ago.

He was last seen wearing a dirty white T-shirt and dark trousers."

"Do you have any pictures, Chief?" a voice called.

"Yes," Peck said. "Through the cooperation of the St. Louis Police Department and United Press International, a picture of the suspect was transmitted to us several hours ago. Our photo lab is in the process of making duplicates, and they should be available soon.

"Incidentally, Pepper is also wanted for robbery and homicide in St. Louis. It appears that he, Wray, Dukes, Woods, Rowe, and a man the sheriff's office took in custody before the shooting, by the name of Grear, all came to Los Angeles together after pulling a bank robbery in St. Louis in which a security officer was slain."

"Do you have any leads on where Pepper may be?" a voice called from the audience.

"No, gentlemen," Peck conceded. "We have no idea. That's one of our motives in having this news conference. We need your help, in the sense that you can make Pepper very well known. Well enough, perhaps, that he'll have no place left to hide. Needless to say, he is to be considered armed and extremely dangerous. He didn't hesitate to shoot an armed officer, so he's a threat to anybody. We encourage you to advise those with any information about him to contact the police immediately. All information will, of course, be kept strictly confidential.

"Gentlemen," Peck continued, picking up the papers in front of him. "I have an appointment. Inspector Brock will take over and answer any questions I may have missed. But I would like to say this before I finish. Last night there was some friction between the men of my department and certain members of the news media, very probably some of you here today. We, as policemen, walk a thin line between cooperation with the press and the necessary performance of our duty. There will always be a conflict between the two. It's unavoidable. Last night the officers of Southwest Division had a member of their team killed and others seriously injured. As long as we continue to recruit policemen from the human race, they're going to get emotional when one of them gets killed or injured. It'll be a damn sad day for this city when they don't. So I'm not apologizing for what happened, just explaining why, and I'm certain most of you are professional enough to understand. Thank you very much for your time and cooperation."

Peck walked to the right side of the platform; the TV lights and cameras followed; several cameras flashed as he disappeared behind the blue curtain.

Immediately, the reporters moved toward the bank of temporary telephones installed near the rear of the auditorium.

"Well, ladies and gentlemen," said Frank Miller as he stepped in front of the TV camera near the front of the auditorium, "you've just heard chief of police, James Peck, give the police version of the shooting that rocked South Los Angeles last night, leaving eight men dead and several others seriously injured. Why did it all happen? Where will it all end? Perhaps we'll never . . ."

Field Deputy LeBlanc eased back in his chair after turning off the television set in the Ward living room. He finished a note on the yellow pad in his lap, then turned off the tape recorder. "Peck played his audience well," he thought. "The dedicated-cop routine, duty till death, and all that other shit. But those bastards elected Jacob Ward mayor of Los Angeles last night."

He glanced at his watch. It was one-forty-five.

Back in his office, Peck read the latest situation report.

"1320 hours; Southwest Station desk reports fifth bomb threat. No further."

"1325 hours; Central Receiving Hospital: hospital detail reports bomb threat via telephone. Requested officers for security. Central Division supplied same. No evidence of bomb."

"1335 hours; police-car windshield broken by thrown bottle; Vernon and Vermont. No injuries. No arrests."

"1340 hours; administrator of Daniel Freeman Hospital called Southwest commander and reported hospital receiving bomb and arson threats. Security detail at same increased to eight men plus sergeant. Inglewood P.D. advised."

"Rosson, get me Inspector Foster on the phone," Peck called to his aide.

"Yes, sir."

The phone buzzed. "Yes."

"Inspector Foster on line fifty-eight, sir."

"Okay." Peck pressed the blinking button.

"Foster, this is Peck. How are things going?"

"I've never seen anything like this," the inspector said. "I just took a ride in Air 3 over Wilshire, Southwest, Newton, and Seventy-seventh Division, and not to sound melodramatic, but it looks like the calm before the storm. The streets are nearly empty."

"I think it's shock and curiosity," Peck said, mulling it over. "Maybe they're watching television or listening to the radio."

"I'll buy that," Foster said. "I've issued an order for Southwest, Newton, and Seventy-seventh Division to wear helmets on patrol."

"Fine," Peck said.

"We've got another problem, Chief," Foster said. "Penworth, the administrator of Daniel Freeman Hospital, has called three times in the past hour. He's complaining of bomb and arson threats and problems with some of his nursing staff about Bennett. He's all but asked us to get Bennett out of there."

Peck leaned back in his chair, rubbing his eyes with thumb and forefinger.

"Here's what we'll do. I'll call Central Receiving and see if one of our doctors will go down to Daniel Freeman and examine Bennett. After I get that report back, I'll give you the decision on moving him."

"Very good, sir."

"Foster, only you and I know about this now, and that's the way I want it to stay."

"I understand."

"We can't afford any leaks. And if Penworth calls back again, I'll handle him."

"Yes, sir."

"If we decide to go ahead, we'll do it at exactly three P.M.," Peck said. "That's when Ward will be starting his news conference, and most of the black community will be watching In the meantime, Inspector, you lay out what you think is the best route and security procedures."

"Yes, sir."

Detective Lieutenant Purington had returned early from a weekend at Lake Arrowhead. After reading through Stryker's and West's reports, he came to the door of his office. "Okay, shove off, you two. Go home, get some chow and a good night's sleep. You've got a long week ahead of you."

When both objected, Purington said, "Look, I know you may not believe it, but we've got other detectives in this city. Now, go home."

"Well, see you tomorrow, guy," West said as they parted in the parking lot.

"Right." Stryker yawned, walking toward his blue Firebird. When he opened the door, the warm air from the car's interior boiled out to greet him.

He slipped off his suit jacket, then removed the tan shoulder holster and slid it under the bucket seat. The seat burned from the glare of the afternoon sun, and he nearly hit a Volkswagen parked behind him as he backed out of his spot. "Damn, I am tired." He glanced at the car's clock. "Two-twenty; been here nearly thirteen hours. Getting old, I guess."

Traffic on Western Avenue was light as Stryker traveled northbound, cursing the traffic engineer who had planned the traffic-light sequence on Western Avenue. Slowing to a stop at the intersection of Western and Exposition, he could see that the traffic signals for the next two blocks were already green. "As soon as I move, they'll change," he thought. The light flashed to green. Tromping on the accelerator, Stryker raced toward the green light. He had traveled three-quarters of a block and was just about to shift to third when the green light switched to amber. "You bastard," he said aloud, downshifted, and rolled to a smooth stop.

After losing the battle with two more red lights on Western, Stryker finally hit the freeway and began to move. He was toying with the idea of writing a letter to the city traffic engineer to tell him how screwed up his system was. He was convinced such a rotten system caused more accidents than it prevented.

But the rush of cool air relaxed him, and in the back of Stryker's mind he realized that this game of anger with trivial things was his way of getting rid of frustrations. If he allowed himself to think of Conrad's bloody body, or Bennett's, or Casner's, his stomach would churn with anger, he wouldn't sleep or eat, and eventually his ulcer would bleed again, maybe for the last time. So he filled his mind with other targets: the traffic lights, the telephone company, and billboards. He'd learned five years ago, when he lost his first partner, that if he carried the job home with him, it would eat him alive.

McKnight was driving. Stryker had spotted a license with a want on it. They were following the hot Mustang in their unmarked Plymouth and had radioed for a black-and-white to intercept, but the suspects had spotted them for detectives. At the red light at Hoover Boulevard and Twenty-eighth Street, the Mustang suddenly made a screeching left turn and sped south. About six car lengths back, McKnight gunned it up to fifty, and, tires smoking, jerked the wheel all the way to the left at the intersection.

"Traffic on the right!" Stryker screamed as the Plymouth went into a four-wheel lock skid. They were spinning to the right—sliding; Stryker vividly recalled the little red Corvair, the terror on the face of the young woman driving, and the little girl standing beside her mother on the seat, holding a black doll to her chest. McKnight was killed in the crash; his wife was five months pregnant at the time. She lost her child eighteen hours later; it would have been their first. Four days afterward she was found hanging in the bathroom. On the mirror she had written in lipstick, "Now we will all be together."

Stryker had spent day after day in his apartment staring out the window. He had decided to quit the department. One day a construction crew showed up and started erecting something on the grounds in front of his building; he realized it was a huge billboard; he was furious.

"Who in the hell's going to pay one-seventy-five a month to look at the back of a billboard," he demanded of the apartment manager. Carried on by his anger, he recruited several other residents of the complex and threatened to move out unless the construction stopped.

Before he realized it, Stryker was elected chairman of Save Our Community, formed to combat the construction of the billboard. He was swept up into a round of lobbying with councilmen, visiting the construction company's offices, and gathering signatures on petitions. He stopped feeling sorry for himself.

Elm Drive was a quiet, tree-lined street with modern two-story apartment complexes on one side and Vista Mesa Park on the other. The park was a rolling green acre of grass, trees, and bushes with a small blue lake in its center. Some boys playing an undermanned game of softball moved to the side as Stryker drove into the street.

He pulled into the driveway, then welcomed the subterranean coolness as he rolled down the ramp into the dim garage.

Wrapping shoulder holster and pistol in his suit jacket, he walked toward the courtyard. Two women were sunning themselves at the far end of the pool. He gave both a "fair" rating. Children played with an inflatable duck in the shallow end. The water looked cool and inviting. Maybe a swim later.

FM music came from the bedroom. He pushed the door quietly, closed it behind him, tossed jacket and gun to the couch, and after slipping off his shoes, crossed to the partly open bedroom door. He paused at the entrance.

Connie sat on the edge of the bed with her back to the doorway, folding T-shirts, shorts, and socks into an open dresser drawer.

Her long blond hair hung in loose waves to the middle of her back. As usual, she wore no shoes, and her lavender mini-dress was cut low in the back, showing her deep brown tan.

"Too bad all burglars aren't as pretty," Stryker said.

She jumped up, holding a pair of black socks. "John Stryker, damn you, you scared the hell out of me!"

"What are you doing, woman?"

"Just supporting my local police." She smiled, tossing the socks into the open drawer, then pushing it closed with a bare foot.

She put her arms around him and leaned her head on his shoulder. "You look tired, John." The soft scent of her perfume made him tingle.

"I am." He breathed heavily, running a hand through her hair. He slid a hand under her chin, tilted her head back, and looked into her blue eyes.

She ran a finger along his cheek, feeling the stubble of his beard. "Was it bad?"

"They don't call me out for good news."

She was silent a moment. "Hey, John, I've got some potato salad and corned beef in my apartment." She had learned early in their relationship not to pry. "How about some?"

"Sounds like a clue." He smiled. She was unbuttoning his shirt and pulling it off as she spoke.

"Okay, mister," she said, "you stretch out here and unwind, and I'll go get your chow."

She guided him to the bed and knelt over him as he stretched out on his back. "I'll be right back." She gave him a brief kiss. Stryker changed the kiss to a longer one. His arms circled her and pulled her tight against him. She responded for a moment, then pushed away. "Not on an empty stomach, dear, it's bad for your health."

He slapped her on the butt as she moved away. She smiled, then stuck out her tongue and left the room.

Connie returned in about ten minutes, carrying a TV tray with the potato salad and a corned-beef sandwich. Stryker was now lying on his stomach with his face buried in one of the bed pillows.

"Avon calling," she said softly. He didn't answer. "Damn." Setting the tray on the dresser, she closed the venetian blind. Then, turning off the radio on the dresser, she knelt beside the bed, brushed the graying hair at his temple, leaned forward, and kissed him gently on the cheek. "You don't know what you missed, fella," she whispered.

It was ten minutes to three. She put the potato salad and sandwich in his refrigerator, walked to the living room, lay down on the couch, and picked up a novel she had half-read. Holding the open book against her chest, she stared at his gun and holster at the other end of the couch. She nudged it with a toe. "What's the police department got that I haven't?"

The "Ward for Mayor" campaign headquarters on West Adams was teeming with newsmen, awaiting the three-o'clock press conference. Most of those present had also attended the press conference at Parker Center earlier in the day.

Young campaign workers were busy setting up folding chairs in the old market that served as campaign headquarters. They all wore black arm bands. A photographer for the *Times* had several of them pose near a large poster of the councilman.

Black cloth draped the speaker's platform and the entrance to the market. The reporters who had been so noisy at Parker Center were quiet now, and most were already seated while camera crews and technicians were setting up.

"I'm sorry I couldn't inform you of this sooner," Inspector Foster began, knocking his pipe ashes into an ashtray, "but we've decided to move Bennett. Daniel Freeman has had several bomb and arson threats since Bennett's arrival. They're also having a problem with some of their minority nurses. Not all, just some," he said, looking up at the group gathered around the conference table at the command post—Captain Gunning, several sergeants, and the lieutenant in charge of the day watch at Southwest. "Anyway"—he began packing his pipe —"Freeman is just too damn big for us to provide security. So we're moving Bennett."

Gunning wasn't surprised. Nearly an hour before, Foster had requested that a city ambulance be sent to the command post, and there were maps of Los Angeles and Inglewood spread out on the table, with staggered red lines running across them.

"Chief Peck has had Bennett examined by a doctor from Central Receiving, and the doctor gave the go-ahead for the ride.

"Lieutenant Duffey, you'll send a black-and-white with two officers along with the ambulance to the emergency entrance of Freeman. The security officers there will wheel a decoy patient from Bennett's room to the ambulance, which will then proceed to the Police Academy.

"Everybody will use red lights and siren," Foster added. "We want to draw attention. If the motorcade should catch a rock or bottle, or get sniped at, it should call for help but keep rolling. I want no stopping under any circumstances."

The lieutenant nodded, making notes.

"Now, Duffey, after the ambulance leaves the hospital, you are to arrive there. That'll be about three-fifteen. Your transportation is parked at the Coliseum. It's a hearse."

The group laughed.

"Don't worry, Lieutenant," Foster said, "you'll probably only ride in a hearse once more after today." The men laughed louder. Foster drew in on his pipe and exhaled the smoke up toward the ceiling of the van, where it circled slowly in the humid air. "We have two Negro officers who'll be acting as driver and attendant. You'll go to the service entrance at Freeman, where our doctor will be waiting with Bennett. Here's the route." He flipped the map around to face Duffey. Duffey leaned forward and studied the red line. "Got it?"

"Yes, sir," Duffey answered.

Foster took a long drink from the styrofoam cup in front of him. The coffee was cold, flat, and bitter.

"Damn"—he made a face—"no wonder so many cops have ulcers."

LeBlanc gripped the sides of the rostrum tightly, his face showing the strain of the night. A band of black was pinned to the sleeve of his black suit.

"I won't start this press conference by saying, 'Good afternoon,' as Chief Peck did, because it is not a good day for the black community. The police may consider it a good day when they slay the unarmed son of a black councilman, but we do not.

"Councilman Ward will not be here this afternoon. Mrs. Ward, who was visiting her family in Philadelphia when her son was slain, is returning to Los Angeles this afternoon at about three-twenty. It was Councilman Ward's desire that he and his wife not be disturbed upon her arrival." He paused, looked into the audience through the glare of the camera lights. "I hope you ladies and gentlemen of the press will honor that request.

"I have here," LeBlanc said, holding up a sheet of typed paper, "a statement from Councilman Ward. I will read it now."

The untimely death of my son is the most tragic event of my lifetime. But the tragedy is not only mine.

My son was at the age where I could see manhood in his eyes. He was fast developing into a dynamic black man who would share the task of improving the quality of life in the black community. But we have been robbed of his participation by the sound of gunfire, the sound we hear again and again in our community.

I make this pledge to the memory of my beloved son, and to those whose faith elected me to public office. I will fight regardless of the odds, I will fight until the individuals responsible for his death are brought to justice.

We will not settle for Chief Peck's simple explanation. We will not settle for the district attorney's excuse of insufficient evidence. We will not rest until the murderer of my son is punished.

Two unarmed black men were shot in the back by a police officer. If our chief of police can call it unavoidable, then I call Chief Peck an arrogant white racist.

I summon all decent people in this city, be you white, brown, yellow, or black to join with me in demanding that the attorney general of the United States immediately launch a federal grand-jury investigation into this act of murder perpetrated by members of the Los Angeles Police Department.

I ask that the attorney general immediately direct the Federal Bureau of Investigation to intervene and assume the responsibility of investigating the incident before valuable evidence is lost or destroyed.

We have lost other sons and brothers—Malcolm, John, Martin, Bobby. Now it is Jacob Jr. We must keep the faith. We mourn their loss and shed our tears, but we must, for their sake, fight on.

LeBlanc put the paper down slowly. The room was quiet. The audience sat hushed.

LeBlanc looked into the audience.

"We are suspending all campaign activities for the next ten days, and we call upon Mayor Abbott to join with us, out of respect for Jacob Jr. and Councilman and Mrs. Ward."

"You deceitful bastard!" Mayor Abbott shouted at the television set.

"Dennis!" His wife spoke crisply from behind him. "Your daughter has friends in the other room."

Abbott reached for his cigarettes. "That two-faced black bastard. He knows I offered to suspend all campaign activities. Now he's got the gall to use it against me."

"You needn't shout," his wife said.

LeBlanc continued, "The Ward family will permit a public viewing on Monday, from ten A.M. until ten P.M., at the Heller Mortuary, at 2601 West Manchester. Interment will be on Tuesday at Glen Forrest Lawn in West Los Angeles. Services will begin at eleven A.M.

"Councilman Ward will not make any public statements or permit any interviews until after Tuesday. Thank you."

LeBlanc picked up the papers from the rostrum. Reporters from the audience moved forward to the platform. "Mr. LeBlanc, has the councilman . . . ?" "Has Mayor Abbott been in touch . . . ?" "Have you sent a . . . ?"

LeBlanc raised an arm. The questions ceased. His eyes drifted over the group. The reporters were uncertain; their questions remained unanswered. He was pleased, very pleased; but his face showed nothing but restrained grief and anger. "Gentlemen, you have heard the councilman's statement. I cannot speculate on how he might answer your questions."

And he left the platform.

"Inspector Foster, line forty-three," a voice called from the switchboard in the command-post van.

Foster pushed aside a situation report, picked up the black phone. "Inspector Foster."

"Inspector, this is Lieutenant Duffey. The package has been delivered with no damage."

"Very good, Lieutenant," Foster said. "Stand by there until Sergeant Mason and his security detail arrive from Daniel Freeman."

"Right, sir."

Foster noted the time on a yellow pad: "3:34 P.M. Bennett transfer complete."

"Bennett's now at Central Receiving," Peck said to his two deputies, hanging up the phone. "That was Foster."

"Are you going to announce that to the public?" Deputy Chief Searcy asked.

"No." Peck smiled. "You are. Prepare a statement and present it at about five this afternoon. By that time our security will be tight. Explain that our motive was the concern for other patients' safety and so on. You know how to handle it."

"How about answering Ward?" Crown asked sharply.

"Yeah, I'd be interested to see how an arrogant white racist like yourself replies to that," Searcy said.

Peck smiled. "I've been called a helluva lot worse."

"I think most people are smart enough to realize that his statement was ninety percent emotional and the rest shock," Searcy said. "If you try to answer the charges, they'll know they hit a nerve. I say ignore it."

"Crown, what's your opinion?"

"Well, if he were just another man on the street, we wouldn't need to respond; but he's not," the deputy chief said thoughtfully. "He's an elected official of this city, and a candidate for the city's highest office. Being that, one helluva lot of people listen to what he says, and most who listen believe him. Even if they *don't* believe him, they'll expect you to defend yourself."

Peck considered. He studied the picture of his son on the desk. It showed the boy sitting in the cockpit of a green helicopter wearing a flight helmet and giving a thumbs-up gesture. He wondered how he would have reacted if it were his son who was dead.

"No," he said, looking up, "I'm not going to answer. I agree with you, Searcy, it was a father feeling pain who made the statement. I'll make no reply."

After the Ward press conference, black arm bands appeared all over the city. In the black community, car headlights were turned on.

The afternoon dragged on, without incident. The police radio was unusually quiet. Even the usual weekend family and neighbor disputes were nonexistent. Playgrounds were empty. An odd tension seemed to build in the stillness as the late-afternoon sun sank, turning the sky deep purple as the street lights flickered on.

It was almost nine-thirty when one of Southwest Division's black-and-whites, southbound on Hoover Boulevard at Forty-eighth Street, spotted the red Mercury. Perhaps it was the driver's window being down about four inches, the way it was parked at a slight angle to the curb, or just that unexplainable sixth sense a policeman develops that made the two officers suspicious. They jotted down the license number as they passed, and requested a want. While they circled back toward the car, the communications clerk typed the number onto the typewriterlike computer. "761-Adam Sam Union, wants only."

The coded electrical impulses traveled five hundred miles up the coast of California to Sacramento to another computer operated by the State Department of Motor Vehicles, searched its memory banks, and returned the information to Los Angeles as the officer released the microphone button. It all took approximately six seconds.

The information returning appeared on a small television video screen in communications. The clerk's voice was tense as she broadcast the information: "3Adam98, your license, 761-Adam Sam Union, is a Southwest stolen. DR Number 76-104-719, with a request to stake and notify Southwest detectives. Wanted for possible 187P.C. of a police officer. Vehicle is a 1970 Mercury, Cougar two-door, hardtop, red in color, with VIN Frank 76977431Adam7."

When the officers received the information, they immediately broadcast a Code Five and concealed themselves in an alley three-quarters of a block from the Cougar. They called the watch commander, who told them to stand by until he contacted the detectives.

Stryker awoke at about eight-fifteen. After taking a shower, shaving, and eating Connie's corned beef and potato salad, he felt almost human again.

He and Connie were stretched out on the living-room floor with pillows from the couch, watching *Sunday Night at the Movies* when the phone rang. Stryker's eyes opened. "Who?" he thought. He raised to an elbow. Connie didn't move. He stretched, grasping the phone cord, pulled the white phone toward him, picked it up on the sixth ring. "Stryker."

"John, this is Kraft. I think we've got your man's car."

"Where?" Stryker sat up.

"Forty-eighth and Hoover. 3A98 spotted it about ten minutes ago. They're sitting on it now, until you decide what you want done with it."

"I'll be there in about thirty minutes."

Connie sat up slowly and gave him a cold glare as he spoke.

Kraft's voice on the phone was eager. "This one looks good, John. DMV shows it's from 5607 South Overhill. That's only two blocks from the scene of the shooting."

"Be there as soon as possible," he said, hanging up the phone.

Connie's back was to him. "Hey, woman. I have to go to work," he whispered.

She sat with her knees drawn up, her chin resting on them, her arms circling her legs. "I think I'll go find a nice insurance man or maybe a banker," she said.

He massaged the back of her neck. "Look at Darrin Clark," she said, referring to the detective in the film. "He takes his women everywhere with him."

"Especially to bed."

"Go on, John. Go to work. Go catch another bad guy."

"Hey," he said, bending close, "next week I'll take a couple of days and we'll go to Vegas. Okay?"

"You told me that last week, and the week before that we were going to Mexico," she said, twisting toward him.

He broke off their kiss when the thought of having another detective team handle the stakeout tugged at his mind. "You're right, woman. You might as well find that insurance man."

She bit him gently on the neck. "Shut your mouth, John Stryker."

"Watch your flick now, I've got to call West," he said. She kissed him on the forehead and then returned to the television.

Stryker dialed West's number. Holding the receiver cradled on his shoulder, he tied his shoes.

"Hello," a deep female voice answered.

"Hello, Mom," Stryker said. "This is John, the son you don't talk about."

"John Stryker," she laughed, "you're the world's worst."

"How's the arthritis?" he asked, rolling down a shirt sleeve and buttoning it.

"Oh, not bad, John, not bad at all," she said. "How are you doing with your smoking?"

He smiled his small grin. "Ratted on me again, huh?"

"Well, John," she said warmly, "if you expect to raise a big healthy family, you're going to have to take care of yourself. You're not getting any younger, you know."

"I'm not out of gas yet," he said. "Is your two-hundred-and-ten-pound dependent about?"

"Just a minute. He's out in the backyard with Lisa."

"Lisa again, huh?"

She laughed softly. "Just a minute, John."

West ran his finger along Lisa's smooth brown cheek as she lay on her back in the cool green grass of the backyard. They hadn't spoken for several minutes.

Her eyes were closed, her soft face framed by lustrous black hair. West leaned over her and kissed her full lips. She responded.

"Grant . . ." his mother called. "Grant, telephone, hon."

Lisa laughed as their lips parted. She tried to muffle the laughter with her hands.

"You've got a warped sense of humor, girl," West said, rising.

"I wasn't laughing at you," she assured him as he stood towering over her.

"I know," he said, smiling down. "Come on,

let's go see what Stryker wants. It's got to be him. Nobody else has timing like that."

They joined hands and walked toward the house. West brushed some grass off Lisa's back as they reached the back porch.

"Yeah, John," West said in mock disgust.

"Hope I didn't disturb your peace." Stryker laughed.

"Very funny," West said. "What's got you in this good mood? Your rich uncle die?"

"No, better than that," Stryker said. "They've found Pepper's wheels."

"Where?" West asked eagerly.

"Forty-eighth and Hoover, about fifteen minutes ago."

"How do you know it's his?"

"It was taken from 5607 South Overhill last night."

"Sounds good. Think he'll come back to it?"

"Odds are a thousand to one that he won't. Do you wanna bet he doesn't?"

"No. See you at the station in about fifteen minutes."

"Right."

When Stryker arrived at the station, West had already been there five minutes. He was sitting in the coffee room talking with several patrol officers when his partner came in the rear door.

"Hey, Gomer. Come on, let's talk to Kraft," Stryker called to him.

"I already have," West said, joining Stryker in the hallway outside the coffee room. "He said 98's parked in the north-south alley just west of Hoover at Forty-eighth."

"Okay." They walked down the hall toward the

watch commander's office. "Let me tell him how we'll work this, and then we'll get down there."

They moved to the side of the hallway to allow two uniformed officers, with three handcuffed arrestees, to pass.

"Hey, man, look here," one of the suspects, a tall, dark, bearded Negro, said to one of the officers leading them, "I've got a right to take a piss, haven't I?"

"Okay," the uniformed officer answered, "as soon as we get you uncuffed."

"The constitution guarantees the right to piss?" West whispered to Stryker.

"Sure," Stryker said, then to the officer, "What have you got?"

"Kidnap-rape," the officer said as he directed the tall, bearded suspect into the holding tank.

Stryker looked hard at the trio through the large, unbreakable window in the tank. He and West were haunted by several unsolved kidnap-rape-homicides. These three were candidates, and he would remember to talk to them later.

They went into the watch commander's office.

"Hello, Phil," Stryker said to the uniformed lieutenant behind the desk.

"Hello, John," Kraft answered, looking up from the arrest report he was reading. "Be with you in a minute." Two uniformed officers stood in front of his desk waiting.

Stryker and West stood in the corner of the office. Through the glass wall, West watched the officer in the holding tank fill out a field interview card on two of the kidnap-rape suspects. Stryker removed a cigarette from an inside jacket pocket and was about to light it when they heard a crash, then the sound of a door banging against a wall.

West raced into the hallway; Stryker followed.

The tall, bearded Negro was running toward the rear door. West ran after him, shouting, "Stop him!"

The hallway filled with officers racing for the door. Outside, in the semidarkness, an officer yelled, "There he goes!" and followed the tall, bearded Negro toward Santa Barbara Avenue.

The suspect charged across the street through the traffic. One car slammed on the brakes and swerved to avoid hitting him. As West rounded the corner of the station, he saw the Buick slam into the officer, who crumpled like wet cardboard in a crash of glass and metal.

West tore past the car as the suspect faded into the darkness nearly three-quarters of a block away. When West turned the corner, still running full speed, the street was empty. "Son-of-a-bitch!" he breathed, his chest heaving. As he stood looking down the block, a dog began to bark. West smiled; the guy was here somewhere; he only had to wait. He moved slowly and quietly to the mouth of an alley, and hid in the shadow of a garage. A siren wailed nearby. He thought of the officer lying in the street; he was sure he must be dead. There was a sudden crunch of dirt in the alley, and as West flattened himself against the garage, the suspect appeared at the mouth of the alley. He paused, gulping the air. West lunged, and the tall man screamed in sudden fear. The scream died as West's forearm tightened around his neck. West pressed until he felt the body go limp. Then he let go, and the man collapsed onto the street, jerking and twitching from lack of oxygen.

In a few seconds, officers appeared everywhere, on foot and in cars. Stryker pulled up in the green Plymouth as the suspect was loaded into a black-and-white.

"Come on, hero, I'll buy you a coffee," he called from the car.

"Sounds good." West climbed into the car. "How's the guy who got hit?"

"Just a couple of busted ribs, it looks like. He'll be okay. Shit, he got up and chewed out the driver after you ran by."

"What the hell happened in there?"

"The bad guy kicked the officer in the nuts and split. He's in worse shape than the one who got hit by the car."

Kraft lost the toss with Stryker to see who would buy coffee. He dropped the coins into the machine and carried the steaming white cups to one of the tables in the coffee room.

"Well, John, how are you going to work it?" He sat down at the table.

Stryker picked up his coffee and sipped it.

"I've got lots of people tonight, since we're on tact alert, so I can give you whatever you want," Kraft added.

Stryker set his coffee down, took out a cigarette, and began to search his pockets for a match.

"Why don't you take some time and think it over," Kraft teased. "I'd hate to pressure you for a decision right now."

Stryker flashed a smile at Kraft as he lit his cigarette. "West and I will handle it alone," he said, exhaling smoke. "Pepper's no amateur. If he's going to come back to the car, he'll be damn careful. If we put more people down there, it will just increase his chances of spotting them."

"I'll buy that," Kraft agreed.

"When and if he shows, we'll yell for help," Stryker added.

"Okay," Kraft said. "How about 98? You going to get him out of there, too?"

"Right," Stryker said, sipping the coffee. "As soon as we get in position, we'll advise them to pull out."

"Let's do it," West suggested, slapping his palms together as he entered the coffee room.

Stryker downed the remainder of his coffee. "Thanks for the coffee, Phil."

"Yeah," the lieutenant complained, "if I minted my own coins, I wouldn't have to buy either."

"Don't be bitter." Stryker smiled as he and West went out the door.

"Keys," West said, extending an open palm as Stryker and he walked toward their green Plymouth.

"Why?" Stryker asked, making no move to give up the keys.

"Because de folks down 'bout Hoover and Forty-eighth ain't use' to seein' no white folks park on their block at eleven-thirty at night," West answered.

"What the hell do you want me to do, get in the trunk?" Stryker handed the keys to West as they reached the Plymouth.

"No, just slouch in your seat until we get into position."

"Sometimes I think you'll make a half-ass detective someday," Stryker said, opening the passenger door.

West smiled as he slid in behind the wheel.

He was backing the Plymouth out of the parking spot when Inspector Foster called from the station door, "Stryker, wait a minute." He walked toward their car, pipe in hand.

"You still here, Inspector?" Stryker said, surprised.

"Yeah, I caught a catnap a few hours ago," Foster said, leaning a forearm on the car door near Stryker's open window. "You fellows going to stake the car at Forty-eighth and Hoover?" Foster asked, drawing in on his pipe.

"That's it," Stryker answered.

"Well, John," Foster said, removing his pipe from his mouth and glancing into its unlit bowl, "I've never been one to tell a field officer how to handle a situation, and I know you don't need advice, but I've got a favor to ask."

"We're listening, Inspector."

"You both know the department is taking a lot of heat as a result of the shooting," Foster said. "A little heat never hurt us. It helps teach us to think on our feet, but to help get the egg off our face in this case, it would be nice to talk to Pepper. So, if by chance he comes back to that car, try to bring him back breathing."

Stryker smiled. "West and I always bring 'em back alive, Inspector."

"Well, if he wants to play rough," Foster said, "then he's bought his ticket, but if you can, let's book him and let the courts bury him."

"Right, Inspector," Stryker assured.

"Okay," Foster concluded, returning his pipe to his mouth. "Good luck." He slapped the hood of the Plymouth and walked back toward the blue command-post van.

"Let's drive past Forty-eighth and Hoover first and take a look at where the car's parked. Then decide where we'll sit," Stryker said, as West turned onto Hoover Boulevard from Santa Barbara.

"Right."

West slowed the green Plymouth as they approached the intersection where the Cougar was parked. The car was on their left as they passed. The two men turned their eyes to the left, but not their heads, and after passing it they were careful not to turn back to look.

After passing the intersection, West drove on for another six blocks to be sure they wouldn't be seen turning back.

"Let's park on Forty-eighth on the west side of Hoover," West said.

"Why?"

"That puts us across the intersection from the Cougar. When and if Pepper shows, he'll be looking at us through a lighted intersection, which will make us harder to see. Also, I spotted a parking space there, behind two other cars, just west of Hoover on the south side of the street. That space had a tree next to it on the sidewalk, and the lights in the houses nearby were all out. Gives us a dark background."

"What do you mean, us?" Stryker said. "I'm the one that needs the dark background. You sure as hell don't."

"Eat your heart out." West smiled as he slowed the Plymouth to turn onto Forty-eighth Street from Vermont, several blocks west of Hoover.

West eased the Plymouth into the spot they had agreed on. He turned off the headlights and then the ignition. The spot was excellent. The limbs of the large elm on the sidewalk overhung the street, casting a dark jagged shadow over their car, adding to the street's darkness.

Parked in front of them were a Ford station wagon and an aging Cadillac. Beyond, there were thirty feet of curb to Hoover Boulevard. The first car on the other side of Hoover on Forty-eighth Street was the red Cougar.

Light from the street lamp mid-block east of the Cougar on Forty-eighth provided back lighting for any pedestrians walking toward Hoover. Stryker and West would find them easy to spot.

Stryker opened the glove box, where the radio

was concealed. He picked up the mike. "3W6 requesting 3Adam98 meet this unit on frequency six," he said softly.

There was a brief pause; then the female RTO answered, "Roger, 3W6. 3Adam98, meet 3W6 on frequency six."

Stryker changed the frequency selector to one marked F-2. "3W6 to 3A98," he called.

"98 here, go, 3W6."

"3W6 is on base now, 98. We thank you for watching the store."

"3A98 to 3W6, roger. We saw you pull in. There's been no activity. If you need anything, give us a call. 3A98 out."

Stryker changed the frequency selector back to its original spot, turned the volume low, and closed the glove box.

They heard the black-and-white's engine start and then fade as it backed down the alley.

The only sounds now were the occasional metallic clangs of their car's engine cooling, the electric relay switches in the traffic signal at Forty-eighth and Hoover, as they clicked on and off, and a dog barking occasionally far in the distance.

Their eyes were now adjusted to the dim lighting provided by the inadequate, antiquated street lamps. Stryker slouched in his seat and rested his knees on the dash, with his head propped against the back of the seat. He pitied West, whose big frame just couldn't find comfort behind the steering wheel.

Fifteen minutes passed.

"You know what I'd like?" West said softly.

"The night off," Stryker answered in a low tone.

"A pizza," West said.

"A pizza!" Stryker laughed. "Jesus Christ, West, haven't you ever seen any detective movies?"

"What's that have to do with my pizza?" West

asked, watching Stryker's relaxed silhouette in the darkness.

"In a situation like this, all those tinsel-town dicks always check their guns to make sure they're loaded, wipe the sweat from their foreheads while they listen to the suspenseful music, and here you are screwing up the image by thinking of pizza."

"To hell with their image. I'd still like to have a pizza."

"Maybe Pepper will have a pizza on him when he shows." Stryker chuckled.

West straightened slightly in his seat.

"Got something?" Stryker whispered.

"Yeah, a ped about three-quarters of a block away from the Cougar, on my side," West answered quietly.

"Can't see him from here yet," Stryker said without moving.

West watched the moving shadow as it passed along the parked cars. "He's big," West said in an excited, expectant tone.

Stryker didn't reply as his eyes searched for movement.

"He's moving slow," West said quietly. "Seems to be using a lot of caution."

"I see him now," Stryker said.

The pair watched the large shadow as it moved slowly westward along the darkened street.

"Goddamn," West mumbled as the shadow walked beneath a street lamp.

Stryker smiled his small, tight grin and resumed his relaxed position. The shadow, now in plain view, wore a bathrobe and slippers, and led a large boxer on a chain. The dog zigzagged back and forth on the sidewalk, sniffing, smelling, raising a leg every few feet.

They spent the next hour and a half discussing women, food, cars, and religion.

"I sat beside this snake in the eighth grade," West said. "She had the biggest set of lungs you ever saw below high-school senior. I was always asking her to help me with my math problems, and she would lean over my shoulder, you know. She'd lean forward, and I'd lean back. We never did solve any math problems, but I didn't care."

Stryker chuckled. "Yeah, I know what you mean. I had this good-looking art teacher who always stared over your shoulder. She came up behind me once and laid a hand on my shoulder, while I had a paintbrush in my mouth. I turned and painted the tip of the right one blue."

West laughed.

"I offered to wipe it off, but she wouldn't let me," Stryker added.

They were still laughing quietly when they saw a large dark figure dart across the street, several cars in front of the Cougar.

The laughter stopped.

"Where's he at now?" West asked in a hushed tone.

"I've lost him, too," Stryker answered. "Where in the hell did he come from all of a sudden?"

"Either out of a house or from between them," West offered as a guess.

"There he is," Stryker said as the large figure appeared beside the red Cougar. "Get ready."

He was tall, heavy, and Negro; from where Stryker and West sat, that's all they could tell. He looked toward the lighted intersection. A car approached. Stryker and West heard it, and so did the suspect. He crouched between the Cougar and another car as the car they had heard crossed the intersection and then faded into the night.

"As soon as he stands up, we'll take him," Stryker whispered as he slid a hand to the door handle.

"I got my running shoes on," West said.

They waited.

The suspect's head and shoulder appeared above the Cougar. Stryker pressed on the door handle. They heard another vehicle approaching. A big one. "Goddammit," Stryker said, as a yellow-and-white city bus pulled into the intersection. Its air brakes hissed as it rolled to a stop; then it crept forward slowly as its driver anticipated the signal change.

"No . . . no . . . you stupid bastard." The slowly rolling bus cut off their view of the car and suspect.

It seemed as if several minutes passed, but it was only thirty seconds until the signal changed to green. The bus's engine roared, and it rolled forward. West's heart pounded heavily.

As the bus moved away, they saw the spot where the Cougar had been parked. Empty. "Go! Go!" Stryker shouted. He could see the Cougar's taillights, now nearly a block away.

West turned the ignition key. The Plymouth's engine roared as he jerked the selector into drive and stomped on the accelerator. The Plymouth's tires burned, as West sped after the fading taillights.

"Keep your headlights out," Stryker shouted. "Maybe we can get on him before he knows we're coming."

West nodded agreement as he raced the Plymouth down the street, narrowed by cars parked on both sides, slammed hard into a dip in an intersection, bounced, and came down with a bang.

The taillights disappeared when the Cougar reached Figueroa Street. "He turned right," Stryker yelled while bracing himself with an arm on the dash.

West turned the Plymouth hard to the right without slowing as the reached Figueroa. The red Cougar was two blocks ahead, waiting at a red light.

As West closed the gap, the suspect suddenly floored the accelerator and popped the clutch, and the Mercury leaped forward through the red light.

Seeing the puff of blue smoke from the Cougar, Stryker shouted, "He's running!" He opened the glove box and grabbed the mike. "3W6, we're in pursuit!"

West braked as they approached the red signal, and looked to his left. A pair of headlights approached. They were several hundred feet away. "Clear on the right," he heard Stryker shout. West felt the moistness growing in his palms as they gripped the steering wheel. He flicked on the headlights, took the pressure from the brake pedal, and returned it to the accelerator at the same time, pulling the selector to low range. The Plymouth responded with a deep belly roar and surged forward. The other car flashed by the rear of the Plymouth, missing it by inches as they crossed the intersection.

Stryker grinned tightly at West.

"All units, all frequencies, stand by. 3W6 is in pursuit," the link operator broadcast. "3W6, what is your location?" the calm voice of the link asked.

West pushed on the brake pedal with both feet three-quarters of a block from the next red light to slow down or stop, if necessary, at the intersection. The howling, screaming sound of the smoking tires filled the night.

"Okay on the right," Stryker shouted. The Plymouth began to slide to the left. West counter-steered, removed the brake pressure, and sped through the intersection.

"3W6, we're southbound on Figueroa approaching Slauson. In pursuit of a 1970 Mercury red Cougar. California license 761-Adam Sam Union. 187 suspect. Be advised this unit has no red lights or siren."

"Roger, 3W6," the link said immediately. "All units, 3W6 is southbound on Figueroa approaching Slauson. In pursuit of a 1970 red Mercury Cougar. California License 761-Adam Sam Union. Possible 187 P.C. suspect. Be advised, 3W6 has no red light or siren. Any unit in the vicinity intercept and assist 3W6."

The Cougar's brake lights came on as it approached Slauson Avenue. Blue-gray smoke poured from the tires as the car jerked back and forth. The traffic light here was green. The car turned hard to the left, skidded violently to the right, and crashed into the curb. A hub cap spun through the air as the car rocked and righted itself. Then the driver regained control and sped the damaged Cougar eastward on Slauson.

West pumped the Plymouth's brakes, reduced his speed, and took the corner on the inside, gaining valuable seconds. As he straightened after the turn, the Cougar again braked, preparing to turn left onto the northbound Harbor Freeway.

West was accelerating as Stryker advised communications of their location and direction, when a black-and-white with its red lights flashing and the electronic siren screaming passed them on the right.

The black-and-white was eastbound on Slauson when the patrolmen heard the pursuit broadcast.

As the patrol car passed the Plymouth, the officers saw the Cougar turn onto the freeway. The patrol car skidded, turned wide, nearly disappearing in the smoke from its tires, and shot up the freeway ramp after the Cougar.

Stryker heard the patrol car advising the link that it had taken over the pursuit. When West got the Plymouth onto the freeway, the black-and-white was riding the bumper of the Cougar about half a mile ahead.

West watched the speedometer climb to 105 as they streaked up the freeway. Another black-and-white screamed past and fell in behind the first. West looked in his rear-view mirror. At least three other sets of red lights were closing in fast.

"He's going to take Adams," West yelled to Stryker. The Cougar whipped to the right and shot onto the exit ramp.

The suspect braked and down-shifted as he neared the top of the ramp and saw the three police cars parked at various angles around it, red and amber lights flashing. He had no place to go. He tramped harder on the brakes. The Cougar whipped back and forth violently, and its tires billowed out blue smoke as they slid on the pavement.

It struck the curb, blowing out the left-front tire, then spun to the right, jumping the curb into a bed of ice plants, and spun several more times, sending the slippery, wet green plants flying in all directions. Then the Cougar stopped dead.

The train of pursuing police cars filled the freeway off ramp as they slid to a stop. Stryker, West, and the patrol officers ran toward the Cougar.

The car's headlights aimed slightly skyward, its right turn signal sending out an amber flash every few seconds. The suspect was not in sight.

"Watch your ass," West warned as they converged on the Cougar.

"Don't move," an officer ordered, aiming his

flashlight and pistol toward the driver's open window.

Stryker moved to the passenger side. The suspect was stretched across the two bucket seats in the front, his face covered with his hands and his knees drawn up. His body shook as if he had been dipped in ice water. The uniformed officer kept his flashlight on the suspect as Stryker opened the door.

"Don't kill me, please don't kill me," the suspect cried over and over.

Stryker leaned into the car, grabbed the suspect's fat wrists and pulled. "No . . . no . . . don't," he screamed as Stryker dragged him out of the car and onto the slime of the crushed ice plants.

West grabbed a wrist as the suspect met the ground. Stryker held the other and put his knee to the man's throat. Stryker leaned close. "If you don't shut that big mouth, I'm gonna push my knee all the way to the rear of your shirt collar." He leaned on the knee to demonstrate. The suspect's scream turned into a gargling sound, and his eyes bugged. Stryker relieved the pressure. "Got the message?" he asked, looking down into the tear-filled brown eyes. The suspect nodded.

One of the uniformed officers gave the suspect a cursory search for weapons as Stryker and West controlled him. "He's . . . clean," the officer said.

"Let's sit him up," West suggested, and they pulled him up to a sitting position. West removed his handcuffs, snapped the wrist he held, pulled it to the center of the suspect's back, and then snapped the other.

They stood up. West brushed mud and ice plants from the knees of his dark suit. "I'll be goddamned. I just put this on clean, and look what you got me into."

Stryker lit a cigarette, drew in, exhaled, and answered, "You would have screwed it up worse than that in the backyard with Lisa. So don't bitch."

"Well, what do you think?" West asked, looking down at the suspect, whose head was now bowed between his legs, sobbing loudly.

"It ain't Pepper. That's for sure," Stryker said in disgust. "He can't be more than twenty years old."

"Want us to impound the car, Sergeant?" asked a uniformed officer.

"Yeah, go ahead. That'll save us a lot of time."

"You guys 3A98?" West asked the officer and his partner as they walked into the darkness toward their black-and-white.

"Yeah," one answered.

"You guys did a good job running this bird down," West said.

"Just like the Mounties." The officer smiled.

"Well, let's get him back to the station," Stryker said, looking at the man still sobbing on the ground.

"Right." West reached down and grabbed the suspect under the arm. "Let's go, Tiger," he said, pulling the fat man to his feet.

A sergeant approached from the freeway off ramp and met Stryker and West with the suspect on the way back to their car. "Good morning, gentlemen," he said, "I see you've got your man."

"No, not quite," Stryker grumbled. "All we got is the world's unluckiest car thief."

"Yeah," West said, "over seven million cars in this city, and this mental giant has to try and steal the one we're staked on."

The sergeant smiled a wide, gentle grin. "Well, that's life in the big city."

"Thanks for the philosophy," Stryker said, grinding out his cigarette in the ice plants. "Sergeant

Willis," Stryker added as he and West turned to leave, "ask 98 to put a hold for prints on the car. They're going to impound it for us."

"Right," the sergeant called as he walked toward the group around the Cougar.

Stryker opened the rear door of the Plymouth. "Get in and slide to the other side," West said, still holding the suspect by the arm only. After the suspect was in the car, West fished the car keys from his pocket and handed them to Stryker. "Drive carefully, now."

They laughed.

The suspect, hands locked behind his head, rested his forehead on the back of the front seat as Stryker wormed the Plymouth in and around the black-and-whites on the off ramp, headed for Adams Boulevard.

"What's your name, man?" West asked.

The suspect mumbled a reply. West, not hearing the answer, reached out and pulled the young man back to a sitting position.

"Don't beat me! Please, I'm sorry!" He crowded into the corner of the seat. West could see real terror on the boy's face.

"Listen, man," West said, "you've been watching too many flicks or talking to the wrong people. This isn't 1950. Nobody's going to beat you. We haven't got any rubber hose or lead gloves; now, quit acting like some ten-year-old girl and tell me your name."

The suspect wiped his nose on the shoulder of his plaid shirt. "Sherman Roberts," he said in a high, broken tone.

"How old are you, Sherman?" West asked.

"Nineteen."

"Where's home at?"

"On Forty-eighth Street."

"There's a lot of houses on Forty-eighth Street," West said. "Which one is yours?"

"The gray one," the suspect answered timidly.

Stryker smiled as he turned the Plymouth onto Exposition Boulevard.

"No, man, that won't do," West said, trying not to laugh. "I mean, what number?"

"941," the suspect answered.

"Okay, fine, now just relax until we get to the station."

The suspect nodded but continued to breathe heavily. The smell of his sweat filled the hot interior of the Plymouth.

They were silent for the rest of the ride to the station. The police radio in the car's glove box continued to blurt out orders to other police cars throughout the city. "12A35 a screaming woman at 841 East Eighty-third Street, Code Two; 3A9, a 459 silent at 2907 South Hoover, ten minutes on the man; 7A31, a family dispute, possible gun involved, 2107 West Boulevard."

West watched the frightened boy. His head was bowed again, and he shivered as if it were freezing. How, West wondered, did anybody become so frightened of the police?

"3W6, out to Southwest Station," Stryker said into the mike as he eased the Plymouth into a space behind the station.

The detective squad room was deserted, desks strewn with reports, overflowing ashtrays, and empty coffee cups. West led the suspect to their desk, unlocked one side of the handcuffs, and relocked it around the steel frame of a chair, which allowed the suspect one free arm and comfort. "Sit down, Sherman," West said.

The heavy young man sat down, his brown eyes wide with fright.

West sat on the edge of the desk. Stryker, standing on the other side of the desk, took out his cigarettes. "You smoke, Sherman?" he asked.

"Yeah, but I don't have any," he said, staring at the floor.

"Have one." Stryker tossed the pack to the table.

The suspect shook a cigarette from the pack as Stryker lit his own. Then Stryker leaned across the table with his lighter. The suspect's hand trembled as he held the tip of the cigarette in the flame.

"You want a coffee?" Stryker asked West.

"Yeah, sounds good."

"Okay, I'll get it while you warn Sherman, here." He went out into the hallway.

"Okay, Sherman, you got anything with your name on it?" West said.

"No, sir."

"All right," West said. "Empty your pockets onto the table so I can see what you've got."

The suspect dug in his trouser pockets and spread the contents on the desk. West surveyed the assortment. One natural comb, one white handkerchief yellowed with dried mucus, two dimes, four pennies, a small pocket knife with a broken handle, and a pack of Trojan prophylactics.

"That's everything," the suspect said, obviously embarrassed.

"Okay, fine," West said. "Have you ever been arrested before in L.A.?"

"Yeah."

"What for?"

"GTA."

"When?"

"June, 1969."

"Where?"

"Seventy-seventh Division."

"That's the only other?"

"Uh-huh."

"Okay, Sherman, listen up," West said, removing his field officer's notebook from an inside pocket and glancing at the printed warning on its cover. "You have the right to remain silent; anything you say can and will be used against you in a court of law. You have the right to speak with an attorney and to have the attorney present during questioning. If you so desire and cannot afford one, an attorney will be appointed for you without charge before questioning."

He looked across the table at the suspect, who sat listening intently. "Do you understand each of these rights I've explained to you?"

He nodded.

"Do you wish to give up the right to remain silent?"

The suspect looked at his fingernails, caked with black dirt. He bit one. "Yeah, I give that up."

"Do you wish to give up the right to speak to an attorney and have him present during questioning?"

"Yeah, they don't do any good. When I got busted before, I got me a public defender. He musta forgot I was part of the public. He was a long-haired, moustached fruit. He didn't do shit for me. Except blow in my ear all the time."

West smiled. "You can have any attorney you want."

"No, I don't want none."

Stryker returned carrying three cups of coffee. Lieutenant Kraft was with him.

"How do you get Scrooge here to buy coffee?" Kraft asked as Stryker set the three coffees on the desk.

"If he doesn't buy, I have my mother knit him another sweater."

Kraft laughed.

"Sherman, this one is yours," Stryker said, pushing one of the cups in front of the suspect, who looked at Stryker with a surprised expression.

"Lots of cream and heavy on the sugar, right, Sherman?" Stryker said.

"Yeah, man. That's it. How'd ya know?"

"I get paid to know," Stryker told him.

West and Kraft knew Stryker's method. Let the kid relax, give him a cigarette, some coffee, make a little talk, and soon he forgets who arrested him or who was going to put him in jail, or what answering the questions meant to him. It seldom failed. Stryker and West were expert at it.

"Hey, hey," Stryker said, seeing the pack of prophylactics on the desk, "these yours, West?"

"No, not mine," West said.

"We've got a lover around somewhere," Stryker said.

"How about you, Sherman," Stryker said. "You the lover?"

The suspect looked at the floor as a broad grin appeared on his face. "Well, I take care of my business, ya know."

"Old Sherm the stud," West said, sipping on his coffee.

"You mean old Sherm, the fucking car thief," Lieutenant Kraft broke in. The smiles disappeared.

Kraft was playing the heavy, as Stryker had asked him to do in the coffee room. West picked up the act. "Hey, man. Now, wait a minute. There's a big difference between joy riding and grand theft auto. Sherman here had just taken the car."

"Well, he's driving a hot car that was stolen after a homicide. If it had been me chasing him, I'd more than likely shot him," Kraft said, glaring at the suspect.

"Hey, man," the suspect said in a wide-eyed, frightened tone, "I didn't know that car was used in no murder. All I seen was this big dude park it last night and leave it in a hurry. He didn't lock it or nothing. I was sittin' on my porch, ya know. Hey, man, all I did was . . . I mean, all I wanted to do was go for a little ride. Ya know. I didn't know that dude had pulled no murder. I'm tellin' the truth, man."

"What time did you see him park it, Sherman?" West asked.

"Shit, he's not going to tell you the truth," Kraft snapped. "He fits the description. Book him, murder one."

"Look, Lieutenant," Stryker said, "this is our investigation, we'll handle it our way."

"Yeah, well, this clown is lucky it's not mine," Kraft growled. "Or I'd sure as hell turn the screws down tight." He gave the suspect a look of disgust, turned, and walked into the hallway.

"Don't worry about him, Sherman," West assured the suspect. "My partner and I will handle this our way; but don't try to bullshit us, or we'll hang you out to dry. We'll be fair and honest with you until we catch you lying, and as sure as hell, if you do, we'll find out. Do we understand one another?"

"Yes, sir."

"Okay," West said, as Stryker leaned against a nearby desk and continued to drink his coffee. "Now, again. What time did you see this guy park the car?"

"It was about two, Sunday morning, I think."

"Where'd he come from?"

"He came down Hoover, ya know?"

"You mean south?"

The suspect looked at the ceiling. "Is that toward Fifty-fourth Street?" he asked.

"Right!" West said.

"Yeah, he was goin' south."

"You mean he came south on Hoover and turned left onto your street?" West said.

"Is that toward Fifty-fourth Street?"

"Forget it," West said.

Stryker grinned.

"Tell us what this guy looked like," West said, leaning his big frame back in the metal chair.

The suspect finished the sticky-sweet coffee, wiped his broad lips with a dirty shirt sleeve, and said, "What?"

West shook his head, looked at the floor, and then to Stryker.

"Pay attention, goddammit," Stryker ordered.

"Yes, sir," the heavy suspect said, straightening in his chair.

"Now, what did this dude look like?" West asked again.

The suspect dug in his nose with a finger, removed a small, black ball, and wiped it on his trouser leg. Stryker smiled as West looked away.

"He was big."

West stood. "How big compared to me?"

"Yeah, yeah, 'bout the same."

"How about his weight?"

"He was fatter."

"Where?"

"His belly, ya know, and he had fat arms, too."

"Okay," West said, sitting down. "What was he wearing?"

"Nothing."

West looked at the ceiling and mumbled an inaudible profanity.

Stryker turned toward the wall.

"Say . . . what?" the suspect asked with a puzzled expression on his round brown face.

"What was the guy wearing?" West asked, spreading his palms on the table, looking directly into the suspect's face.

"He wasn't wearin' nothing," the suspect said. "Just a white T-shirt and some pants."

"Okay, fine." West's impatience was leaking into his low tone. "Where did he go after he parked the car?"

"He went back out onto Hoover."

"Then where?"

The suspect looked at the ceiling again, then to West. "He went south."

"You mean toward Fifty-fourth Street?"

"Is that south?"

"Yeah, that's south."

"South, yeah, man, he went south."

"Could you see where he went?"

"Yeah, he went south on Hoover, toward Fifty-fourth Street," the suspect said proudly.

"I know that," West said, leaning back in his chair. "But, could you see where he went?"

"Sure, he went south on Hoover toward Fifty-fourth—"

"Okay, okay, forget it," West ordered, getting up out of his chair. He stretched his arms over his head and then covered his mouth as he yawned.

"What's wrong, Nature Boy, getting tired?" asked Stryker.

West glanced at his watch. It was two-ten A.M. "Yeah, same thing happens every day about this time."

"Better see a doctor," Stryker said.

"I'll do that if I ever get enough time off."

"Well, what do you want to do with this character?" Stryker asked as he watched the suspect squeeze a white pimple near his left ear.

West glanced at him. "Let's book him and go home."

"Sounds good," Stryker agreed.

"I'll get the arrest reports," West said. "If we're lucky, we can be out of here in an hour."

"Yeah, out in one, and back in five." Stryker moved to the chair West had vacated.

"Look at the money you're making," West added, walking toward the hallway.

"You going to book me now?" the plump suspect asked.

"Soon," Stryker said.

"I knew I'd get caught," the suspect said in a sorrowful tone as he again eyed his dirty fingernails. "Some guys steal cars all the time and don't get caught. I take just two lousy cars and get busted both times."

"Who are you trying to bullshit?" Stryker said sharply.

The young suspect glanced at him, wiped his nose on his sleeve again, and said, "Five, I took five, but I know a lot of guys that took a lot more than that. Ya know?"

"Yeah, I know," Stryker said.

"I tried to buy a car, but I ain't got no job. I worked at a restaurant for a while, but they fired me 'cause I sweat too much, they said." He sniffled, wiped the runny nose with the back of his hand. "You ever been broke?"

"It's been awhile," Stryker said, looking at him. The suspect wiped his nose again as a tear spilled down his round face, running toward a fold in his neck.

Monday morning dawned dull, hot, and smoggy in Los Angeles. One of Helen Conrad's friends removed Wayne's shirts from a clothesline in the backyard. The Conrad children were not playing outside today, she told two little boys who leaned over the fence. They couldn't understand why.

On the morning news, Bill Hart told of a fist fight between a white and a black officer in the Seventy-seventh Division after the black officer appeared for roll call wearing a black arm band.

The crowd at the Heller Mortuary on West Manchester swelled to several thousand by nine-thirty. The public viewing of Jacob Ward, Jr., began at ten, and the line snaked eastward all the way to Western Avenue. The police, because of the size of the crowd, had blocked traffic on Manchester between Western and Crenshaw. Only Negro officers were being used at the intersections. The crowd was quiet, the line endless, the movement slow and solemn.

Charles Peerless, a black state congressman from South Los Angeles, called a press conference in the state capital. He charged that the death of Councilman Ward's son was a conspiracy by the white power structure to intimidate the councilman into withdrawing from the race. He called on Mayor Abbott to fire Police Chief Peck and asked blacks across the nation to join with the councilman in the fight for justice.

Stryker and West returned to work at eight-thirty after three hours' sleep. They spent an hour on the phone with St. Louis detectives about Pepper. There wasn't much, and there was nothing that would help them find Pepper in Los Angeles. He had been in and out of jail since he was eighteen; he had lived in New Jersey, Texas, and Missouri, and he had a criminal record in all three states, mainly for robbery and rape.

He had been twenty-six years old when he

acquired the ugly purple scar. It happened in Newark, New Jersey, outside the Metropolitan Hospital. He had forced his way into a nurse's car, forced her to drive to a vacant lot, and attempted to rape her. She had struggled, gotten hold of a pair of surgical scissors, and slashed him across the bridge of the nose.

The two detectives carefully searched a second time through patrol logs and field interview cards hoping to turn up a prior contact with Pepper or with one of the dead suspects—any connection that might lead them to where he was hiding. They looked through traffic citations, comparing license numbers and names. They read and reread the patrol logs for the week past in search of such a contact. They found none. They started over.

By early afternoon West had talked to the yellow-cab dispatcher who was on duty early Sunday morning to check for a possible pickup on Hoover after Pepper abandoned the stolen Cougar. He also phoned the bus driver who had made a run northbound on Hoover at two Sunday morning. But nobody had seen anything. Pepper had vanished.

Stryker was reading the morning watch patrol logs for the third time when he found the name. He had missed it twice before. It was on 3A71's log. Near the bottom on the front of the log at 0105, the patrol officers had written, "Observed two possible 459 suspects, Slauson and Western, Better Foods Market, investigated. No evidence 459; suspects questioned and released; see two field interviews; Kennedy + (1)."

"I got something," Stryker said loudly, pleased with himself.

"Sure as hell hope it's not contagious," West said from the other side of the desk.

Stryker turned the patrol log on the desk so

West could see. "Look here"—pointing to the name Kennedy on the log. "That could be the kid that got blown up with Ward. At least, it's the same name."

West was cautious. "But I've got the field interview cards for that night, and I've got nothing on Kennedy."

"With all the shit that happened, maybe they forgot to turn them in."

"Could be," West said. "It's happened before. Let's give them a call."

Stryker dialed the first number, tapping his foot impatiently as he waited. After eight rings he hung up and dialed the other. On the third ring, a female voice answered.

"Hello."

"Mrs. Thompson?"

"Yes."

They talked for a half-minute; then Stryker hung up the phone. "He's in court. Division Twenty." His finger ran down the department directory under the sheet of plastic on the desk. "485-7196."

"County Courthouse."

"Division Twenty, please."

Stryker listened as the extension rang. Three, four, five times. "Division Twenty, Hughes," a voice answered.

"This is Sergeant Stryker, Southwest Detectives. I'm trying to locate Officer Thompson. He's down there today."

"I'm sorry, we're at recess right now, and he's not here," the bailiff said.

"Goddammit," Stryker said angrily. "How in the hell do you know he's not there if you haven't checked?"

"Now, look, Sergeant—"

"No, you look," Stryker shot back. "I'm not calling there to ask Thompson what the hell he's doing tonight. I'm calling about a homicide, and if you don't get off your fat ass and look for him, Hughes, you'll be pumping gas in Resume Speed, Indiana."

"Just a minute," the bailiff said wearily. Stryker could hear the voices in the crowded courtroom, and then, above them, the bailiff, "Officer Thompson . . . is Officer Thompson, LAPD, here?"

"Goddamned courtroom marshals," Stryker said, barely covering the mouthpiece. "Fat and lazy bunch of lounge lizards."

"Thompson," a voice answered.

"Thompson, this is Stryker. We were looking over your log for Sunday morning, and at 0105 you and your partner F.I.'d two 459 suspects at Slauson and Western. One was named Kennedy. Do you recall it?"

"Yeah, I remember them. They were loitering around the market, so we checked them out. They were clean. I remember the one dude saying they were hitchhiking to Santa Monica, to some party. Some problem?"

"Yeah, we can't find the F.I.'s. You turn them in?"

"I thought so. I kept the log. If I didn't turn them in, they may be in my uniform pocket in my locker."

"What's the number?"

"Seventy-three. How come they're so important?"

"We think maybe it was Ward's kid and his playmate you interviewed."

"Jesus Christ. I never thought of the connection."

"It's understandable," Stryker said. "Everybody was a bit shook that night. Don't sweat it."

"Well, they should be in my locker."

"Did you and your partner believe these two when they said they were hitchhiking?"

"Yeah, sure, or we wouldn't have cut them loose. They were cooperative, no bad-mouthing or anything. If it was Ward's kid, he never indicated it. You know, most guys that are somebody tell you right off. Like my old man's a judge or I know So-and-so, you know."

"I know," Stryker agreed. "We'll check your locker, Thompson. If we don't find it, we'll call you back."

"Okay, Sarge, I'll stick by the phone."

Stryker hung up. "It's in his shirt pocket in his locker—maybe."

They got a master key from the watch commander and went to the locker room on the second floor.

Stryker inserted the key and unlocked the metal door. There was a centerfold from *Playboy* taped inside. The Bunny-of-the-Month was a tall, shapely blond spread on a soft green rug in front of a fireplace. Stryker eyed the picture. "Wonder if she's all blond," he said.

"The F.I., the F.I.," West suggested.

Stryker, smiling, reached for the blue uniform shirt hanging in the locker. He patted the left pocket and felt paper. Unbuttoning the pocket, he removed the F.I. cards.

West watched over his shoulder as Stryker read:

Name:	Kennedy, Preston R.
Residence Address:	4308 11th Avenue, Apt. #7
Sex:	Male
Descent:	Negro
Hair:	Black
Eyes:	Brown
Height:	Six feet
Weight:	174

Age:	18
Residence Phone:	292-0841
Social Security Number:	198-32-6107
Location of Interview:	Slauson and Western
Business Name, Address and Occupation:	Student, UCLA
Clothing Worn:	Light green sweater, short-sleeved; dark green bell bottoms; black sandals.
Physical Oddities/ Complexion:	None/Clear
Persons with Subject:	Ward, Jacob M., Jr.
Circumstances of Interview:	Susp(s) obs. loitering abv. location poss. 459. Invest. NO459. Q&R/ Claim hitching to party/Santa Monica.
Officer(s) Reporting:	M. Thompson & J. Walker 3A71

"Well, now we know how Ward and Kennedy got in the Chevy." Stryker studied the card. "I can't see Pepper and his crew offering these two a ride, though."

"Maybe Pepper will explain it."

"Yeah, right, when we get him," Stryker said caustically. "Just hitchhiking to a party, and who picks them up? . . . Pepper! That fat bastard got us into all of this."

"Too bad it was Ward Junior and not Senior," Stryker said, studying the F.I. card.

"What in the hell is that supposed to mean?" West said, giving him a puzzled look.

"That means it would have solved a lot of problems if it had been the old man instead of the kid."

"Why?" West questioned. "You worried about having a black mayor?"

"You're goddamned right I am," Stryker said.

"Jesus Christ," West muttered. He stared at the floor. "Your sheet is showing."

"Get off my ass," Stryker said, standing up. "Look at all the other cities with fucking black mayors," he said angrily. "They appoint all their asshole brothers to every commission there is, and in four years the city is fucking broke, the police corrupt, and everybody is up to their ass with Mafia hoods."

West stood with his face a foot from Stryker's. "Bullshit!" he shouted. "What in the hell are you saying? That no matter what, White Is Right? How many blacks you ever see in the top ten? One goddamn woman. What color was Oswald? What color was James Earl Ray? What color was John Wilkes Booth, Benedict Arnold? How many blacks are in the fucking Mafia, since you brought it up.

"That goddamned Abbott," West continued heatedly, "is no prize. The son-of-a-bitch can't do much wrong if he's never in the fucking city. He's no goddamned mayor, he's a piss-poor roving ambassador with a pocketful of city money. He earns his salary about as much as these welfare Christians you're always bitching about. His only defense in this whole goddamned election is that he's white, which must mean he's better than Ward. You know what you can do with this fucking—"

The door to the locker room swung open. Two patrol officers walked in. West fell silent. He stood breathing hard, looking into Stryker's blue eyes. The patrol officers gave the two a puzzled look as they passed.

The stare continued for a few seconds, until Stryker smiled. "Come on, let's knock it off and get back to work," he said. "Maybe we can put Pepper in the top ten."

West rubbed the sweat from his forehead with the back of his hand, then smiled too, relieved it was over.

At three o'clock, Mayor Abbott walked into the glare of the camera lights in the press room of City Hall, and sat down at the polished oak desk bearing the city seal.

His gray suit hung loosely on his tall, thin frame; he looked as if he'd be more at home repairing a lawn mower. It was an image he liked.

"Good afternoon," he said. "I have no prepared statement—I think you've had enough of those in the past forty-eight hours; but I do have an announcement, and then we'll have a few minutes of questions. I spoke with Councilman Ward several minutes ago, since I felt he had a right to know this before we released it to the public."

"Abbott clears announcement with Ward," the *Times* scribbled on his pad.

Abbott glanced at the notes which he had removed from an inside pocket, then looked up at the reporters. "Just about an hour ago, detectives in the Southwest Division discovered evidence which has proven that Jacob Ward, Jr., and Preston Kennedy were not involved in any criminal activity. Just minutes before the shooting, they had hitched a ride from the other suspects at the intersection of Western Avenue and Slauson."

"Councilman's slain son guilty of no crime," the *Times* wrote. "Police admit shooting innocent youth," the *Sentinel* recorded.

"This fact was established by a police field interview card, a brief form used by patrol officers for interviewing possible criminal suspects in the course of daily patrol.

"Two patrol officers interviewed young Ward and his companion in front of a supermarket a few minutes before the shooting.

"That's it," Abbott said bluntly. "Questions?"

"Mayor Abbott . . . Mr. Mayor . . . Mayor . . ."

"Mr. Hart," Abbott said, running a hand back along his hair.

"Mayor Abbott," Bill Hart said with a smile as he stood, referring to a prepared question on a pad he held. Abbott leaned forward. He disliked Hart, whose handsome face and polished voice made him one of the city's most listened to television commentators.

"The people of this city are no doubt concerned," Hart said in his familiar dramatic tone, "about the wide gap between the two theories existing on this tragic event. The police say the shooting started after the suspected car thieves opened fire on them and that Councilman Ward's son and young Kennedy were shot and killed by accident. On the other hand, five residents of South Los Angeles have come to the press and stated they witnessed this event." He paused for effect. "And they claim that the occupants of this suspected stolen car opened fire only in self-defense after they had been fired upon by the police."

"Well . . ." Abbott began.

"I'm not through, Mr. Mayor," Hart said, gesturing brusquely.

Abbott reddened slightly, waited.

"Further, Mr. Mayor," Hart continued, "these witnesses say that Jacob Ward, Jr., and young Kennedy were the first to be slain."

A pause. "Are you through, Mr. Hart?"

"For now, Mayor Abbott," Hart answered, sitting down.

"Number one," Abbott said, controlling his anger, "I don't recall the police department presenting any *theories*. What they *did* present was a *factual* account of the events as they occurred, based on eyewitness accounts and physical evidence.

"Number two, this was not a *suspected* stolen car, it was a *known* stolen car. It was on a list of stolen cars the two officers carried in their patrol car.

"Number three, I would expect you, as a responsible representative of the news media, to direct these eyewitnesses to go to the police and report what they saw. . . ."

"Mr. Mayor," Hart said, standing.

"I know what you're going to say," Abbott said, not allowing Hart to interrupt. "You're going to claim these witnesses are afraid to go to the police."

Hart sat down.

"Well, I think that's a damn lie," Abbott said. "I believe, as most people do, that the only reason these individuals don't go to the police is because they are liars."

Several flash bulbs whitened the room. Hart sat toying with a pencil, his lips pressed in a straight line.

"Now, Mr. Hart," Abbott said, "just to make sure we don't close the door on any possibilities, will you please have these individuals come to me with their stories, or to the district attorney, or to any responsible public official, and we'll gladly listen. Next question."

"Mayor Abbott"—the short, stocky reporter in the front row removed a chewed cigar from his mouth—"Sam Donald, Detroit *Dispatch*." Abbott smiled at his bluntness. "Mayor, how do you feel about the request for a federal investigation into the Ward death?"

Abbott could feel the water trickling down his back. His hair was dark with sweat, his shirt collar stained. "Well, I have every confidence in the agencies in this city and county to conduct a thorough and impartial investigation into the incident. But in answer to your question, no, I have no objection to a federal investigation. We have no secrets, and if the Justice Department thinks this matter warrants an investigation, we'll certainly cooperate with them. I have no doubt that they would arrive at the same conclusions the police department has already presented.

"Mr. Flute," Abbott said, pointing a finger at the tall, bearded Negro.

The mayor liked Gregory Flute, even though the two men had had many heated disagreements. Abbott had lost several battles with him. Once the mayor had even tried to enlist him, but when he offered Flute the position of commissioner of urban affairs, Flute had refused, saying that the voice of his paper was more important to him. He was not only the *Grit*'s star reporter; he was its publisher.

The black community liked him, respected him, and most important, listened to him.

"Mayor Abbott," Flute said, removing his dark horn-rimmed glasses. "How can you justify the police department being fully mobilized and concentrated in the black community when the calls for police service are known to be down some forty percent since the shooting Sunday morning?"

"Mr. Flute," Abbott said carefully, leaning forward, resting his arms on the desk, "that's a good question that Chief Peck could best answer, and I wish he were here to answer it."

The reporters laughed.

"Since the chief isn't here, I'll do my best," Abbott went on. "Yesterday afternoon, I asked him basically the same question.

"The chief said, and I quote him, 'The only way to control a riot is to prevent it.' That's what the show of force is—a preventive measure. Sure, some are going to resent it, but they're probably the same ones that would be out with the gas cans if the police weren't there."

"Councilman Ward is a loved and respected man in the black community, and he's been hurt by the death of his son. When an entire community feels frustration and anger, you have a very explosive situation. You and I know this, and so does Chief Peck, and he's the one responsible for keeping the peace. If it takes policemen on the street to prevent a riot, then I back him when he puts them there.

"If by chance we did have a riot erupt now, who would win? And what would the winner have— ashes! It would be a war in which both sides would lose."

"Thank you, Mayor," Flute said respectfully.

The mayor glanced at the clock on the wall. "One more question, and then I must go." He pointed to an attractive young brunette. "Yes, miss."

"Mayor Abbott," she said, standing, "will you attend the Ward funeral?"

"No," Abbott said flatly. "Councilman Ward and I are not close friends, as most of you know. I think my attendance would be awkward for the councilman. No, I will not attend."

The mayor stood. The camera lights dimmed. "Thank you," he said. He picked up his notes and moved to the door, where his secretary stood, holding it open. She winked her approval as he passed.

The long, dim hall was quiet when the elevator door slid open. The uniformed officer had been leaning against the wall, but he stood up quickly and blocked the way of the woman who stepped off.

"Who are you visiting?" he asked politely.

"I'm Helen Conrad," she said softly. "I'm here to see Steve Bennett."

"Yes, ma'am, he's in room eight."

"Thank you." She smiled.

His face burned as he watched her walk slowly down the hall.

Another officer sat outside the open door, a steel-gray shotgun against the wall beside him. His partner waved from the end of the hall, and he allowed Helen to pass.

Joy had been at the hospital since six. They were talking about the baby. When she told Steve that Martin had a bowel movement in his bath, Steve smiled for the first time since being shot.

Joy grasped Steve's hand tightly when Helen came in.

"Hello, Steve, I'm Helen Conrad." She took his free hand between her white-gloved ones.

Pushing himself up, he said, "Hello, Mrs. Conrad, it's nice to meet you."

"This must be your wife."

"Yes, this is Joy." They were silent for an awkward moment.

"How do you feel, Steve?"

"I'll be fine," he answered quietly. He felt a heavy weight of guilt. "Mrs. Conrad, I'm sorry I—"

Helen interrupted. "Please, Steve, I didn't come here to have you apologize for Wayne's death. I know what happened. I'm here because you are a friend of Wayne's."

A tear rolled down his cheek. She turned to Joy. "How's the baby?"

"He's fine," Joy replied. "I think he misses Steve."

There was another pause. "I don't want to take up any more of your time," Helen said politely. "Steve, get well soon."

"I'll walk you out." Joy rose.

In the hall, Helen said, "Wayne's funeral is tomorrow. I'd like you to come."

"Yes, of course I will. Good night." Joy took her by the shoulders and kissed her gently on the cheek.

"Good night." Helen turned and walked quickly to the elevator. The clicking of her heels on the polished floor was the only sound.

Joy watched her go. Steve and Wayne had been close friends, yet this was the first time she had ever met Helen Conrad. She felt very black.

Councilman Ward and his wife visited the Heller Mortuary just after dark. The public viewing was halted to allow them privacy. The two sat for an hour in silence, near the open polished casket.

Jacob Jr. was dressed in a charcoal suit. His hands were placed one on top of the other, his head resting on a white satin pillow. The soft white light from above gave his young face a look of contented sleep. The area around the casket and along the walls of the room was covered with flowers.

"I'm ready to go home, Jacob," Sarah said, breaking the long silence.

Without answering, Ward stood, offering his hand to his wife. They walked to the side of their son's casket and stood silent for a moment. Finally Sarah reached out and ran her hand gently along her son's cheek. "Good night, my baby," she whispered. She leaned forward and kissed him softly on the forehead.

As the Wards left the funeral home, the huge line outside, which still continued to grow, moved forward again slowly. The director of the mortuary told the councilman that the crowd was too large to complete the viewing by ten P.M. Ward consented to continuing it.

Sarah sat erect, a sober look of calm on her face, staring ahead as her husband headed their polished Cadillac northbound on Western Avenue. Ward glanced at her as he lit one of his black, twisted cigars. He did not understand her calmness of the past two days, but it was a comfort to him.

He stopped for a traffic signal at Vernon and Western. As they sat waiting for the light to change, a black-and-white patrol car pulled alongside and stopped. Sarah looked at the driver, a young Negro.

The officer sat relaxed behind the wheel of the police car, watching the activity in a gas station on the corner. The other officer, Sarah noticed, was also black, perhaps ten years older than his young partner. His hair was cut short, and he had a small, well-trimmed moustache. A thin light scar ran from the base of his left ear, along his cheek, toward the corner of his mouth. Realizing her stare was making them uncomfortable, Sarah looked away.

"Jacob," she said in a sober tone, "is this our enemy? Are these the ones who practice genocide?"

Ward glanced at the patrol car.

"You're twisting what I've said," he answered, without looking at her.

The signal changed, and the patrol car pulled away. The Wards were silent the remainder of their ride home.

"Jacob," Sarah said, as they entered the house, "let's have a coffee in the kitchen and talk, the way we used to do. I'll tell Bonnie we don't want to be disturbed."

Ward glanced at his watch.

"Jacob," she said calmly, "forget the time. Forget telephone calls and think of us for a change."

"All right, hon." He nodded, taking her hand. "Let's have a coffee."

They sat in the built-in dinette in the kitchen of the big house. Ward lit another of his cigars as Sarah poured the coffee.

"Remember that little kitchen we had when we lived in Normandie?" Sarah said.

"Yeah, only too well." Ward slipped off his coat and loosened his tie. "It was about the size of a closet, with a leaky old gas stove and an icebox."

Sarah sipped the hot coffee. This smiling, broad-shouldered man, with his coat off and tie loose, was different from the Jacob Ward she saw and heard on television. "Do you remember the night I heard that prowler at the back door?"

Jacob laughed. "That's the night I nearly went to jail for being a sex-crazed rapist."

"Well, they would have been right about the 'sex-crazed.'" Sarah smiled. Ward always warmed to Sarah's smile. Her white, even teeth were dazzling; her lips were soft and smooth.

"You made me what I was, Sarah."

"If you'd left the door unlocked when you went out, you wouldn't have been locked out in your shorts."

"How was I to know your damn dog would pull it closed?"

"I didn't have anything to tie her to but the doorknob."

"I'll never forget these two officers who drove down the alley and found me banging on the back door," Ward said, smiling. "Cunningham and Schwartz."

"Well, if you hadn't run, they might never have seen you."

"No man likes to be seen in his shorts," Jacob said. "Even in his own backyard. And I'd have gotten away if it hadn't been for that damn clothesline."

"You're just lucky I got up and came out."

"Damn Cunningham." Ward smiled. "He laughed and laughed, like some horse."

"Wouldn't you?"

"I suppose," he said, laughing. "Those were the days." When their laughter died, they were quiet for a long while, Ward staring into his coffee cup, Sarah watching him, trying to read the thoughts behind his piercing black eyes.

"Those were the days," he said again. "And now they're gone."

Sarah reached across the table, took his big hand in hers. "They don't have to be, Jacob, they really don't have to be."

He searched her eyes. "Everything's different, Sarah, everything's changed."

"No, Jacob," she said firmly. "The only thing that has changed is you."

He looked away.

"Listen to me, Jacob. I saw this happen to my father. First he became a successful lawyer, then a judge, then a congressman. He had no time for Mother or any of us children. He had a brilliant career. And he was a very lonely and unhappy man."

"Oh, for Christ's sake, don't lecture me, Sarah." Ward frowned and pulled his hand away.

"Please, Jacob. I love you, and I don't want you to destroy yourself."

He leveled his eyes to hers. "You think I'm the cause of J.D.'s death?"

She met his gaze. "If I hadn't run away to Philadelphia, and if you hadn't let him move out of the house, he'd be here tonight. If we had been the husband and wife we used to be, we would have been the parents J.D. needed." A tear slowly made its trace in her makeup.

Ward stared at her.

"We can take the easy way out and blame the police," Sarah continued. "But we both know they couldn't help what happened, and they certainly didn't cause it." She paused. "I know it broke J.D.'s heart when I went to Philadelphia. He thought we were going to get a divorce, and I seriously considered it. For J.D.'s sake, let's put it back together. I'm not asking you not to run, but run as the good and decent man that you are, Jacob, and not as the father of a black martyr. Our son deserves better than that, Jacob." She began to sob. "He deserves more . . ." She couldn't continue. She bowed her head in her hands.

Ward studied her for a long moment. Then he got up, walked around the table, and sat down beside her, putting his arms awkwardly around her shoulders. "We'll do it the right way, hon," he whispered. "We'll do it the right way."

"Russell, are you here?" Ward called as he entered his study.

LeBlanc turned away from the lighted aquarium. "Yes, sir."

Offering him a folded blue paper, Ward said, "I want this delivered to Officer Conrad's widow as soon as possible. I don't know the address, but I'm sure you can get it."

LeBlanc cautiously took the paper. Eyeing it, he

reached inside his dark suit jacket for his glasses and slipped them on. "May I read it?" he asked with exaggerated politeness.

"I want you to read it, Russell," Ward said, turning toward his desk.

LeBlanc unfolded the paper and read it quickly as Ward sat down at his desk and lit another cigar.

Finishing the note, LeBlanc removed his glasses. He carefully refolded it. Throwing the note onto the desk, he said in an uncharacteristic high-pitched voice, "I'll . . . I'll not be part of this sellout!"

Ward drew in on his cigar, "Sellout?"

"That's right," LeBlanc said, leaning over the desk. "Sellout. Abbott, Peck, your wife, they've all got to you, and now you're ready to step back into line like all the rest of the white man's niggers. Go ahead, Uncle Tom, kiss their ass, but don't expect me to hand you a towel to wipe your mouth with."

Ward crushed his cigar in a brass ashtray and stood up.

LeBlanc stepped back from the desk.

"Anything else, Russell?" Ward said quietly.

"Yes," LeBlanc shouted immediately. "You haven't given a goddamned thought to the rights of the 600,000 blacks who looked to you to fight harder for a few basic rights that the white man has enjoyed for—"

Ward suddenly brought his fist down on the desk. "Now you listen to me, you self-righteous asshole," he hissed. "You talk about winning a few basic rights—why, you spoiled bastard, *you* never rode on the back of a bus, *you* never had to step off the sidewalk when a white woman approached, and *you* never picked cotton for thirty cents a bale until your hands bled."

LeBlanc stared.

"Your father died at fifty-two from cleaning six

office buildings a night," Ward continued, glaring at LeBlanc, "just to get your ass through law school. Did it take the National Guard to get you in that school, Russell?" Ward shouted, his voice shaking. "You're goddamned right it didn't, because we took care of that while you were still in grammar school. And you've got the audacity to stand there and tell me—tell me—that I've sold out. Why, you son-of-a-bitch, you have yet to earn the right to call yourself a black man."

"Jacob," Sarah said sharply, appearing in the doorway.

Ward was silent, breathing hard.

She looked at them. "I think enough has been said."

Ward sank slowly into his chair.

LeBlanc moved to the desk, avoiding a look at Ward, picked up the note, and left the room.

Two plainclothesmen watched the blue van drive slowly up the street.

"What do you think, partner?" the officer behind the wheel whispered in the darkness.

"He's looking for something," said the other, sliding down in the seat. "Let's see where he stops."

The van had nearly passed the Conrad home when it stopped abruptly, backed up, and pulled to the curb.

"Get ready," one of the officers said, removing his revolver from a shoulder holster. His partner did the same. The driver of the van cut the motor and turned off the lights. A slender Negro man stepped out of the van. He slipped a shiny metallic tube into a rear pocket and closed the door gently.

"Only one."

"Yeah," came a hushed reply, "it's a dude, and he put something in his back pocket."

"Right. We'll take him when he crosses the street."

The man had just passed the front hedge when the larger of the two officers leaped over the hedge and hooked an arm around his neck. He choked out a muffled scream as the officer threw him violently to the grass. When the suspect was handcuffed, the officer released his stranglehold.

"Don't make a sound," he cautioned, but the black man was completely unable to speak. He sat on the ground gasping for breath. They searched him. The metallic tube was a flashlight.

"Hey, man," the tall Negro finally said, still choking and coughing, "I ain't got but seven dollars, but you can have it."

The officers stared. Then one reached into his pocket and held out his badge case.

"Oh, wow, man," he sighed with relief, "I thought I'd bought it. Look, I don't know what this is all about, but I ain't done nothing."

"Let us be the judge of that," the standing officer said. "First, let's start with your name."

"Earl Davis, I'm twenty-nine, I live at 3706 South Menlo and I work for . . ."

"Whoa, whoa . . . Let us ask the questions, okay?"

"Oh, yeah, man," the suspect said earnestly. "But I knew you'd be asking for that stuff."

"Okay, what brings you out here tonight?"

"I work for Kings Special Messenger Service and I was making a delivery."

"Where?"

"To that house over there. Their name is Conrad. It's here in my pocket, man."

The officer reached and felt the paper in the pocket. "He looks legitimate, partner."

One helped Davis to his feet. The other unhand-cuffed him.

Davis massaged his wrists.

"Listen, we didn't know who you were. From where we sat, you—"

"Hey, man," Davis interrupted with a grin, "you don't have to tell me. I've been around. I know you don't go jump on no dude without him doin' something. I ain't going to make no waves."

"You're okay, Earl," one of the officers said. There was relief in his voice.

"No sweat," Davis said, brushing his slacks. "Now, can I deliver my message?"

"Right."

"I've got to make tracks. I've got this fox, a number-one fox, ya know, waitin', and I don't want her to wait too long." Davis trotted back across the street.

They watched him go.

"Jesus," one said finally, "close."

One of the police wives staying with Helen opened the front door when the bell rang. She relaxed when she saw the two metro officers standing near the hedge. Davis handed her the envelope.

After signing, she carried it to Helen, who sat quietly with another woman in the family room.

Helen's fingers trembled, despite the sedatives she had taken. She unfolded the blue paper.

Dear Mrs. Conrad:

My wife and I extend our heartfelt sympathy to you and sincerely hope it may help bring you comfort at this trying moment.

The words do not come easily as I write this note, for we too have suffered the loss of a loved one.

Your husband's bravery in the face of over-

whelming odds exemplifies the highest stan-
dards of the law-enforcement profession.

He was a public servant, one so dedicated
to his ideals that he paid the ultimate price to
protect and to serve.

I, as a councilman of this city, am proud
that Wayne Conrad was a police officer for the
city of Los Angeles.

> Sincerely,
> Jacob D. Ward, Sr.

Local weathermen blamed the unusual August
rain on tropical storm Beth. Cool ocean air poured
into the Los Angeles Basin just after midnight,
meeting the warm static air resting there. The result was a gray, cloud-clogged sky whitened by
flashes of lightning. Deafening claps of thunder
made the city tremble.

Tuesday's darkness gave way to a dull, gray light
as dawn spilled into the wet streets. A light cool
drizzle continued. Forecasters promised it would
give way to the familiar California sun by midafter-
noon.

At nine o'clock, the first few policemen arrived
at the gray stone church in West Los Angeles. In
spite of the light rain, motorcycle officers also appeared. Their numbers continued to grow until
there were hundreds.

Shortly before nine-thirty, the news teams appeared and began to erect their equipment across
the street. One of the major television networks was
scheduled to provide live coverage of both the Conrad and Ward funerals.

Two motor officers stood by their polished cycles,
drenched from the light rain, watching the technicians erect their cameras. "Live coverage of a
funeral, kind of ironic, isn't it?"

His partner, wiping rain from his chin, nodded in silent agreement.

The black polished limousine, with rain beaded on its waxed surface, slid to a smooth stop in front of the crowded church. The wife, dressed in black, and the three children stepped out. They moved quickly to the open doorway; the youngest and smallest of the children, a brown-haired three-year-old boy, holding his mother's hand, flashed a wide grin and waved to one of the motor officers standing in the morning rain. The officer waved back, then dropped his hand quickly to his side. He stood, head down, staring hard at the pavement.

The police had cordoned off three blocks of West Manchester in South Los Angeles near the Heller Mortuary to provide the Ward funeral motorcade room to assemble. The crowd of mourners and the curious now numbered in the thousands. The television crews attempted to provide coverage from the street level, but due to the crush, they had been forced to move to the top of a market across the street.

Meanwhile, the police quietly established a staging area in a vacant furniture warehouse at Eighty-second Street and Arlington Avenue, just a few blocks from the mortuary. Several hundred officers sat in and around the warehouse, waiting.

Inspector Foster, still acting as field commander, was relieved to find that the rain had started early in the morning. Rain was always a deterrent to violence.

When Chief Peck and Deputy Chief Searcy arrived at the Conrad funeral, the church, though crowded, was quiet but for the soft organ music and an occasional sob. They had come late after meeting with Inspector Foster about policing the Ward funeral. Now they stood along the wall near the rear of the church with other officers.

The six uniformed pallbearers moved into position beside the casket and stood at rigid attention. As they gripped the handles and lifted, a young voice called out, "Mommy, what are they doing with Daddy?"

Helen knelt beside her three-year-old son. "Timmy," she said softly, "Mommy wants you to be quiet now, and when we get home, we'll have some Kool-Aid and talk about it."

"But, Mommy . . ."

The six pallbearers moved in a slow, reverent pace toward the doors at the rear of the church.

As the Conrad funeral wound its way through the streets of West Los Angeles en route to the Pine Crest Memorial Park, it passed the beautiful Westwood campus of UCLA.

Three students, still hilarious and high from a night of wine and pot, stood rain-soaked on the curb, waiting for a break in the traffic. A girl, her long hair dripping, huddled between two boys, smiling up at them, moving slightly to an inner beat, rolling softly from one to the other. The escorting motor officers rolled by, the cortege moved by, tires hissing on the wet pavement.

"Hey, look," the young girl laughed, "it's the Pig Patrol."

"They're here to arrest everybody," one of the boys said. He raised his arms. "Don't shoot, coppers —I surrender."

"Look—the pigs are gonna plant someone in the grass." He cocked his fingers. "Tat-tat-tat, coppers —you'll never take me alive!"

They all laughed raucously. "Get screwed, pigs," the girl shouted. The cars and motorcycles rolled by.

"Fuck the pigs," the tall boy sang, raising his middle finger. The other two joined him. "Fuck the pigs, fuck the pigs."

The cars rolled on, the hundreds of officers in the motorcade frozen in silent rage, hoping somehow their silence would speak.

When the coffin carrying young Ward appeared, a low, involuntary moan rose from the thousands outside the Heller Mortuary. The weeping started when the councilman, his head bowed, his arm around his wife's shoulders, walked down the white steps to a waiting limousine.

At Forest Lawn, the California Highway Patrol estimated the crowd at eleven thousand. Residents as far away as a mile could hear the crowd singing "We Shall Overcome" at the conclusion of the graveside service. The reporters at the scene were awed and frightened. They could sense the burning anger and frustration behind the tears.

On the evening news, Bill Hart narrated the video tape of the Ward funeral. "For many Los Angeles residents, it was the most moving event since the funeral of John F. Kennedy. For many, it was much less. While most black and many white city employees took the day off to attend services, Mayor Abbott spent the day at work in his office. Final rites were also held for slain police officer John W. Conrad, one of the officers involved in the shooting death of young Ward."

The headlines of the evening papers read, "RECORD TURNOUT FOR WARD FUNERAL," "BLACK COMMUNITY BIDS J.D. WARD JR. FAREWELL," "FUNERAL MOTORCADE JAMS L.A. FREEWAYS," "CITY STOPS IN RESPECT"; and further down the page there was the story of the Conrad funeral: "SLAIN OFFICER LAID TO REST," "COP INVOLVED IN

WARD DEATH BURIED," "POLICEMEN FROM SOUTH-
ERN CALIFORNIA ATTEND FINAL RITES FOR FELLOW
OFFICER," and "COP KILLED IN WARD DEATH
BURIED TODAY."

As the weatherman promised, the familiar sun
appeared late Tuesday afternoon and began to erase
the wet from the asphalt and concrete. But the city
was still damp late in the day when the shadows
lengthened and lights blinked on across the wide
basin.

For the police, the city was still far from normal.
The unnerving quiet continued.

On Wednesday, the Watts Summer Festival, de-
layed two days for the Ward funeral, finally got under way. Traditionally, the mayor cut the ribbon
which opened Will Rogers Park, where the festival
was held. But this year Raymond Kupps, the senator from California, replaced Mayor Abbott at the
ceremony. Senator Kupps smiled and waved to the
crowd of several hundred spectators as he climbed
onto the speaker's platform.

"Who's that, brother?" a Negro with a large Afro
asked.

"Fugg, I don't know, man," came the answer.
"Another white missionary down here to save us
poor black folks."

They laughed.

"Greetings, brothers and sisters." Kupps smiled,
raising his right arm, fist clenched.

"Oh, for Christ's sake," said Gregory Flute,
standing near the speaker's platform.

"I'm very pleased to be here with you this morning." He paused, expecting applause. None came.
He continued, "This year our festival is more important than ever. Tragedy has swept through our
community, tearing at our hearts and leaving us

with a feeling of frustration and a sense of great loss.

"This is the feeling that some would like to have prevail in the black community. It shall not. We shall overcome." He paused again, as his text instructed him to do. The crowd was silent.

The senator had another two pages of his speech left, but he folded the papers. "Thank you, ladies and gentlemen," he concluded lamely.

There was spattered applause as the senator left the speaker's platform and headed for the silk ribbon. Miss Watts, a shapely black girl in a tiger-striped bathing suit, handed him a pair of oversized chrome scissors. "It is with great personal pride that I—"

"Come on, man, cut it," a voice called from the crowd.

The senator frowned slightly. "It is with great personal pride that I cut the ribbon opening the eleventh annual Watts Festival."

Cameras flashed as the senator snipped the ribbon. He forced a stiff grin. The crowd surged by him into the park as a rock band began to blare.

The chairman of the Festival Committee shook hands with the senator and invited him into the park. Kupps said he had a pressing engagement, and headed quickly for his waiting car.

As his driver turned the big car onto the freeway, Kupps removed a white handkerchief from a rear pocket and wiped the dust from his polished shoes. "You can't talk to that kind of people," he said to his aide.

Early Wednesday afternoon, Chester Bradshaw, the United States attorney in Los Angeles, announced that he was satisfied with the Los Angeles

Police Department's investigation of the shooting, and saw no need for federal intervention.

Late Wednesday afternoon Russell LeBlanc announced that Councilman Ward and his wife had left the city for an undisclosed destination, seeking privacy and rest. They would return to the city the following week.

Senator Kupps was upset when he learned of Ward's departure. He had counted on Ward's cooperation in an investigation of the shooting. When he telephoned and asked LeBlanc to speak for the councilman in announcing the investigation, LeBlanc courteously explained that Councilman Ward did not want his people to have any part of an investigation. He believed that his son's death was accidental.

"Listen, LeBlanc, you don't know that for sure. And we've got to act now, while this thing is still hot."

"I cannot go against the councilman's wishes, Senator," LeBlanc said firmly.

Kupps hung up in anger. "They're all alike," he said with disgust.

Chief Peck, satisfied that the crisis had passed, canceled the mobilization. After four days of working twelve-hour shifts, normal duty was a welcome relief to exhausted officers. It was even more of a relief to their families.

Stryker and West spent Wednesday and Thursday retracing their few leads to locate Pepper. They reinterviewed Johnny Grear, talked to the officers who had arrested him, pounded doors around the scene of the shooting in the hope of finding a new witness, and ran down a number of suspects that citizens had reported as looking like Pepper. Nothing. They were frustrated and tired.

PART

TWO

On Friday morning, shortly after four A.M., Stryker and West were called out of bed to handle a homicide. They met at the station and drove to the scene on South Raymond.

Chuck Johnson and two officers were already conducting a preliminary investigation when Stryker and West arrived.

A few neighbors curious enough to get out of bed in the early morning stood near two patrol cars parked in front of the small duplex. The front door of the house stood open; they could hear a baby crying.

Sergeant Johnson was on the telephone. "Okay, thanks," he said, hanging up. " 'Morning, fellows."

"How's it going, man?" West said as they came in.

And Stryker asked, "What have you got?"

"Looks like the Pisser," Johnson said.

Stryker and West stared and said nothing.

One of the most vicious murderers Los Angeles had ever seen, he had terrorized the South End for nearly four months. Striking between the hours of midnight and five A.M., he had already taken two lives. This appeared to be the third. His victims were women in their late twenties or early thirties, living alone.

After raping his victims, he forced them to perform oral copulation. Then he slashed their throats and wrists with what the police believed to be a straight razor.

The police had nicknamed him the Pisser—he urinated on his dead victims and on their beds.

He hadn't struck in Southwest Division before, but now he was Stryker and West's problem.

"The victim," Johnson said, glancing at his field officer's notebook, "is Sophie Christian, female, Negro, twenty-seven. She lived here with her ten-month-old daughter. Her throat and wrists were cut."

"How'd you people find out?" Stryker questioned.

"3A9 got a call to see the woman, an abandoned child. The lady next door heard the baby crying for several hours, and she thought maybe the mother had split. Our guys kicked the door in after nobody answered. They found the body in the bedroom."

After a moment, Johnson said, "You know what that son-of-a-bitch did?"

"What?" West said.

"He stood on a chair in the baby's room and pissed all over her."

Stryker said nothing.

West shook his head in disbelief.

"Landry's cleaning the kid up now," Johnson said.

"Let's take a look at the body," Stryker said.

"In here." Johnson led them toward a bedroom. The stench of stale urine met them as they walked down the short hall.

"We haven't been in the room," Johnson said, stopping at the doorway. Stryker stepped past him into the small room. West followed.

The young mother lay face down on the bed, nude, on a white sheet. Her face was buried in a pool of drying blood. One hand lay at her side;

the other hung from the bed. Both wrists had been slashed. The arm hanging from the bed looked as if it wore a scarlet glove. Several flies crawled over her bloody wrists and neck, and a dozen others buzzed loudly in the dim room. A stain of urine yellowed the white sheet around her legs. A small yellow puddle rested in the depression between the small of her back and her buttocks.

A single window in the room was open. Its pale green curtain swung in the morning's gentle breeze.

Stryker stepped closer to the bed. He reached out, took the body by the ankle, and shook it gently. "Been dead awhile; she's stiff."

West stood silently and surveyed the room. He thought of Lisa first, asleep alone in her apartment, and a chill swept over him. Then he shook the thought off. "No sign of struggle or ransack," he said aloud.

Stryker nodded. "Okay, partner," Stryker said, "call SID, photos, prints, and the coroner."

"Right."

"And, Johnson, call another unit for security around the outside. If our bad guy left a footprint or something outside, we don't want a curious neighbor screwing it up."

"Have 'em here in five minutes," Johnson said.

Stryker went back to the living room. A young Negro officer sat on the couch rocking back and forth, holding the sleeping baby girl carefully in his arms. Stryker studied the baby. He thought the kid was ugly.

After two and a half hours, Stryker and West completed their investigation. The body was removed by the coroner, the house sealed.

"Do you wanna get some breakfast?" West asked as they climbed into the car.

"Christ," Stryker said, "you could eat shit in a graveyard."

"*This* beautiful body," West said, as he started the car, "does not run on air."

"Well, I'm not hungry," Stryker said, slumping in the seat. He closed his eyes as West pulled the car into gear.

At the station, West breakfasted out of the vending machines in the coffee room. Stryker drank two cups of coffee and bought another pack of cigarettes.

At nine o'clock they appeared in Division Forty, Superior Court, for a preliminary hearing on a robbery-homicide. They waited for over an hour until the judge granted the defendant a continuance —his attorney had failed to show.

They went to the coroner's office for the autopsy results on the Pisser's latest victim; then to Parker Center, the main police building, to pick up the photos of the murder scene and see if the latent-prints office had been able to make any of the prints they had lifted. They hadn't.

They skipped lunch and returned to the South End to interview Sophie Christian's neighbors, hoping to find someone who might have seen or heard something, anything unusual. After two hours they returned to the station. Nothing.

"About time you guys came to work," Lieutenant Purington said as they passed his desk in the squad room.

"Fuck you," Stryker snarled, removing his suit jacket.

West spread out the multitude of reports. Stryker spun one of the eight-by-ten photos of the murder scene around, studying it.

"Stryker, West," Purington called, crossing the room to them.

"Whatever it is, Tom, we didn't do it."

"I know you didn't, that's the problem," the tall, slender lieutenant said, leaning on the end of the desk.

Stryker continued to study the photo, hoping Purington would see he didn't want to be bothered.

West pushed his big frame back in his chair and waited.

Purington looked at Stryker. "The captain is screaming for a report on the homicide-rape you two handled this morning."

Stryker looked at West. "That's a pisser, isn't it, partner?"

They both laughed loudly.

"No offense, Lieutenant," Stryker said, trying to look sober.

"No offense taken, but I need that report," Purington said. "Get on it."

"You'll have it in half an hour."

"That's worth a coffee, if you make it," Purington promised.

"Hell," West said, "for a free coffee, he'd reroute the Mississippi River in half an hour."

3Adam58, a Southwest Division patrol unit, was an hour away from the end of a busy day. End of watch was four P.M. They had just finished a quick cup of coffee and returned to their black-and-white when they received the call.

"3Adam58, see the woman, an attack report. 907 West Fifty-third Street. Code Two."

The officers acknowledged and rolled. 907 West Fifty-third street was a graying, white, two-story frame house with a wide front porch. The narrow strip of green that was a front yard was litter-strewn with broken glass, beer cans, and a variety of paper.

The two officers parked in front of a neighboring

house, walked to 907, climbed the four steps to the porch, and knocked on the rusted screen.

"Come in," a female sobbed.

One of the two cautiously opened the torn screen door. The woman, wearing only a short slip and bra, sat crying on a soiled brown couch. She was perhaps thirty years old. Her face was hidden in her hands; long black hair hung over her shoulders. Her brown skin was smooth, and her figure, though a few pounds heavy, was shapely. Her ample breasts heaved in the low-cut bra as she sobbed.

"Anybody else in the house, lady?" the first officer asked, as he eyed her figure.

She shook her head without looking up.

"Okay, you wanna tell us what happened?" the senior officer said, motioning his partner to check the adjoining rooms.

She reached for a Kleenex and mopped her eyes. "That fat motherfucker raped me."

"Does he have another name?" the officer asked in a disinterested tone.

"His name's Red. That's all I know him by."

"You ever sleep with him before?"

"No."

"How long have you known him?"

"He's a friend of my stupid-ass husband. He's been here since last Sunday. Hasn't been out of the goddamn house until today."

"When did he rape you?"

"About half an hour ago. I just took my bath, and I was goin' back to my room to get dressed. Ya know?"

"Go on."

"Well, Bee-Bee Balls had been drinkin' all day, and he's pretty high, and he sees me."

"Were you wearing anything?"

"What difference does that make?"

"None to me, lady, but I have to put it in the report," the officer lied, wondering how she looked naked.

"I was wearing a towel."

"Okay, what happened next?"

"After he sees me, he comes to my room. He says, 'Hey, baby, you've been wavin' that cute ass under my nose all week, and now you're going to get what you've asked for.' I tell him to get his ass out or my old man would kick his when he gets back. Then he tore my towel off and pushed me on the bed. He said he didn't give a shit about my old man. Said I'd like it so much I wouldn't tell."

"Go on."

"Well, I started to scream, so he punched me in the mouth. See?" She pointed to a bloody lip. "So, he says if I do it again, he'll kill me. Mommy didn't raise no fool, so I shut up and let him do his thing."

"Did you believe that he would kill you?"

"Hell, yes, he's got two guns. I've seen them."

"Where's he keep them?" the officer said with new interest.

"Upstairs in his room. The one on the left. Keeps them under the mattress."

"Where is he now?"

"Fat Boy said he was going out to get some more booze. He told me not to get dressed, because he wasn't done."

"You and your husband own this house?"

"Yeah."

"May we have your permission to take a look at the guns?"

"Yeah, I want you to take them, and I want this dude arrested," she said angrily.

"We'll do what we can," the officer promised. "Partner, go take a look under that mattress."

The second officer disappeared up the stairs.

"What's your name, ma'am?" the officer asked, removing his notebook.

"Cleo."

"Last name?"

"Frey, Cleo Frey."

"To establish that a rape has occurred, Cleo, it will be necessary for you to submit to a physical examination by a doctor. Are you willing to do that?"

"Yeah, I'm willing, if that's what it takes to put Fat Boy in jail."

"Fine. Why don't you get ready to go, then?"

She stood up. "I'll be ready in a few minutes."

The officer watched as she crossed the room. As she climbed the stairs, his partner came down carrying a revolver.

"Look at this," he said, holding it up. It was a thirty-eight special, blue steel with a four-inch barrel. The grips were a hard, black rubber.

"Looks like a service revolver, doesn't it?" He held the gun carefully by the trigger guard.

"Sure as hell does," the other answered, digging in his shirt pocket for his notebook. "If we're lucky, maybe it's Bennett's. I got the serial number of his at roll call on Monday. Let me check."

His partner laid the pistol carefully on the coffee table, opening the cylinder to expose the serial number.

The other thumbed hurriedly through his small notebook. "Here it is," he said in an excited tone. "K-773510."

"Jesus Christ, that's it," his partner breathed.

"Doing anything this weekend?" West asked as he stuffed reports into a brown case envelope.

"Yeah, Connie and I are going to Vegas tonight. Go up and win a few coins." Stryker smiled.

"You mean lose a few coins, don't you?"

"Well, it shouldn't cost too much."

"What's it going to cost Connie?"

Stryker smiled. "Man cannot live by bread alone."

West smiled a wide grin. "I think I'll take the phone off the hook and lie around the house all weekend."

"You mean you're not going to play with Lisa this weekend?" Stryker said, jotting his name and serial number on a 5.10 report.

"I didn't say that." West grinned. "Mom's going to Riverside tonight to visit a sister, and somebody's got to take care of me."

"Lisa should be able to take care of you," Stryker said, inserting the 5.10 in an envelope.

"Stryker, West, Steele, Boyd, Kline, Cook," Lieutenant Purington called in a loud voice from the head of the detective squad room. "All of you people, come here."

Stryker and West pushed their paperwork aside and joined the detectives around the lieutenant's desk.

Purington looked up at the six. "3A58 just recovered Bennett's gun."

Stryker's pulse raced.

"Where did they get it?"

"Wait a minute, dammit," Purington said. "Let's start at the beginning. 58 received a radio call to see the woman, an attack report at 907 West Fifty-third Street.

"The victim told the officers that she knew the suspect only as Red, and that he moved in with her and her old man last Sunday night. She also said this Red had two guns hidden under his mattress. They checked and found only one. It was Bennett's.

"Red, according to our victim, is drunk. After raping this broad, he took her car and left. He told her he was going after another bottle and that he'd be back.

"The car he's driving is a 1967 Ford Galaxie 500. It's a green two-door hardtop. California license NNC-453.

"Stryker," Purington said, "this is your caper, so you run the show. I want you guys to go get him."

"Okay, here's how we'll do it," Stryker said without hesitation, glad that Purington was done with his spiel. "Steele, you and Boyd take the intersection at the west end of the block, park on Fifty-third on the south side facing east, as close to the intersection as you can get.

"Boyd, you drive. Steele, you're the wrong color for the neighborhood, so you stay down, out of sight.

"I want both of you to take off your jackets and ties. These damn suits are as easy to spot as a uniform."

"Okay, we've got it."

"Good. Kline, you and Cook take the intersection at the east end of the block. Park on the north side of the street facing west, as close to the intersection as you can.

"Both of you are the wrong color, so stay out of sight as much as possible."

"Got it," Kline said.

"West and I will take the house," Stryker continued. "We'll stake in the front room. When he shows, we'll let him get out of his car and onto the lawn, and then we'll take him.

"If he smells us and decides to rabbit, we've got a car facing east and west. It won't matter which way he runs, we'll have him.

"Any questions?"

There were none.

"Okay, let's get down there and get that black-and-white the hell out of there before he shows.

"One final point," Stryker added. "Let's stagger our arrival at three-minute intervals. If we all roll in there at one time, we're going to have the neighbors out eyeballing. West and I will go first, then Steele and Boyd, and then you, Kline."

It was nearly five o'clock when Stryker and West arrived at the house. They parked their Plymouth in the alley at the rear and entered through the backyard.

"This is Cleo Frey," the patrol officer said as they entered the living room. "The gun's there on the coffee table."

"You touch it?" Stryker asked.

"Only the trigger guard."

"What time does your husband get home?" West asked the woman, who now wore a tight blue sweater and bell bottoms.

"He gets off at eleven," she said, eyeing West. "He works at Imperial Meat Packing in Compton."

"Okay, fellas," Stryker said, "take her and shove off. If Pepper gets back, he'll never come near with that black-and-white out front."

"Right, Sarge," the senior officer said. "Okay, Cleo, let's go."

"Take her to the station after you're done at the hospital," Stryker added.

"Good luck," one of the officers called as they walked onto the porch.

"Thanks," West answered.

Stryker pulled a torn leather foot stool up close to one of the two front windows and sat down. "You might as well get comfortable. It may be awhile." West was at the far end of the room thumbing through a copy of *Ebony*.

"The other guys in position yet?" he asked.

"I can see Kline's car," Stryker said. "Looks like it's empty. Which is good." His eyes searched the west end of the block, looking for the other detective unit. "Yeah, there's Boyd," he said, recognizing the familiar black face. "Looks like he's sleeping."

"Knowing Boyd"—West smiled—"he probably is."

"Steele's probably the one sleeping. Stretched in the back seat." Stryker grinned.

West, unable to find anything to sit on, sat on the floor next to the other front window.

"Think we'll have to kill him?"

"Got me," Stryker answered dryly. "It's all up to him."

"Anyway you look at it, he sure screwed up our weekend," West said.

Stryker said nothing.

"I sure could use some chow," West said.

"Christ," Stryker said, shaking his head.

A car turned into the block from the west. West saw it first. "One coming."

"No good," Stryker said as it came into view. A car carrying a family rolled by.

They relaxed.

West watched two boys struggling down the far side of the street with a large bag of soft-drink bottles. "Based on personal experience, I'd say it took 'em about two hours to collect those."

Stryker looked up at the two. "Naw, not unless they're beginners," he said. "I could scrape up that many in forty minutes when I was a kid."

"Yeah," West said. "I can guess your method. Steal them from one store and sell them to another."

"You're wrong. I sold them to the same store."

West smiled. "Ever steal anything besides bottles?"

"Yeah," Stryker said, watching the quiet street. "I took a pair of sunglasses once." He smiled. "I broke 'em the same goddamn day."

"When I was ten," West said softly, "I fell in love with this yellow-and-blue dump truck at the five-and-ten. It cost ninety-eight cents. That's more than my old man made a day. I took it, and Mom caught me in the backyard with it. Worse than getting caught was having to take it back."

Stryker said nothing as he sat listening, pulling a few strands of thread from his frayed trouser cuff.

"Yeah, being poor was hell," West added.

"Don't say that like you're the only one who knows what the hell poor is," Stryker said, turning toward him. "Many a day I wore my cleanest dirty shirt to school."

"Didn't mean it that way." Their eyes met.

"Good," Stryker said, grinning slightly. "I thought you were going to ask to borrow some money."

Their conversation stopped when West saw the green car turn onto the block from the west end. "Green one coming," he said, pushing away from the window.

Stryker glanced to the end of the block. "It's him," he whispered.

Both men drew their guns. West knelt on one knee near the window. Stryker pushed the footstool away and moved to the side of the screen door. He wanted to be first.

"I'm still hungry," West said as they watched the green Ford roll slowly toward the house.

Stryker smiled his small, tight grin. "I'll buy us a prime-rib dinner after this is over."

"You'll find some way to get out of it," West said.

As Pepper turned the Ford onto the block, he noticed the white Plymouth parked at the curb. If he hadn't been drinking, he would have immediately known it was the police, but now he was dulled by liquor, and he was careless.

He looked closer at the Plymouth as he passed. "Only one dude in the car, and he's sleeping."

Boyd, his jacket and tie off, was slouched behind the wheel of the Plymouth, resting his head on the seat. He opened his eyes after Pepper passed. The car's outside mirror gave him a good view of the intersection behind him. After Pepper had passed, Boyd whispered, "Get ready, Steele, it's him."

Pepper's thoughts were on Cleo. "That bitch is still laying around naked on the bed, waitin' for Big Red. She be all rested and ready." He laughed softly. He wheeled the Ford into the curb in front of the house and stopped.

Stryker stood with his back to the wall. He had one hand on the screen door; the other held his thirty-eight. His breathing was now rapid and shallow.

West, kneeling near the window, watching, cautioned softly, "Okay, get ready, he's stopped."

Kline and Cook, at the east end of the block, now had guns in hand, waiting for Pepper to get out of his car.

Pepper turned off the ignition.

"He's shut it off," West whispered.

Stryker smiled.

Pepper reached to the right and picked up the cold six-pack of beer. Reflexively, he glanced into the rear-view mirror. His heart jumped. He stared hard at the white Plymouth. Now, instead of one sleeping Negro, he saw that there were two people in the car, and one was white. Cops!

He dropped the six-pack to the floor and twisted the ignition key. The starter whined.

"He's going to run," West shouted.

"That son-of-a-bitch," Stryker snorted, pushing the screen door open and bolting onto the front porch. West followed.

The Ford's engine started. "Police officers, don't move," Stryker shouted, raising his arm and pointing the thirty-eight at Pepper.

Their eyes met. Stryker saw the scar on his shining, sweaty face as Pepper grabbed for his waistband.

Stryker fired twice as Pepper raised the thirty-two automatic. His first shot shattered the speedometer in the Ford, showering Pepper with the plastic that covered it. The second passed in front of Pepper's stomach, under his left arm, and buried itself in the armrest.

Stryker's misses gave Pepper the time he needed.

His face twisted as he pointed the thirty-two and jerked the trigger. The gun fired. He pulled again and again, firing all six shots.

The first shot struck West high in the left chest. The second struck him again as he reeled backward.

West, not believing what had happened to him, fired his revolver twice as he collapsed. One went skyward, and the other struck the porch roof. Then he was lying on the porch's rough floor watching the light fade and hearing the faraway sound of Stryker shooting and cursing. He wondered if he were dying. Then he could not hear or see or wonder.

Pepper threw down the automatic and pulled the

Ford into gear. It lunged forward as he tramped hard on the accelerator.

Stryker leaped from the porch, continuing to fire.

The Ford's back window disintegrated, but the car didn't stop.

Boyd and Steele, at the east end of the block, saw the six-second gun fight.

"Get on it, he's running!" Steele shouted. Boyd had the Plymouth rolling.

Stryker lowered his empty gun in disgust as the Ford gained speed toward the end of the block. "You fat, miserable bastard," he shouted in helpless anger.

As the Ford raced toward them, Kline and Cook pulled their car into the street, blocking it, and scrambled out the left side as Pepper bore down on them.

Just short of the detective car, Pepper wrenched the Ford violently to the left. The front end jumped as it struck the curb with a bang. Pepper tightened his sweaty grip on the steering wheel as the car bounced and crossed the sidewalk, crushing its way through a hedge into a front yard. Pepper fought to maintain control as the heavy car slid in the grass. He turned hard to the right. The Ford responded. It dug across the yard, smashing a hedge, a white picket fence, and a bicycle.

Kline and Cook fired as the Ford crashed through the yards, passing behind them. One of the shots shattered the side window of the Ford. Flying glass tore into Pepper's face, and blood poured from a dozen punctures. Another shot flattened the right-rear tire. The Ford sped on, reached the intersection, jerked left, bounced onto the street, and sped north. Kline and Cook scrambled to their car.

In their Plymouth, Boyd and Steele raced down

the block, intending to follow Pepper's route around Kline's car through the torn-up grass.

Otis Jefferson was sitting in his kitchen with a cold beer, listening to the Dodgers and Pirates. He was startled first by the sound of gunfire and then by a loud crash in his front yard. He put down his beer and rushed to the front door.

"Hey, man," Jefferson yelled when he saw his flattened fence and the deep tire ruts in the lawn. "Goddamn drunk!" he shouted. Seeing the twisted wreckage of his son's bike, he pushed open the screen and ran onto the lawn.

"Look out!" Steele screamed. It was too late to stop.

"Christ!" Boyd wrenched the wheel violently to the right, slamming on the brakes.

Kline saw the Plymouth turn toward them. "Look out," he yelled. Brakes screaming, the Plymouth slid toward them at a slight angle, Boyd now jamming on the brakes with both feet, twisting the wheel hard to the right.

The Plymouth slammed into the car blocking the street. The sound of crunching metal and breaking glass echoed off the houses.

Otis Jefferson stood in his front yard barefoot, his mouth hanging open.

"Son-of-a-bitch," Stryker screamed as he watched the two cars collide. Holstering his gun, he turned back to the porch. "Come on, West, let's . . ." He stood frozen. His jaw fell, and he began to shake. "No . . . no . . . no," he shouted again and again, stumbling to the porch where West lay. Stryker knelt, swinging angrily at several large black flies in the pool of deep red blood around West's shoulder and head.

He turned West's head gently. West's face was relaxed and without expression, his mouth slightly open. Stryker gritted his teeth as his fingers searched frantically for a pulse. "Come on, come on, goddammit," he mumbled. "Don't die . . . don't die."

Unable to find a pulse, he dropped the wrist and leaned an ear to West's chest. He listened, hearing nothing. "Come on, partner, come on, breathe, please, goddammit." Then, slowly, the faint thump of a heartbeat. He took West's hand in his. "Hang on, partner. Hang on."

From the end of the block where the two cars had collided, three of the four detectives ran toward him.

"Steele," Stryker screamed. "Steele, he's shot. Get my car, it's out back."

Steele looked down at West. "We'd better wait for an ambulance, John," he said. "He looks bad."

"He's going to be all right," Stryker said, looking at West's relaxed face. "He's going to be all right."

Boyd knelt beside West. "Let's see what we can do for this bleeding," he said, pulling back the open jacket. The pale blue shirt below was blood-soaked. Boyd carefully removed West's tie and unbuttoned the shirt. He pulled it back, exposing the left side of his chest.

Stryker watched in silence. Blood spurted from a pencil-sized hole, just above the breast. An occasional air bubble interrupted its steady flow. Boyd reached to his rear pocket, removed a white handkerchief, and pressed it over the wound.

A crowd gathered on the sidewalk. They peered at the porch, whispering and pointing, some laughing. Another group formed around the smashed cars. The white Plymouth, its radiator smashed, sent a trail of white vapor skyward.

"I put out a broadcast on Pepper," Steele said.

"He shouldn't get far. Who knows, maybe he's got some lead in him."

Stryker said nothing as he continued to watch West.

Sirens whined in the distance. The ambulance was followed by six black-and-whites and several motor officers.

"Finally, you slow bastards," Steele breathed as the ambulance pulled up to the house.

One of the attendants was out and opening the rear door before it rolled to a stop. Joined by another, they slid a metal-framed stretcher from the rear and raced up the porch steps. The ring of officers moved to allow them through.

"Okay, fellas, move back."

Boyd released the pressure he held on the soaked handkerchief. He looked at Stryker, who seemed not to hear the attendant. "John," Boyd said, standing up, "come on, these guys will take care of him."

Stryker stared, his face strange and expressionless. He released West's hand and stood up.

Chief of Police Peck sat in his office, penciling out final instructions for Deputy Chief Searcy, who would act as chief while he was out of the city.

Peck and his wife, Nancy, were spending the weekend in San Francisco. Peck did not often get away, and they both looked forward to this rare escape. The intercom buzzed. "Yes?" he said, pushing a button.

"Sir," his adjutant said, "we've just received a report from Southwest Division that an officer has been shot trying to apprehend the suspect in the Bennett shooting. There's no report on the officer's condition or his identity. We do know the suspect escaped."

"Thank you, Rosson," Peck said.

He pushed back in his chair, staring blankly at his desk. Suddenly he swung a clenched fist, striking the desk top a powerful blow. A coffee cup danced into the air and fell, spilling coffee over the memo he had just written.

Policemen and the two attendants carried West from the porch to the waiting ambulance. Stryker and Boyd climbed into the rear with the stretcher.

Ignoring department policy, two motor officers provided escort as the ambulance raced to Morningside Hospital at Manchester and Western Avenue several miles away.

Stryker and Boyd walked with West as he was wheeled into the treatment room.

Immediately, a tall Negro nurse pushed Boyd aside and began cutting at West's shirt. "Doctor, we've got a critical GSW," she called in a loud voice.

Another nurse pushed by Stryker and placed an oxygen mask over West's relaxed face.

"You two wait outside, please," a Negro doctor ordered as he joined the nurse.

"He's a policeman," Stryker said as he watched the trio cut at West's bloodied shirt.

"Well, now he's a patient," the doctor barked. "Wait outside."

"You smart bastard," Stryker said angrily.

The doctor turned toward him.

"This one is sucking," a nurse interrupted, uncovering the wound in West's chest. The doctor leaned over, looking at the wound. "Get a Vaseline gauze on this, and get me his blood pressure."

"Come on, John," Boyd said, pulling Stryker by the arm.

Stryker followed reluctantly, "Goddamn ape,

probably got his degree from a correspondence school," he muttered childishly.

Boyd didn't answer.

As they walked into the hallway, Steele and Kline pushed through the emergency entrance assisting Cook, whose right arm hung limp at his side. His face showed the pain.

"In all the excitement, we forgot to put this guy in the ambulance." Steele smiled.

Cook forced a grin. "Any word on West?"

Stryker shook his head. "They just went to work."

"Come on, Al." Kline guided Cook toward the treatment room.

"I'll wait out here," Steele said. "Hospitals make me sick."

The trio walked the short distance to the waiting room at the end of the hall and plopped into the soft leather chairs.

They had been sitting quietly for five minutes when Stryker stood up. "We haven't called his mother," he said, looking surprised.

Steele straightened from his slouch in the leather chair. "We shouldn't call. That would scare the hell out of her. Boyd and I will go get her."

"You know where she lives?" Stryker asked.

"I do," Boyd said.

"Let's go, then," Steele said, standing up. "Get a coffee. We'll only be a few minutes."

Stryker watched the two walk down the hall; then he walked to a vending machine and dropped in a dime. He wished it would rain. The city was more sane when it rained. He sipped the hot coffee as he walked back to the waiting room.

He was studying a painting of a mountain stream winding its way through the rocks when Lieutenant Purington came in.

"How's he doing, John?"

Stryker closed his eyes. He wanted to be alone. "No word yet. They've been working on him for about twenty minutes."

"Is it bad?" Purington asked.

Stryker sat down. "How in the fuck would I know? I'm no doctor."

"What happened?"

Stryker leaned forward with his elbows on his knees, clasping his hands together. He had been shaken badly. "Something spooked him before he got out of the car. I don't know what the hell it was," he said. "Anyway, when he started to rabbit, West and I ran to the porch. I fired twice, and he fired back. West went down. I fired four more, but he drove off. I don't know if we got a piece of him or not." He downed the remainder of his coffee.

"We found his car," Purington said.

"Where?"

"Forty-eighth and Figueroa. We've got men searching the area now."

"That son-of-a-bitch is overdue," Stryker said. "He's shot two policemen, killed one citizen, and he's still running around loose."

"We'll get him."

Stryker stood. He heard voices in the hallway. A camera crew and reporter walked into view.

"Little action this afternoon, huh, fellows?" The tall, well-dressed reporter smiled as they entered the waiting room. The camera's floodlights glared on as the man shouldering it panned across the room.

"Get that shit out of here," Stryker snapped.

"What?" The reporter looked shocked.

"I said, get that shit out of here," Stryker repeated in a slow, deliberate tone.

"Now, look here, fella," the reporter said, looking at Stryker. The floodlights dimmed.

Purington stood up. "Let's move outside," he suggested.

The reporter turned to Purington. "I don't like this man's attitude, Lieutenant. We always do our best to cooperate with your department, and I think a little courtesy is in order."

Stryker glared.

Purington repeated, "Let's talk about it outside." He closed the door behind the TV crew and turned to Stryker. "That was uncalled for, John. Calm down."

"Get off my ass, Tom," Stryker said, pointing a finger at him.

Purington went back in and explained to the television people that Stryker's partner was seriously wounded and that Stryker was naturally overwrought. They understood.

While he briefed them on the details of the shooting, more reporters arrived.

The nurse in charge of the floor told Stryker that West was now in surgery. She had no information on his condition. Stryker insisted she check for them, but she refused. As soon as there was any word, she'd let them know.

Stryker paced.

He was looking at his watch for the third time in ten minutes when he heard the sound of high heels in the hallway. He moved quickly to the door.

Steele and Boyd flanked the woman, and even though she was crying softly, she held her head erect, covering her face partially with a small handkerchief. She was tall and shapely, with full, thick black hair. Her eyes, reddened from crying, were an intense, piercing brown. Though he had never seen her, Stryker knew she was Lisa.

"Lisa, this is John Stryker, Grant's partner," Boyd said.

"Hello, John," Lisa said, extending a hand.

Her hand was warm and soft. "Hello, Lisa. Let's find a spot where we can talk without an audience," Stryker suggested, looking toward the glass doors at the end of the hall, where a number of reporters and photographers stood on the outside, watching.

"You wouldn't have believed that bunch when we came in," Lisa said, looking at the group.

"Yeah, I would." Stryker smiled.

He led Lisa to a door labeled "Employees Only" and pushed the door open. It was dark. He ran a hand along the wall. Finding the switch, he turned it on, and the overhead fluorescent lights flickered on.

"Must be the nurses' lounge."

Lisa sat in a soft red chair, Stryker on a couch opposite her.

"How is he?"

"That big ox will be okay." Stryker smiled. "It'll take more than a bullet to kill him. If he ever dies of anything, it'll be from indigestion."

Lisa smiled back. Stryker was everything West had told her—tough, unemotional, and cool. She liked him. Her fear eased.

"Where's Mom tonight?" Stryker asked, leaning forward.

"She went to Riverside to visit her sister. She'll be back Sunday afternoon."

"Right, I remember now, West mentioned it earlier."

"Do you think we should call her?"

"No. Not yet. Let's wait until he's out of surgery."

Lisa nodded agreement. There was a moment's pause; then she asked, "Where did Grant get hit?"

"Left side of his chest. There's not much up there, just some muscle and bone."

"Who did it, John?"

"Frederick L. Pepper. He's better known as Red Pepper."

"Grant told me about him when he shot Officer Bennett. Is he——?"

"No, he got away," Stryker interrupted, looking embarrassed.

Lisa was sorry she had asked. She took a pack of cigarettes from her purse and shook one out. Stryker produced his lighter.

"Care for one?"

"Thanks," Stryker said. "I smoked my last, half an hour ago."

Lighting his, he looked at it. "I'm going to quit smoking one of these days."

"So I've heard." She smiled.

"Mom told you too, huh?"

"She worries about you as much as she does Grant."

"Yeah, she's some mother," Stryker said, drawing on the cigarette.

"You know, now that Grant's been shot, maybe I'll get to see him for more than just a few hours at a time," Lisa said suddenly.

Stryker smiled a small grin.

Lisa watched him. "Rotten thing to say, wasn't it?" she said calmly.

"No, I understand," he said, wondering what it would be like to make love to her. The thought made him feel guilty.

"The department," she said, "is like another woman. Grant loves it, worries about it, and spends more time with it than he does with me."

Stryker thought of trying to explain, but decided not to.

"I'm jealous of you, too," she said. "No matter

what we're doing, when you call, he drops everything."

"He's a good policeman, Lisa," Stryker said soberly. "But don't tell him I said so."

She smiled, failing to understand the male logic. "I won't," she promised.

Stryker glanced at his watch. It was twenty minutes to seven.

"How long do you think it will be?"

"I'd guess maybe another half-hour."

She crushed her barely smoked cigarette. "We're going to get married, you know."

"I know."

"How come you've never married, John?"

"Nobody's ever asked me."

She smiled.

"How about a coffee?"

"Sounds fine."

"Black with a little sugar, right?"

"Right," Lisa answered. "How did you know?"

"I'm a policeman; I get paid to know."

Boyd opened the door to the lounge. "Hey, the doctor's out here. He's going to give us the scoop."

Stryker and Lisa joined the others in the waiting room.

The doctor looked tired. His white tunic was sweat-stained at the collar; small lines creased his brown skin at the corners of his eyes. He rubbed his chin with the back of his hand.

"West, is it?" the doctor asked, looking at Boyd.

"Right."

"Well," the doctor said, massaging his neck, "he's out of danger."

Lisa put her hands to her face. The others smiled. Stryker, standing beside Lisa, showed no emotion.

"One of the bullets," the doctor explained,

"entered the left chest muscle; it penetrated the left lung and lodged itself against the inside of the fourth rib, embedded in the rib muscle.

"I didn't remove the bullet, because he had already lost a considerable amount of blood, and X rays show that it's presenting no problem. So he's got himself a new souvenir, at least for a while.

"We went into the chest, tied off some small arteries, and repaired torn muscle tissue. He had bled internally quite a bit, but we were able to control it.

"The second bullet passed through the fleshy part of the upper left arm, grazing the tricep muscle but doing no real damage. All that was required was some cleaning and a few sutures.

"What it all amounts to is that the patient suffered two gunshot wounds. Though a lung was punctured, no other vital organs were injured, and we can expect complete recovery.

"Now, if you'll excuse me, I've got to get back to work."

"Dr. Hunter," Lieutenant Purington said, "how long till we can see him?"

"He's heavily sedated now, and won't be coherent for perhaps another twelve hours. We want his breathing and activity low until the left lung clears itself.

"But," the doctor added, glancing at Lisa, "I'll permit one of you five minutes with him. . . . Now, I must go."

He turned and walked toward the treatment room. Stryker followed. "Doc"—the doctor paused —"I just wanted to say I'm sorry for mouthing off," Stryker said.

"No need to, I understand."

"When he's back on his feet, we'll come down and buy you a cold beer."

"Sounds good." The doctor grinned.

"Take care," Stryker said, slapping him on the shoulder.

"John," Lieutenant Purington said, as Stryker rejoined the group in the waiting room, "Internal Affairs wants you for an interview."

"Oh, Christ," Stryker said wearily.

"I'm going back," Purington said. "I'll give you a ride."

Lisa, standing near, smiled as Stryker turned to her. He couldn't think of a thing to say. She squeezed his hand gently. "Thank you, Sergeant."

Stryker smiled slightly, turned, and walked with the lieutenant down the hall toward the door.

Lisa stood watching until the two men reached the glass doors. As they opened, she saw the flash of cameras in the evening darkness.

"Ready to go see him?" Boyd asked.

"Yes," she said.

"You two go ahead," Steele said, moving toward a chair.

"I know," Boyd said, "hospitals make you sick."

At the station, Stryker learned that the search for Pepper had failed. He dented a metal file cabinet with his fist when they told him. The punch left him with bloody knuckles.

He reconstructed the shooting six times for the two sergeants from Internal Affairs. The two-hour interview ended when Stryker told them his wife and two kids were waiting for him at home. One of the sergeants said, "Yeah, I know how it is. I got three of my own." Stryker kept a straight face.

Tired, angry, and frustrated, he cursed the heavy Friday-night traffic as he pushed his Firebird through it, headed home.

When he finally arrived at his apartment, he

found Connie asleep on the couch. Her bags, packed for the trip to Las Vegas, sat near the door.

He turned off the television and walked quietly to the bedroom, sat down on the edge of the bed, pulled off his jacket, and tossed it to a chair. He pushed off one shoe and then lay back for a moment. He fell asleep with the question in his head, "Was it my fault?"

The headlines in Los Angeles on Saturday morning read: "POLICE BLUNDER LEAVES ONE OFFICER SHOT, TWO POLICE CARS DESTROYED"; "OFFICER WOUNDED IN POLICE FOUL-UP"; "SUSPECTED FELON ELUDES POLICE IN SHOOTOUT"; and "GUNFIRE ERUPTS IN BLACK COMMUNITY, ONE OFFICER NEAR DEATH AND TWO POLICE CARS DESTROYED."

Lisa couldn't believe what she read. She had heard Lieutenant Purington's account of the incident, but somehow the press had gotten it all wrong. She just couldn't understand it.

Chief Peck returned to Parker Center early Saturday morning. He met with deputy chiefs Searcy and Crown for two hours, setting up task force CAT.

The concentrated-attack team combined the department's most talented investigators. Their sole assignment was to find Frederick L. Pepper. Peck and his deputies had chosen twenty detectives drawn from all the divisions of the department. Deputy Chief Crown was to head the force. Peck gave him Saturday to organize personnel; he wanted the CAT in action by Sunday morning.

A choking, gagging cough brought West to consciousness. The walls and ceiling swung and blurred as he forced his eyes open. His stomach knotted, sending a bitter foul taste to his mouth as a wave of nausea swept over him. He coughed again, harder, flooding his mouth with a salty, bloody slime from the damaged lung. He gagged, and the pink, red-spotted fluid spilled from his mouth and down his neck.

A nurse mopped his chin. He struggled to focus on her face, but her image faded as the walls closed in.

"Just try to relax, honey. You're going to be fine." She brushed the beads of perspiration from his forehead.

His chest and shoulders burned as if a lighted match had been held to him. Through a gray cloud he could see Stryker looking down at him. "Hang on, partner, hang on," he heard him calling in a distant voice.

"Is he dead, John?" West whispered, his voice crackling, congested.

"John's not here, hon," the nurse said.

"Is he dead, John?" West looked up wide-eyed at the nurse. "Is that son-of-a-bitch dead?"

She pushed the call button.

Stryker and Connie were at the pool when the phone in his apartment rang.

"Are you going to answer it?" Connie asked, swimming to where he sat in the shallow end.

"No," he said bluntly, leaning back in the cool blue water.

"But it may be important."

"It's not," he said, as the phone continued to ring.

"How do you know, if you don't answer it?" she said, wiping water from her face.

"Wanna bet your—"

"No, I don't," she interrupted, moving toward the pool's edge.

He watched her breasts bounce in the red bikini as she raced across the patio and up the steps.

After she disappeared into the apartment he turned his attention to a gray sparrow straining hard to get airborne with a discarded cookie. He was offering the sparrow silent advice when Connie called him from the top of the stairs.

"John, telephone."

He didn't move.

"John, dammit."

Stryker reluctantly left the pool, pulled a towel over his shoulders, and walked toward the stairs.

Connie stood in the kitchen pouring coffee when he walked into the apartment. She stuck her tongue out as he flashed her a heated look.

"Stryker," he said dryly, picking up the telephone.

"Stryker, this is Inspector O'Connor."

"Good morning, Inspector."

"I know what you're thinking, and I'm not going to disappoint you."

"You never have, Inspector."

O'Connor laughed on the other end of the phone. "Anyway, you've been selected to be a member of CAT. I want you at Parker Center tomorrow morning at 0700. We'll meet in assembly room number two."

"What the hell is CAT?" Stryker asked.

"Cat is a four-legged, furry animal that likes mice," O'Connor said. "It's also the name of a task force organized to get Pepper off the street."

"Task force, huh?" Stryker said bitingly. His case had just been taken away from him.

"The chief thinks it's necessary," O'Connor explained.

Stryker said nothing.

"By the way, how's West doing?" O'Connor asked.

"He'll be fine in a couple of weeks."

"Good, that's real good. Tell him I said hello, when you see him."

"Sure will."

"See you in the morning."

"Right." Stryker hung up the phone. "Son-of-a-bitch."

After lunch in a Mexican restaurant that Connie suggested, they drove to Morningside Hospital. Connie, nervous about meeting West, asked, "What will I say to him?"

"Try 'hello,' " Stryker suggested.

"You're a big help, John Stryker."

He eased the car into the hospital's rear parking lot. Connie moved the rear-view mirror to check her image in it. She ran a hand over her blond hair, smoothing it.

"Come on, woman," he said impatiently.

As Stryker pushed open the door to West's room, he saw Chief Peck standing with his back to him, and Deputy Chief Searcy at the foot of the bed. Stryker pushed Connie through the door ahead of him.

Lisa, standing on the right side of West's bed, smiled as they entered. "Hi."

"Hello," Connie answered nervously.

Chief Peck turned toward the door, stepping out of West's view. The head of his bed was in a raised position. West managed a grin.

"Chief," West said with some effort, "this is my partner, Sergeant John Stryker."

Peck extended a hand to Stryker. "Glad to meet you, Sergeant." Peck gripped Stryker's hand firmly.

"I'm pleased to meet you, sir," Stryker said in a voice which sounded high-pitched to him.

Peck turned back to West. "Well, we've got to run. Is there anything we can do for you?"

"Yes, sir, there is," West said with some reluctance. "The doctor here tells me I'll be in the hospital for possibly three weeks. If that's true, I'd like to move to Central Receiving, so I'll have someone to swap stories with."

Peck smiled. "I can't see any problem in that." He looked to Deputy Chief Searcy. "Searcy, can you take care of that?"

"Sure," Searcy answered. "I'll see how soon we can do it. Shouldn't be any problem at all."

"Miss Giland, nice to have met you," Peck said to Lisa. "Take good care of this character."

"I will, sir."

Peck nodded, turning toward the door. Searcy followed. Stryker pulled the door open for them.

Pausing in the doorway, Peck turned. "Sergeant, got a minute?"

"Yes, sir," Stryker said, following the two into the hallway.

As the door swung shut, Peck asked, "Have you heard about CAT?"

"Yes, sir, Inspector O'Connor called me about noon."

"Do you have any idea where Pepper may be?"

"No, sir, I don't, but he couldn't have moved far without being seen."

Peck gave him a long look. "Where would you start?"

"Where we found the car," Stryker said.

Peck ran a finger along his jaw as he nodded thoughtful agreement. "Okay, thank you, Sergeant . . . and good luck."

"You're welcome, sir."

Stryker ground out his cigarette on the polished floor as the two men walked down the hall; then, seeing a "No Smoking" sign on the wall, he felt guilty.

Connie and Lisa pushed by Stryker as he entered the room. "We're going after some Cokes," Connie said as they passed.

Stryker pulled a chair close to the bed. "What did he want?" West asked.

"He needed some advice on a few things," Stryker said dryly.

West smiled.

"Did he tell you about CAT?" Stryker asked.

"Yeah," West said, pulling at his pillow with his right arm. "Do you think it will work?"

"If they don't get in my road," Stryker said.

Near seven o'clock on Sunday morning, the twenty members of CAT gathered in assembly room two on the ground floor of Parker Center.

Stryker and Steele had been chosen from Southwest Detectives. They sat with the other eighteen men drinking coffee and exchanging ideas on how CAT would operate.

At precisely seven A.M., Deputy Chief Crown and Inspector O'Connor entered the room and walked to the desk at the front. The conversation died immediately.

Opening a notebook, Crown looked at the waiting faces. "Good morning, gentlemen," he said in his usual businesslike tone. "I just talked to Deputy Chief Searcy, and he congratulated me on being the commander of CAT, the first official group of pussies the department has ever had."

The group laughed loudly.

"On the serious side, gentlemen, the sole objective behind the formation of CAT is the arrest of Frederick L. Pepper.

"You gentlemen are the elite of the department's

various talents needed to accomplish this task. That's why you're here this morning.

"I needn't tell you the character of the individual we're after. He is a proven threat to police officers and an even greater threat to any citizen he may come in contact with.

"It's our job to put an end to this threat as soon as possible.

"Inspector O'Connor will explain the mechanics of our operation and tell you your particular assignment. Inspector."

"Thank you, sir," O'Connor said, glancing at the notes spread in front of him. "Basically, we'll be divided into two sections. One, field operations, and the other, research and development.

"I will act as the unit's assistant commander. I'll be the one looking over your shoulder all the time. I'll also coordinate the activity between field operations and research and development.

"We'll start each day with a six-o'clock roll call."

A few moans came from the group. Deputy Chief Crown, sitting with his arms folded, smiled.

"If I can get my ass in here at six A.M., so can you," O'Connor said.

"Now, I want each team to keep a log of daily activities, so we'll have a record of ground covered. These logs will be turned in to me at the conclusion of each day.

"End of watch for us will be when we finish the day's work. Some days that'll be early. Others, it'll be damn late. I don't think we have any clock watchers in here."

"The field-operations unit will be the legs, ears, and eyes for CAT. It will be responsible for investigation conducted in the field, such as finding wits, interviewing them, and running down leads that turn up.

"The research-and-development unit will be responsible for reviewing all physical evidence we have, in addition to finding out more about Pepper than he knows about himself.

"We'll do this by talking to his family, friends, former probation officers, other police departments, prison guards, and anyone else who ever had contact with him.

"Pepper's only one of eleven million people in Southern California. All we have to do is find him.

"Here are the assignments." O'Connor paused to give the group time to prepare to copy.

"Lieutenant Roberts."

"Here."

"Lieutenant Roberts, you're in charge of field operations. You'll have Melonson, Erice, Nardone, Pryor, Dean, Nichol, Barry, Steele, and Stryker working for you."

"Got it."

"Lieutenant Pieper."

"Yo," a voice answered from the rear.

"Pieper, you're in charge of research and development. You'll have Baxter, Barker, Allen, LaBus, Smith, Glass, Strickland, and Hanson."

"Right."

"I have here," O'Connor said, laying a hand on a stack of multicolored papers, "copies of every crime report Pepper has been a part of. There's also a brief biographical sheet and mug shots. I want each of you to get copies and spend the next few hours reviewing them and getting organized for your assignment."

O'Connor glanced at the wall clock. "We'll start business at one o'clock."

After a brief lunch in the cafeteria atop Parker Center, Stryker and Steele began by reinterviewing

Cleo Frey and her husband, who both had been jailed for harboring a known fugitive, Pepper.

They spent four hours in interrogation but failed to learn anything new.

Shortly after midnight on Tuesday, the Pisser claimed his fourth victim in Southwest Los Angeles, a twenty-six-year-old divorcée living alone. Her sister found her lying in a pool of blood and urine in her bathtub. Again there were no leads.

As the news of the latest brutal rape-murder spread across the city, the fear of thousands of lonely women transformed into hysteria. Deputy Chief Searcy, commander of the Patrol Bureau, requested the assistance of the Metro Division to supplement patrol in the black community in an effort to find the murderer. Their major problem was that nobody knew what the suspect looked like.

Civic organizations everywhere demanded quick action. Many groups accused the police department of not devoting the necessary resources to apprehending the murderer because he operated only in the black community.

Councilman Ward, just returned to the city, with the three other black city councilmen called upon Chief Peck to immediately exert all the manpower necessary to apprehend the maniac.

On his Wednesday-evening newscast, Bill Hart disclosed that the police department had assigned its most talented investigators to the task of apprehending the suspect who had shot two Los Angeles police officers.

In his commentary, he said, "This suspect on whom the police are expending so much manpower and talent has wounded two police officers, I repeat, he has wounded, not killed them. Compare this to the homicide-rapist who walks our streets every night. This man has killed four defenseless women. I think most citizens would agree with me in asking that the police department reexamine its priorities."

When Chief Peck arrived at his office Thursday morning, his aide advised him that Mayor Abbott had called twice and wished him to return his call as soon as possible.

Peck was reading the major-incident log for the past twenty-four hours when the mayor called for the third time.

"Good morning, Mayor," Peck said. "I was just reviewing the green sheet, and then I was going to return your call."

"Jim," Abbott began tensely, "I'll get right to the point. I've received a number of calls from prominent citizens who are complaining about this so-called CAT organization and what it's doing. I might add, I was a bit surprised to learn of a secret task force from a television program instead of from you.

"The majority of the City Council has been calling for action. What it all amounts to, Jim, is that whatever is done, or isn't done, is blamed on me as mayor, something that we can't afford in an election year." He paused. "I would like this task force reassigned to tracking down this rapist."

"Well, Mayor," Peck said, choosing his words carefully, "you're misinformed on a number of points, but not as a result of me or my department withholding information.

"The formation of CAT and its purposes was fully explained in our weekly intelligence bulletin, which was delivered to your office on Monday.

"As for CAT being secret, well, we made no public announcement of the formation of CAT, but when have we ever announced that we were conducting an investigation? It's not good police procedure to make our investigations public, though they're far from secret.

"According to Mr. Hart's commentary, all that Pepper is wanted for is wounding two police officers. That's a lie." Peck's voice began to show anger; his face reddened. "In addition to wounding two officers, he has killed one innocent citizen, stolen a car, participated in a burglary, and raped a woman. Now, if that's not enough reason to want him off the street, what the hell is?"

"These are things—" Abbott began defensively.

"I'm not through, Mayor," Peck interrupted. "Hart left the impression that all our efforts are directed at Pepper and nothing at this rapist. The fact is, over forty detectives from Seventy-seventh Division, Newton Division, Southwest Division, and Detective Headquarters are working day and night on that case and on nothing else. What's more, the Metro Squad has been deployed in the South End to supplement our regular patrol.

"Now, one final point, Mayor. You said we can't afford this kind of problem during an election year. Well, perhaps I'd better clarify one point now. *We're* not involved in an election, *you* are. I will not be drawn, nor will I permit my department to be drawn, into this election."

Silence. Peck waited, hoping that his police career had not just ended, but feeling certain that as long as he was head of the department, there could be no compromise.

"Your points are well taken," Abbott said coldly. "But as the chief executive of this city, it's my responsibility to be sensitive to the wishes of its residents. And they are upset about this maniac roaming our streets. So I'm requesting . . . requesting," he repeated, "that you consider reassigning task force CAT to that problem."

"I understand," Peck said, realizing that Abbott's request was an order.

Late Thursday afternoon, after five days of fruitless investigation, Stryker and Steele drove to the intersection of Forty-eighth and Figueroa, where Pepper had abandoned his car, to start over again at the bottom. Maybe the third time around they would find a new witness, or maybe one they had interviewed would remember a vital point.

Steele glanced at his watch. "It's almost six, John; you wanna wrap it up and start in the morning?"

"Yeah, okay," Stryker agreed as he studied the vacant street. "Six days ago, at about this time," Stryker whispered, "he parked that car here and disappeared." His eyes searched the now-familiar block. He and Steele had talked to every resident at least twice. He watched two children, a boy and girl, drawing on the sidewalk across the street with a piece of chalk. "Someone had to see him." Steele was busy completing the log as Stryker turned back to him. "Ready to go home?"

"Right," Steele said continuing to work on the log.

Stryker twisted the ignition key, and the car started. As he pulled from the curb, the city bus rolled up to the intersection and stopped. The bus's vacuum lines hissed as its door folded open and a woman stepped off. The door closed, and the bus pulled away.

The woman, a plump, middle-aged Negro, eyed Stryker suspiciously as she walked down the opposite side of the street. He sat quietly watching her as Steele cursed a mistake on the log.

She approached an ancient, dirty station wagon, opened the door, and got in. She gave Stryker a final go-to-hell look as she pulled away.

He looked up and down the street. It was vacant. Even the two kids were gone. The woman in the station wagon turned right and disappeared. The street was quiet and deserted.

"I've got it," he shouted, pulling the car into drive.

"What?" Steele said, looking up from the log with a shocked expression.

"I know where he went," Stryker said, wheeling the car into the street after the bus.

"Where?" Steele asked, throwing the log to the seat between them.

"On the bus," Stryker said, turning onto Figueroa.

"How do you know that?"

"I saw it."

As the bus pulled into the curb at Fifty-fourth Street, Stryker parked behind it. Getting out of their car, the two detectives raced to the closing bus door.

The engine sent out a cloud of blue smoke as it rolled slowly forward. Stryker ran after it, banging on the folding door, and the driver stopped. The door hissed open.

"Police officers, we'd like to talk to you," Stryker said, looking up at the driver.

The driver, a graying, heavyset Negro, pushed the gearshift to neutral, set the brake, and eased himself out of his seat.

"I'm already running a few minutes behind, fellas."

"We won't take long."

"This about me getting robbed last night?"

"No," Stryker said, "we're interested in the big

dude you picked up at Forty-eighth and Fig last Friday about this time. He had a big scar on the—"

"Yeah." The driver smiled, wiping sweat from his chubby chin on a uniformed sleeve. "I remember him. He had a bunch of cuts on his face, ya know. Like somebody hit him with a bottle, maybe."

"That's him. Where'd you drop him?" Stryker asked tensely.

"I asked him what happened," the driver said, intent on telling his story. "He told me his old lady threw a beer bottle at him. I didn't buy that."

"Where'd he get off?"

"Ninety-second and Figueroa."

"Did you see where he went?" Steele questioned.

"Naw, I couldn't wait. I make over four hundred stops in this big baby every day, so I can't be wasting time, ya know."

Stryker was already on his way back to their car. "Thanks a lot. You've been a big help," Steele said, following after him.

"Glad I could help," the driver answered, watching the two. "I was going to call you guys. I knew he was hot," he called to them.

Steele waved a final thanks as Stryker pulled away into the afternoon traffic.

"Luck like that calls for a smoke," Stryker said, slowing for a red light.

"We going to bang some more doors around Ninety-second and Fig?" Steele asked as Stryker lit his cigarette.

"Do you mind?" Stryker said, rolling through the intersection.

"No, if you head for the station, you're going alone. I'm going to Ninety-second and Fig."

Stryker smiled.

At Ninety-second and Figueroa, they parked in a

gas station on the northwest corner. They sat silently, surveying the area.

"If you were Pepper, where would you go after
you got off the bus?" Stryker asked, grinding out
his cigarette.

"Maybe northbound on another bus?" Steele
guessed.

"Naw," Stryker said. "That son-of-a-bitch isn't
that smart."

"He'd know he had to get off the street as soon
as possible, especially since he was bleeding," Steele
added.

"Agreed."

"Let's try the motel on the corner," Steele suggested.

"I was thinking the same thing."

The two men walked the short distance to the
motel on the southwest corner of the intersection.
A sign hanging over the motel driveway read "Star
Dust." Below it hung a smaller neon vacancy sign
which winked its message to the passing traffic.

A young mini-clad Negro girl stood near the
entrance to the motel courtyard. She smiled as the
two detectives passed. "Hello, officers," she said
with a clean, white grin.

"You're looking good today." Stryker smiled.

"What do you mean, *today?*" she said in pre-
tended insult.

Stryker laughed.

"You guys on the vice squad?"

"No, we're the shoplift detail," Steele answered.

"Were you here last Friday night?" Stryker
asked.

She smiled. "You know how Fridays are. Busy. I
was here off and on."

"How about six?"

"Sorry, honey."

"Well, you win a few and lose a few. Take care," he cautioned.

"How do you suppose she knew we were the man?" Steele asked as they walked toward the motel office.

Stryker glanced at him. "In her business, she knows the man."

The clerk behind the dingy counter in the motel office glanced over the top of the sports page as Stryker and Steele entered the office, then resumed his reading.

The two detectives walked to the counter and waited. After several seconds, Steele cleared his throat. The clerk didn't move; Steele glanced at Stryker.

Stryker picked up a large glass ashtray from the counter and tossed it into the clerk's paper. The paper tore down the center, and the ashtray crashed into the clerk's chest.

"Hey, man," the clerk yelled as he jumped to his feet, rubbing his chest. The ashtray slid to the carpeted floor. "You can't do that shit."

"I just wanted to get your attention," Stryker said.

"Yeah, well, you come in here acting like a bad ass, and all you'll get is a hard time," the clerk said in anger.

"You don't know what the fuck a hard time is, asshole, but if you keep pushing, you're sure as hell going to find out," Stryker said, leaning on the counter.

The clerk said nothing.

"Did you work here last Friday night?" Steele asked.

The clerk tried an insulting grin. "You going to accuse me of some humbug burglary or something?"

"If we wanted to accuse you of something, we'd do it at the station, not here. Now, answer the goddamn question," Steele said.

The clerk leaned back against a cluttered desk, Stryker watching him carefully. "Yeah, I worked Friday. So what?"

"We're interested in the fat man that came in here last Friday with the cut-up face."

"I don't know nothing about no cut-up fat man."

"Okay, partner, he's going to be a smart ass," Steele said, glancing at Stryker. "Let's take him down to the station."

"Get your coat, man," Stryker said in a slow, deliberate tone.

The clerk looked at the floor and then to the two detectives. "Hey, man, if I leave now, I'll get fired. I got me a wife and two kids."

"Don't blame us for your family problems. Get your coat," Stryker repeated.

"Okay, man, he was here," the clerk blurted.

"We wanna see his registration card," Steele said.

"He didn't fill one out," the clerk admitted without looking up. "He gave me twenty and told me to forget he was ever here."

"What room did he use?" Stryker asked.

"I think it was eighteen. Yeah, I'm sure. It was eighteen."

"Have any visitors?"

"I don't know, man. It was Friday, you know. I was busy as hell."

"When did he leave?"

"Saturday morning about ten. A green Olds came in and picked him up."

"Anybody you know?"

"No, I never saw 'em before. He just drove in, picked up the fat dude, and left."

"Did you see what direction they went?"

"Yeah, north."

"What year Olds?"

"Sixty-six, I'm sure. I know my machines.

"License number?"

The clerk shook his head.

"What'd the driver look like?"

"He was black. That's all I know."

"Car clean?"

"Not clean. Not dirty. Ya know."

"What color green?"

"Dark."

"You work tomorrow?"

"Yeah."

"We'll be back then. You make sure you're here," Stryker warned.

The clerk nodded.

"Let's go, partner," Stryker said.

"Pigs, filthy goddamn pigs," the clerk mumbled as the office door swung shut behind the two.

Inspector O'Connor was slumped behind his cluttered desk sipping on a cup of coffee when Stryker and Steele walked in. He set his cup down and sat up.

"We bear glad tidings." Stryker smiled.

"I don't know if I can handle any more good news today, but go ahead and lay it on me," O'Connor said without humor.

Stryker and Steele looked puzzled as they sat down. The inspector was usually cool under pressure and had a keen sense of humor. This mood was very out of character.

"We know where Pepper went after the shooting," Steele said. "We know where he spent Friday night, and we've got information on where he went Saturday morning."

"Fine," O'Connor said flatly. "Write it up and give it to Southwest Detectives."

"What?" Stryker's voice rose in disbelief.

"You heard me," O'Connor growled. "Write it up and give it to Southwest Detectives. They're going to handle it. CAT's been reassigned."

Stryker stood up suddenly. "Who in the hell's idea is this?" he burst out. "We bust our ass for a week digging up a lead, and now we're told to give it away, let somebody else handle it. Bullshit."

On the other side of the desk, O'Connor stood up. "Now, look, Stryker, we haven't got any room in this department for supercops. You're no one-man army. You're a member of a team. You've been told to write up what you've got and give it to Southwest Detectives. Now, goddammit, do it!"

Stryker's face reddened with anger. "You bunch of swivel-chair cops really amaze me," he said. "You sit up here in your goddamn ivory tower playing musical chairs with us working cops, like we were nothing. You go out there and bust your ass for a couple of weeks looking for some asshole that shot up two cops, and when you finally do get a lead, you're told to write it up and give it to someone else. Goddammit, no."

O'Connor sat down and waited for Stryker to finish. He understood how Stryker felt. He had given very much the same argument when Deputy Chief Crown told him CAT was being pulled off the hunt for Pepper.

"What the hell do I tell West?" Stryker gritted, leaning on the desk. "Should I tell him what that son-of-a-bitch Hart said the other night? That when you carry a badge you've got to expect to be a target?

"How about Conrad's wife and kids? What do we tell them?

"And how about Bennett? He's been a policeman for eleven months. What'll we tell him? Maybe next time, when you're killed, we'll investigate that?"

He stopped abruptly.

O'Connor looked up. "I've listened to you," he said. "Now, goddammit, you sit down and listen to me."

Stryker sat down. Steele wished he could leave.

O'Connor leaned forward in his chair, resting his arms on his desk. "At about noon today, Deputy Chief Crown informed me that CAT was being pulled off Pepper and was being reassigned to tracking down the Pisser.

"Since he's a deputy chief and I'm an inspector, I do it. Whether or not I like it doesn't matter a damn. That's the way it is.

"I put up with your blowing off steam," O'Connor said, "only because Pepper got a piece of your partner and you've got a right to get emotional about being pulled off the case. But now, you've had your say, and I'm warning you, if you ever yell at me again, I'll be all over your ass."

Stryker sat hunched over, staring at the floor.

"I want both of you back here tomorrow for six-o'clock roll call," O'Connor concluded. "Now, get the hell out."

Outside in the corridor, Steele said cheerfully, "Well, reach back there and pat your ass."

"Why?"

"Be thankful it's still there after that caper."

Stryker smiled.

When Stryker saw the Friday-morning headline, he knew why CAT had been reassigned. "MAYOR PLEDGES ALL-OUT POLICE DRIVE TO JAIL RAPIST."

The story began: "Late Thursday afternoon

Mayor Dennis Abbott announced he had directed the police department to organize a task force in an effort to deal swiftly with the nighttime homicidal rapist that has terrorized the city for the past five months. Mayor Abbott explained the police task force will comprise the department's most talented . . ."

Stryker tore up the paper and threw it in the trash. Though the headline infuriated him, it restored his confidence in the department's leadership. He knew now that the mayor had ordered Chief Peck to reassign CAT.

But following the public announcement of CAT's new objective, the rapist curtailed his activity, and the police were left with what they had in the beginning—nothing.

Six persons surrendered and confessed to the crimes. They were released or detained for psychiatric examination, all innocent.

A month passed, and the Pisser was quiet. With election day drawing closer, news coverage of the rapist investigation faded, and the mayoral race filled the front pages.

Ward's campaign advisers were surprised and disappointed that he consistently refused to discuss his son's death, except to say that he believed it was accidental. He concentrated his speeches on the problems of the city that had remained unsolved during Mayor Abbott's tenure, and on the mayor's unfulfilled promises of the last campaign.

As Ward's standing in the polls improved daily, Mayor Abbott began to shift his speeches to the subject of law and order, hoping to draw Ward into a debate. If Ward agreed with Abbott that the police, the courts, the laws should be tougher, he was sure to hurt himself in the black community; if he disagreed, the white population would figure him for a soft-on-black-criminals radical. Ward steered clear of the issue.

In mid-September, a gas explosion ripped through three blocks in the heart of Watts. Twenty-seven homes were destroyed. Miraculously, only eleven people were killed. But six of the eleven were children.

When he toured the devastation, hours after the incident, Ward stood on the street and wept. After photos of Ward weeping covered the front pages, and all the news programs showed film of it, the mayor angrily and publicly accused Ward of cheap histrionics; Ward's tears, Abbott said, would not only help him with the blacks, it would get him a big Hollywood vote too.

At a press conference a week later, Ward showed photos of rusted-out pipe which he said had not been properly checked for preventive repair; he produced evidence that response to reported gas leaks was slow. He accused the city's department of inspection and control of gross negligence for its failure to enforce proper maintenance of public utilities.

His accusations caused a huge uproar; when he was first elected, Mayor Abbott had appointed his brother, Charles, as commissioner of inspection and control.

"In Charles Abbott we have a man," the papers quoted Ward, "who managed two bakeries before he got on his brother's gravy train. I'm sure the commissioner's bakery experience qualified him highly for his twenty-thousand-dollar-a-year post."

Mayor Abbott countered by accusing Ward, who was the chairman of the Minority Action Council, of forcing the gas company to hire on a quota system, which resulted in unqualified, untrained workers, low-caliber repair work, and eventually a tragedy.

When Charles Abbott resigned as commissioner, the mayor told newsmen that his brother had accepted a position in private industry before the Watts explosion.

His bed raised, West lay quietly watching the evening news. It was October 1, his birthday, and no one was coming to see him. Well, it was just one of those things. His mother had called to wish him a happy birthday, but she always had choir practice on Wednesdays; Lisa had to drive her mother to visit a relative. Stryker had to work. Even Steve Bennett, across the hall, who had become a close friend, wanted to be alone with Joy to discuss something.

He flipped through the *TV Guide*. When he turned to toss it to the table, he saw Lisa, his mother, Stryker, Connie, Steve, and Joy. They all burst out laughing. "Happy birthday, Grant." Lisa came in first, carrying a bright package, and kissed him on the cheek.

"I should have known it was a conspiracy," he said, beaming, as his mother wrapped her arms around his waist.

"How are you feeling, son?"

"Don't give him any sympathy, Mom." Stryker sat down at the foot of the bed. "Look at him—he's overfed and lazy; just sits around here burning up the taxpayers' money."

"Here"—Lisa handed him the package—"it's from your mom and me."

He broke the ribbon and tore the paper off. "Hey, beautiful!" He dropped the box lid and held up a brown leather shoulder holster. "Thanks, Mom." He gave her a kiss. "You too." He winked at Lisa.

Joy handed him a blue envelope which contained an invitation to dinner at the Bennetts'.

"You don't realize what an expensive gift you're giving, Mrs. Bennett." Stryker laughed. "All I can say is, you'd better hide something so you and Steve can eat the next day."

Connie pulled two large Seven-Up bottles out of her straw bag, and Steve produced Dixie cups from his bathrobe pocket.

"My goodness," Mrs. West said softly when she tasted hers.

"Aw, come on, Mom," Stryker urged, "a little I. W. Harper's good for you—it thins your blood, increases your horsepower, and prevents warts."

They all toasted West. Then West proposed a toast to Steve, who was leaving the hospital the next day.

Stryker proposed a toast to better days, to which they all held their cups high.

That same day, Chief Peck notified Mayor Abbott that he could no longer justify keeping twenty men assigned to the investigation of the homicidal rapist, since the team had exhausted all leads, and the rapist had not struck again. Abbott agreed, but wanted no publicity on CAT's abolition. Late in the afternoon, the members of CAT were advised to return to their regular duty assignments the following day. CAT died a quiet death.

Two days later, after much pleading with the doctors, West was discharged from the hospital. Like Bennett, he was also restricted to light duty assignments.

On West's first weekend out of the hospital, much to Lisa's displeasure, he and Stryker drew the weekend duty.

Weekend duty meant spending Saturday and Sunday in the detective squad room at Southwest Station, handling the telephones, giving booking approvals for arrestees brought in by patrol officers, and talking to any citizens who came in with a problem requiring investigation.

Steve was more fortunate. He had the weekend off, and what's more, Steve's father-in-law had given him two tickets to the Rams-49er game Sunday at the Coliseum.

Game time on Sunday was one o'clock, but Steve was anxious, so he and Joy left for the Coliseum at twelve-fifteen. But there was already a huge crowd waiting at the gates.

Joy, though not a football fan, was in a jubilant mood. The terrifying night was fading from her memory. Steve was back, and she was happy.

They were moving slowly through the excited crowd when Steve saw the back of the big man, about twenty yards ahead. The crowd prevented him from moving closer, but Steve knew the man from somewhere. Where was it? A wanted bulletin, a mug shot, maybe he had arrested him once, he couldn't remember.

Joy smiled warmly up at him, squeezing his hand. They continued to inch toward the turnstile.

He couldn't take his attention off the man ahead. He continued to watch him, hoping for a better look at the face. He cursed himself silently for his poor memory.

Steve and Joy were far behind when the big man reached the turnstile. The attendant took the man's ticket, tore it in half, and handed him the stub. He pushed his heavy frame through the turnstile.

Moving closer, Steve saw a short man in a loose gray suit bump into the big man as he walked toward one of the tunnels to the inside of the Coliseum. If he hadn't been thinking of the big man,

Steve would have recognized it immediately as a wallet theft. "Watch it, you mousy mother—" the big man growled.

The smaller man disappeared quickly into the crowd.

A sudden chill swept over Steve as he heard the voice. He felt the pain, the cool, wet grass rising to meet him, the tugging at his belt, the pain, the horrible pain, and then the big man kneeling over him. The voice, *that* voice, "Black motherfucking pig." It was Pepper.

Joy felt his grip on her hand tighten. "You okay, hon?"

"Yeah, I'm fine." His mind raced. Pepper disappeared into the crowded tunnel.

"Steve, honey, the tickets." Steve looked down. They were at the turnstile.

"Hey, what the hell is this?" the little man in the gray suit cried when the two vice officers grabbed him.

A Southwest Division vice squad always worked games at the Coliseum.

"Police officers."

"Yeah, well flake off, slave. I ain't done nothing."

"We think you took that big guy's wallet."

"Get screwed, dude."

One of the officers gave the suspect a pat-down search. "You always carry two wallets, man?"

"It's none of your business if I carry six wallets, fuzz head."

"You're under arrest for grand theft person," the officer said, pushing one of the suspect's skinny arms into the center of his back.

Steve and Joy finally made their way through to their seats. They were near the fifty-yard line about halfway to the top. Joy noticed Steve had turned strangely quiet. "Steve," she asked, "are you sure you're okay?"

"Yes, honey, I'm fine. Now, stop worrying."

"What are you looking for?"

"I thought I saw somebody I know." He smiled.

The Rams won the toss and chose to receive. The 49ers kicked off, and the game was under way. The crowd of fifty-five thousand roared. Steve continued to search the crowd, hoping.

He knew he should go to a phone and call for help. All his training demanded he summon assistance, but he was certain that he could take Pepper alone. He could take Pepper alone and prove he wasn't just a nigger cop who got his partner killed. "If I have to," he told himself, as his heart pounded like a drum in his ears, "I'll kill him."

Stryker and West were sitting in the detective squad room with their feet propped up, enjoying a cup of coffee in the afternoon lull, when the two vice officers came in with their pickpocket.

"Well, well," Stryker said, as he saw the suspect.

West turned to the approaching trio.

"You know this character?" one of the vice officers asked Stryker.

"Yeah." Stryker smiled, dropping his feet to the floor. "I met Greasy when I was walking a beat down on Fifth Street."

One of the officers pulled a chair out from a desk and sat the suspect in it.

"We eyeballed him making a hit," one of the officers said.

"He's still carrying the victim's wallet. Victim disappeared into the crowd before we could get him, but he'll be down here as soon as the game's over, no doubt."

"Greasy," Stryker said, "this is my partner, Grant West."

"Go to hell," Greasy said.

"West," Stryker continued, "I'd like you to meet Greasy Wilson."

"Go to hell, Greasy," West said.

"Smart bastard," Greasy said.

"Let's see the wallet," said Stryker.

One of the officers dug into the suspect's jacket pocket and retrieved a brown leather wallet. He tossed it to the desk top.

"This your wallet, Greasy?" Stryker asked, picking it up.

"Go to hell."

Stryker opened the wallet and thumbed through it. His amused smile vanished, and his face turned white when he saw the name. He pulled the card out of the wallet. West pulled his chair closer to Stryker's.

Group Insurance Identification Card. Issuing Agent: Los Angeles Police Relief Association, Inc. Room 532, Parker Center.

Signature of member: Steven L. Bennett

Stryker and West stared at each other. "What did the victim look like?" Stryker demanded.

"Well, he was a big heavy dude, maybe two hundred, about six foot or so," one answered. The other nodded agreement.

"It's him," West said, standing up. "Come on, it's Pepper."

"Wait a minute," Stryker said. "He's not going anywhere. He doesn't know he's been made."

West paused.

"What was he wearing?" Stryker asked.

"A black leather jacket is all I remember," one of the officers answered.

"It was three-quarter length," his partner added.

"Who's Pepper?" one of the officers asked.

"He's the mother that put two holes in me," West breathed.

"Put this thief in one of the holding tanks," Stryker ordered. "We'll need you guys, too."

"Come on, partner," he said. "Let's talk to the watch commander. We'll need every damn policeman in the city to find Pepper in that crowd."

There were two minutes remaining in the first quarter, and the Rams were behind 7-0, but Steve didn't know it. He wasn't watching the game. His eyes had continued to search the sea of faces in search of Pepper. As the first quarter ended, a candy vendor made his way up the steps. "Hey, candy!" When Pepper stood up and yelled, Steve saw him immediately. He was only eight rows below, near the aisle.

Steve turned to Joy. She saw the strange look on his face. An icelike chill swept over her. "Steve," she said, her eyes pleading for an explanation.

"Honey," he said, "I've got something to do, and I want you to sit here until I come back." His hard voice frightened her.

"Steve, please." Tears suddenly filled her eyes.

"Joy, promise me you'll stay here," he said sternly.

She nodded as tears trickled down her cheeks.

He pulled away and moved toward the aisle.

Going down the steps toward Pepper, Steve moved a hand to his waistband to reassure himself that the gun was there.

The aisle was jammed with people balancing cups of hot coffee, buying candy. Steve moved slowly through the human sea, never taking his eyes from Pepper's back. His heart pounded in his ears, and the noise of the crowd seemed distant.

Close now, another fifteen feet, and he would have him. He could see the black stubble on Pepper's unshaven jaw moving as his teeth ground hard candy.

As the blond passed, Pepper cocked his elbow, brushing her thigh. She pulled away and continued up the stairs. Pepper smiled as he turned to watch her. He saw Bennett pushing toward him. He didn't recognize Steve—he didn't need to. He saw in Bennett's eyes the look that told him: Cop.

On the playing field, J. J. Silva, defensive left end for the Los Angeles Rams, intercepted a 49er pass and streaked for his goal line, an unobstructed sixty yards away. The Coliseum vibrated as the crowd of fifty-five thousand rose and cheered.

In the turmoil, Steve lost sight of Pepper. When the crowd sat down again, Pepper's seat was empty. Steve searched frantically as he pushed through the milling mob down the stairs. He caught a glimpse of the black leather jacket as Pepper, now at the bottom of the stairs, turned toward a tunnel exit.

Steve began to run through the crowd, shoving people aside.

Pepper was running toward the turnstile when Steve came out of the tunnel exit. The crowd, sparse and scattered outside the Coliseum, turned to watch.

"Police officer, stop!" Steve shouted, drawing his gun as he ran.

The uniformed attendant at the turnstile saw Pepper running toward him and heard Steve shout. "Hold it, fella," he said, stepping in front of the exit.

Pepper did not slow; his meaty palm smashed

into the attendant's face, sending him crashing backward to the ground.

Pepper raced toward the huge parking lot. Steve was close behind.

Reaching a line of cars, Pepper pulled a twenty-two revolver from his jacket, turned toward Steve, and fired wildly.

Steve dived behind a station wagon as he saw Pepper turn with the gun. The small-caliber bullets sounded like pebbles as they penetrated the station wagon's metal and glass. He lay still, his face pressed against the cool chrome of the station wagon's bumper until he heard Pepper's gun stop firing and click three times as its hammer fell on empty shells.

Steve rose quickly and stepped into the aisle between the parked cars, pointing his thirty-eight at Pepper's stomach. "Drop it," he ordered.

Pepper, breathing hard, dropped the empty gun to the asphalt.

They stood silently for a moment, Pepper gulping air like a tired horse, his heavy breathing the only sound, his open mouth showing a piece of green candy stuck between his front teeth. Beads of sweat formed on his forehead and around the scar on his broad nose.

"What now?" Pepper asked in a gruff, breathless voice.

"Just don't move," Steve warned as he fought to control the muscle twitching in the arm that held the gun.

"You ever kill anybody?" Pepper asked with menace.

"Wanna be the first?" Steve hoped it was a convincing tone.

"I think maybe you ain't got the guts to kill anybody." Pepper smiled, stepping toward him.

Steve raised the gun to Pepper's eye level and cocked it. Pepper froze, his face frozen in fear.

"You move another inch, and I'll blow your black head off!"

Pepper stopped.

"What's going on? . . . Call the police!" A group was gathering, peering over parked cars at the two men.

Steve glanced toward them. Pepper lunged.

At the flash of movement, Steve pulled the trigger. It was too late. Pepper forced the gun up, and the bullet streaked skyward. His other hand locked onto Steve's throat.

Steve cried a pain-filled, rasping scream as Pepper's fingernails dug into his neck. He stabbed at Pepper's eyes with his free hand. The small crowd of curious disappeared among the cars.

Pepper gave an animal-like growl as Steve's thumbnail raked across an eye. His large yellow teeth snapped at the fingers.

Steve's arm shook under the weight of Pepper's pull. Pepper was strong, heavy. Two shots rang out as the fingers fought for control of the gun. Steve heard the wail of sirens in the distance. "Hurry. . . . Hurry. . . . Too strong. . . . Too big. . . ."

Pepper banged his forehead into Steve's mouth and nose, bloodying both. Steve's ears rang, and he could feel the warm dampness of his own blood as it ran from his face and down his neck. Pepper twisted the hand that held the gun. Steve clung to it desperately. "Hang . . . hang on. . . . Strong . . ."

Turning his face to the side, Steve bit hard on the hand on his neck. Pepper screamed, and Steve could taste the saltiness of blood as it gushed into his mouth. He tightened his bite. A muscle popped like a broken rubber band as his teeth cut through it.

He was still biting when he felt himself being lifted by a powerful blow from Pepper's knee in his groin. Then he felt the pain.

Nausea and pain swept through him as he slumped. Pepper ripped the thirty-eight from his hand. His hand felt so empty . . . and cold. . . .

A foot smashed into his side. He heard something crack.

If only his hand wasn't empty . . . silly god-damned empty hand. . . . He pushed up to his knees. "Got to get something for my hand."

He saw Pepper through a mask of blood. The blue steel of the thirty-eight's muzzle looked silly. "I'm gonna die . . . I'm gonna die, and I've got an empty hand." A flap of blood and hair sprang from the back of his head, spraying a mist of red. He fell to the ground.

As Stryker and West wheeled their Plymouth into the parking lot, they heard the shot. Steve Bennett was dead.

Pepper turned toward them as policemen poured from their cars with guns in hand. He knew it was over.

West brought his shotgun up to shoulder position. Pepper shouted, "Don't shoot . . . don't shoot." The thirty-eight fell to the ground.

Stryker moved to where Bennett lay and knelt over him. "My god . . . Bennett." His stomach jerked. He moved away, covering his mouth as it filled with hot salty liquid.

West glanced down at the body and looked back to Pepper, standing now with his arms extended skyward, breathing hard.

He closed the distance between them. "Pick up that fucking gun, you scum-sucking, motherfucking—" West yelled as tears streamed down his face.

Pepper stood frozen.

"Pick it up. . . . I'm going to blow your fucking head off!" West shook uncontrollably as the uniformed officers moved in behind him.

"Don't shoot. . . . Please, brother. Don't shoot," Pepper begged.

"Brother!" West screamed. "Brother. . . . Why you—" Stryker pushed the muzzle of West's shotgun skyward as it fired. At the same time, he swung his pistol, smashing it into Pepper's face. Pepper reeled backward and fell.

A patrol officer took the shotgun from West as he turned, collapsing across the hood of a parked car, burying his face in his hands.

Stryker rolled Pepper onto his stomach, handcuffing his hands behind his back.

Standing, Stryker reholstered his bloodied gun. Removing his suit jacket, he put it over Steve's head and shoulders.

"I'm sorry, John," West sobbed. Stryker patted his shoulder. "It's okay . . . it's okay," Stryker said. "Come on, let's get the job done."

West wiped his face on his sleeve and pushed himself up from the car hood.

"Get him in the car," Stryker said.

"Right." West was in control again.

"I'll get things organized here," Stryker said. He moved toward Pepper. "Okay, guys," Stryker ordered the uniformed officers, "move these people back at least fifty yards."

West pulled Pepper up from the pavement and walked him to the Plymouth. He opened the rear door, and Pepper slid in without instruction.

Pepper spat blood from his split, swollen lips

onto the floor of the Plymouth. West removed his notebook from an inside jacket pocket.

"Listen up," West said, as he looked at the printed message on the notebook cover. "You have the right to remain silent. If you give up the right to remain silent, anything you say—"

"3 William 90 to 3 William 6," the radio interrupted.

West paused from his reading, lowering the notebook to his knee. He stared blankly at Pepper, who was now resting his forehead on the back of the front seat. A strand of blood and saliva stretched from his open mouth as it traveled slowly toward the floor, where a small puddle gathered.

"3 William 90 to 3 William 6," the radio repeated after a few seconds' pause. West shifted, reached over the front seat, and popped open the glove box, where the radio was concealed. He inhaled deeply, hoping his voice wouldn't betray him. "3 William 6, go ahead."

"3W6, a patrol unit received a call to 3211 West Seventy-fourth Street to see the woman a possible child left alone. They investigated and found a dead body in the bedroom. It's a female Negro, twenty-five to thirty, throat and wrists slashed, possible rape. Looks like the Pisser. Can you roll on it?"

"No," West answered, his voice shaking.

"3 William 6, it's your case, and if you don't roll, we'll have to call in another team. It's Sunday, remember?"

"The whole goddamn world is crazy," he mumbled, as tears poured down his face. He pushed the mike button. "Yeah, I know it's Sunday, 3 William 90. Call another team. We'll be awhile . . ."

More Big Bestsellers from SIGNET

☐ **FOREVER AMBER** by Kathleen Winsor.
(#J7360—$1.95)

☐ **SMOULDERING FIRES** by Anya Seton.
(#J7276—$1.95)

☐ **HARVEST OF DESIRE** by Rochelle Larkin.
(#J7277—$1.95)

☐ **THE PERSIAN PRICE** by Evelyn Anthony.
(#J7254—$1.95)

☐ **EARTHSOUND** by Arthur Herzog.   (#E7255—$1.75)

☐ **THE DEVIL'S OWN** by Christopher Nicole.
(#J7256—$1.95)

☐ **THE GREEK TREASURE** by Irving Stone.
(#E7211—$2.25)

☐ **THE KITCHEN SINK PAPERS** by Mike McGrady.
(#J7212—$1.95)

☐ **THE GATES OF HELL** by Harrison Salisbury.
(#E7213—$2.25)

☐ **SAVAGE EDEN** by Constance Gluyas. (#J7171—$1.95)

☐ **ROSE: MY LIFE IN SERVICE** by Rosina Harrison.
(#J7174—$1.95)

☐ **THE FINAL FIRE** by Dennis Smith.   (#J7141—$1.95)

☐ **SOME KIND OF HERO** by James Kirkwood.
(#J7142—$1.95)

☐ **THE HOMOSEXUAL MATRIX** by C. A. Tripp.
(#E7172—$2.50)

☐ **CBS: Reflections in a Bloodshot Eye** by Robert Metz.
(#E7115—$2.25)